SANDY
BLAIR

The
Laird

❦— A Castle Blackstone novel —❧

Dedication

*To my own tall and beautiful Highlander,
for being my touchstone in the real world
and my muse through my imaginary one.*

Behold, I send an Angel before thee, to keep thee in the way, and to bring thee into the place which I have prepared.

~Exodus 23:20

Prologue

St. Regis Hotel
New York, New York

Since introducing himself to Miss Katherine Elizabeth Pudding, estate executor Tom Silverstein craved only one thing. *Whisky.*

Aqua vitae. The water of life. Any brand, any age, so long as there was plenty of it.

Shrugging out of his wrinkled suit coat, he could—to his dismay—still picture Miss Pudding, the new heir to Castle Blackstone, smiling benignly from behind her desk as he told her about her inheritance and all it entailed.

She was still smiling when she led him through the doors of the nearest police station, where she insisted he be fingerprinted and interrogated. She did apologize profusely after the police verified his credentials, but it still took him the rest of the day and the better part of the night to convince her it was in her best interests to travel with him to Scotland, to at least see her inheritance.

He tossed his briefcase onto the king-sized bed and reached into the in-room liquor cabinet for the cut crystal decanter labeled Scotch. He drained two finger's worth of whisky in one swallow and refilled the tumbler. Drink in hand, he picked up the phone. His beloved and very pregnant wife, Margaret, answered the first ring.

The relief that came into her voice on hearing his warmed him in a way whisky never would. He asked, "Are ye feeling well, love?"

"Aye, but where have ye been? I've been worryin' myself sick."

Reluctantly, he told his bride—a Highlander with a keen appreciation for the absurd—about his day. To her credit, she did manage an "Oh my, ye poor lamb" and a few commiserating "clucks" between muffled giggles. Imagining her, plump and rosy-cheeked, sitting in her favorite parlor chair with a hand on her belly and tears of mirth rolling down her face, he smiled.

She asked, "Will Miss Pudding come, then?"

"Aye, but we'll not be home for another week."

Margaret sighed. "'Tis just as well. Gives me time to tidy the place up a bit."

An ache suddenly materialized between his eyes. "What has his lordship done now?"

"As soon as you left, he tossed everything the old man owned— from toppers to shoes—into the bailey. Even smashed the telly to smithereens. A shame, that."

Tom hadn't liked the previous heir in the least himself, but to smash the telly...

He squeezed the bridge of his nose in an effort to ease the pain. "It could have been worse."

"Aye, according to your Da, it has been."

"Love, I dinna want you goin' over there."

"Dinna worry, Tom. I'm far too pregnant to tolerate another trip to the castle in that wee boat of yours. I'll send a couple of lads over to snow up the place. But tell me, what does Miss Pudding look like? Will his lordship find her fair? Is she bonnie?"

"Who can tell under all the paint American women wear."

"Tom, I'm no' in a mood—"

"She's attractive, but I suspect she's really quite plain under all the gloss and feathers."

"Oh, dear." After a pause Margaret asked, "Does she at least have red hair? He has a recorded weakness for titians."

"I'm afraid it's kirk-mouse brown, love."

"Augh! I was so hoping for our son's sake..."

"Aye, I know." Since 1408, a Silverstein son had been chosen and educated in law and finance—despite what aspirations he might hold—to serve as executor to the Laird of Castle Blackstone. And so it would be for their soon-to-be-born son, unless...

"If it's any consolation," Tom said, "Miss Pudding's no fool. She asked if Blackstone was haunted."

"What did you say, Tom?"

"I told her I'd never seen a ghost."

"Tom! 'Tis written, as executor, you can't lie to the heir. A 'alf truth—by omission or otherwise—is still a lie."

"'Tis no lie to say I've never seen him. Heard him, aye. Tolerated his insufferable arrogance and temper, aye. But never once has he deemed me worthy of his august presence, so I *didna* lie."

After a sigh and a long pause, she murmured, "Could Miss Pudding be *the one*?"

Margaret's reference to the Gael curse levied on their laird just as he died made the words swim before Tom

3

eyes.

> *Curse ye MacDougall by my will,*
> *forever lost in nether world*
> *to pine for all ye lost most dear*
> *Only by ain token thrice blessed*
> *'tis the way to dreams and rest*
> *will one come to change thy fate.*

"Love, we'll not know the answer to that question," murmured Tom, the twenty-third of his line to serve Duncan Angus MacDougall, "unless he takes her."

Chapter 1

Drasmoor, Scotland

Yawning, Duncan MacDougall, the laird of Castle Blackstone, stretched in his enormous bed then cursed as the residual stench from Robert Sheffield's cigars filled his nose. Eight weeks had passed since the old man's death and still the noxious odor hung about the castle like a shroud.

Who would come now?

He prayed it wouldn't be another cigar smoking fop, but better that than no heir. He feared for his home—where he'd been trapped between life and death for so many lifetimes.

Victoria Regina had just died the last time a young family had claimed Blackstone. He smiled thinking of John and his lovely wife, Mary. He missed their children. Aye, it had been too long since he'd heard a lass giggle or watched a lad play with the lead soldiers now hidden away in the east wing.

But what if Silverstein couldna find a rightful heir? Or worse, what if he had, and the new occupant wanted to convert Blackstone into a bloody tourist attraction?

Duncan shuddered, picturing thousands of stippled and pierced youths with their pot-bellied parents stomping up his stairs and running their sticky hands over what had taken him a lifetime—at the cost of his soul—to acquire. He'd sooner abandon his long held hope for redemption, to suffer the perpetual fires of hell, than bear witness to such a violation of his home.

Wishing his recently departed heir—the one who hadn't been man enough to marry and produce an heir—a well-deserved stay in hell, he threw open the mullioned windows and heard the thudding of an aluminum hull against whitecaps. Over the wave-slapping racket he picked up the familiar high-pitched whine of Silverstein's launch engine.

He craned his neck for a better view of the harbor and cursed seeing a woman, her dark hair whipping in the breeze, sitting next to Silverstein.

God had granted his solicitor the love of a good woman and the gift of a wee babe—something he, a laird, had apparently been unfit to receive, dying unloved as he had and with the blood of three wives on his hands—and look what the daft fool does. He's put the poor woman in his miserable boat!

"God's teeth! In her condition, she should be lying in, not bouncing like a bloody cork across the bay." He started down the stairs. "He'll be shakin' the wee babe loose, for God's sake." Outraged by this real possibility, he raced to the great hall, determined to confront Thomas Silverstein face to face.

Generally, he preferred subtle—and sometimes not so subtle—displays to demonstrate his displeasure rather than materializing before the living. Becoming visible always took far more effort than most offenses warranted, while his temper tantrums were easily done and usually proved both effective and entertaining.

But Tommy Boy had now done the unthinkable; risking his child's life was tantamount to slapping God's face and placing Blackstone on the block. For those sins, his solicitor would pay dearly.

~#~

Katherine Elizabeth MacDougall Pudding clutched her really good designer knockoff tote to her chest without a thought to its prized contents and gasped as a huge, spiked gate suddenly ground down behind her with an ear-shattering screech.

"Don't be alarmed, Miss Pudding," Tom Silverstein yelled as he strode toward the keep tower with the rest of her luggage in hand. "The portcullis occasionally slips its chain. There's a hand crank on the left side to raise it again."

"Ah," Beth said, not caring for the image of herself suddenly skewered by the enormous rusting teeth should the damn chain slip as she passed beneath. Deciding fixing the ancient gate would be number one on her list of things to do, she followed tall and lean Mr. Silverstein through the courtyard—or bailey as he called it.

Frowning at the weeds and withered vines clinging to the fifteenth century stonework, she wondered how some people managed to go through life with taking pride in ownership. It only took a little love and elbow grease to make any place a home.

Not any home, but *her home*. Hers to do with as she wished. In her twenty-four years, these ancient granite blocks would be the first walls she could lay honest claim to.

Until two days ago, the latest place she'd call home

had been an overpriced, roach-infested efficiency in an aging Bronx brownstone, but still the roof, the stairs, and pride of ownership had belonged to another. Even the roaches had a "here today, gone tomorrow and then back again" attitude as if she'd had no say in the matter.

She raised her gaze to the sixteenth century mullioned windows above her. They should have been refracting multi-prismed rainbows as they faced the setting sun; instead they stared back at her, dull and opaque like the eyes of a landed cod.

With a proprietary eye, she gauged the height of the four-storied tower before her and the depth of its windowsills.

"Doable," she muttered, deciding to clean them as soon as possible.

Hell, she'd hung many a time out her fifth floor tenement window risking life and limb to scrub soot off warped plate glass for a clearer view of a brick airshaft. For an ocean view out a leaded window, she could climb a rope with her teeth.

She frowned seeing her castle's thick, arched door hadn't fared any better than the windows. The solid oak was stained by creeping mildew and so cracked it appeared to be made of cork. Mr. Silverstein forced it open with a shoulder and said, "Welcome to your new home, Miss Pudding. Welcome to Castle Blackstone."

Ruminating over the delicious import of his words, Beth followed him in. She grabbed the rope railing with her free hand and carefully climbed the tightly curved, well-worn stones to yet another door.

She walked into what Silverstein called Blackstone's great hall and froze, mouth agape.

Her new living room had to be at least sixty feet in

length and thirty feet in width. Two ornate, soot-covered fireplaces—each as tall as a man—graced the ends. Three huge, wheel-shaped wrought iron chandeliers hung above her, suspended by chains from a barreled ceiling. She felt relief seeing the fixtures had been electrified, but suspected she'd been in diapers the last time they and the twelve-foot high woodwork surrounding her had seen so much as a dust cloth.

Silverstein reached for the door at her back. As he pushed it closed, one of its huge mottled hinges screeched and detached. When he only shrugged, she wondered if a ten-penny spike and a gob of nail glue would be all she'd have at her disposal to hold the door up until she garnered some income.

She had no idea what the "maintenance income" Silverstein alluded to in New York might amount to in dollars—and having only six hundred in her checking account—she began having serious doubts about the wisdom of accepting her inheritance.

Her doubts only multiplied as she studied the chipped stenciling on the lofty plaster and beamed ceiling. Could she keep herself warm, let alone keep a castle in a decent state of repair, on a *maintenance*?

"Mr. Silverstein, how long has the castle been empty?"

"'Tis never been empty, Miss Pudding." He scowled as he waved toward a God-awful mix of contemporary and period furnishings. "Oh! You mean to ask how long have we gone without an heir?"

"Yes."

"Two months."

"Ah, yet it seems like just yesterday," she murmured, sniffing the acrid stench of cigar smoke. She ran a hesitant finger along a filthy window sash. Linda, her best friend and the Director of Housekeeping at the St. Regis-New York, would have a heart attack. "Could we open a window or two to air the place out?"

"Certainly."

It still didn't seem possible. *She* owned a castle—actually, it was little more than a medieval fortification occupying most of the landmass of a dinky isle off Scotland's Highland coast, but a rose by any other name...

Her, an orphan raised by—no, dragged up within—the Big Apple's foster-care system.

And what could she, would she do with it?

According to Silverstein, she had to reside in Blackstone for six months to lay claim to her inheritance. After that, she could return to her job in convention services at the St. Regis, using the castle only as a retreat, or she could reside here permanently. The decision would be hers. But no matter, after a six-month residence, her inheritance would be secure and would pass on to her descendants. Not that she had any hopes of having any.

More than a decade had passed since she'd exposed herself to the hope of being loved, and she couldn't imagine a set of circumstances that could ever prompt her to do so again.

It hadn't taken her long to discover most men liked their women pretty and compliant. She was neither.

Having only a high school education, she'd started her career path as a waitress. While watching prettier women seemingly rise without effort, she'd clawed her way, rung by rung, up three different hotel development ladders to become an assistant director. She didn't resent the pretty women. She envied them. They didn't have to work harder, be quicker and brighter, to get noticed.

Too, if the mirror hadn't made her plainness obvious to her, a frank foster mother had. She'd been only twelve when the woman she'd tried so hard to please—to be loved by—had told her, "You'll never be pretty, so you'd best learn to use make-up. Then, there's an outside possibility someone might consider you attractive."

She shook off the memory. It really didn't matter anymore. She, Katherine Elizabeth MacDougall Pudding, was an heiress. She now owned a tiny island and its broken down castle. The very thought took her breath away.

"Let me show you to your rooms before we tour the rest," Silverstein suggested as he gathered her bags.

"By all means, but I'll take that." She snatched her prized tote from Silverstein's hands and gave the surprised man an apologetic smile. Heiress or not, she still couldn't bring herself to trust the tote's contents to another. What if he dropped or misplaced it? The nearest cosmetics counter sat in Glasgow, a good four hour train's ride away, for God's sake.

"Humph!" His anger forgotten, Duncan watched Silverstein and the stranger make their way up the stairs. He'd been relieved to his marrow to find it wasn't Silverstein's wife he'd seen in the boat, but who is this? He followed, listening to their conversation.

Ah! So this is the new heir.

He glanced at her left hand and his heart nearly stopped. Why had he not been told? A young, *unattached* female hadn't taken control of Blackstone in centuries. The last, a beautiful but viperous titian, had nearly been the end of him. But what if this one...

He scowled watching the woman's lithe form lean precariously to the left as she struggled to carry her heavy bag around the tight curves of the stairway. Why in hell hadn't Silverstein offered to carry it for her? Had chivalry died with his generation?

Duncan stayed just steps behind her. He couldn't have her toppling and dying of a broken neck before he could assess the possibilities.

When the woman made it to the fourth floor landing without mishap, he sighed in relief.

"This is the solar," Silverstein told the woman as he stepped over the threshold, "the master bedroom of the castle. Our previous heir, Robert Sheffield, preferred less spacious quarters and slept in the east wing on the second floor."

Duncan grunted at his solicitor's blatant lie. He'd come into this very room shortly after Sheffield had arrived and found the bloody bastard trying to fondle the then ten-year-old Will Frasier's jewels. Furious with Sheffield, Duncan had frightened the piss out of both his heir and the poor boy. His next inclination had been to pitch the old blighter headlong down the steps, but having accumulated enough blood on his hands for one lifetime, he'd contented himself with terrorizing Sheffield for the next two decades. The old fop hadn't so much as dared look at another lad or venture above the second floor landing during the entirety of his residence.

"I hope you find it to your liking," Silverstein continued. "'Tis quite extraordinary. The tapestries on either side of the bed were produced in the late seventeenth century by one of your predecessors, Lady Katherine Stewart MacDougall. The bed is original to the castle. 'Tis over-sized because Duncan Angus MacDougall, the first Laird of Blackstone, was a huge man. Supposedly, he stood six and one half feet tall, much like Robert the Bruce."

Duncan snorted. There was no *supposedly* about it. He did stand six and one-half feet tall and weighed seventeen stone, if anyone cared to know. And Tom knew better than to compare him to the Bruce. *Hummph!*

Waving around the room, Silverstein concluded, "And the windows, Miss Pudding, offer a spectacular three hundred and sixty-degree view."

Pudding? Which one of his cousin's mangy descendants had had the audacity to rut with a Sassenach—an Englishman? Matters had definitely deteriorated further than he'd surmised.

"It's lovely," Miss Pudding murmured running a hand over the hunt scene carved into his headboard. She then gently pressed the mattress. "But please call me Beth."

"Beth it is, but don't be distressed if most about call you *my lady*."

"Oh?"

Silverstein smiled. "The honorarium comes with the castle. We tend to keep to the old ways as much as possible here. Within the next day or so, most from Drasmoor will be out to welcome ye."

"Ah." She wandered to the open window. Staring out, she murmured, "It's still so difficult to believe, Mr. Silverstein. That all this...," her hand fluttered, encompassing the room and the view, "could be *mine* in just six months' time. For so many years, I've not had so much as a pot to—"

Hearing her voice crack then falter, Duncan moved

closer to the now silent woman staring out his window. He studied her face as she tried unsuccessfully to blink away tears. What caused her to weep? From her silent shaking carriage, he suspected she wasna a woman who cried easily and he hoped for her sake that it wasn't too often. 'Twas not a pretty sight.

She'd bitten her bottom lip to the point of scarlet and strange black streaks now stained the flat planes of her cheeks. When she shivered, he felt heat radiate off her and instinctively stepped closer, only to be bathed in a strange scent, an exotic mix of sweet and soft. He fought the unaccountable urge to reach out and touch her. How curious.

"Shall we tour the rest of your domain now?" Silverstein asked from across the solar, "And please call me Tom. There's no point in our standing on ceremony. We're likely to have a long, complex relationship."

Duncan frowned at the comment, but the woman, Beth, silently nodded as she hastily brushed her tears away. She heaved a huge sigh and faced his solicitor, this time with a smile.

"I'd love to see the rest of my *home*."

When she put the emphasis on the word *home*, Duncan Angus MacDougall grinned for the first time in decades.

Alone and hungry, Beth wandered into the bowels of her keep to the kitchen.

Here, at least, she wouldn't have to worry about contracting some nasty disease. Someone had taken the time to scour the large whitewashed room to a high shine. Even the battered tin pots above the hearth glowed.

There were no wall-mounted cabinets in the basement kitchen; just an enormous center table surrounded by stools, an ancient, multi-drawer spice chest and a few old appliances. The cavernous room's only charm came by way of a six-foot high by eight-foot wide fireplace, complete with wrought iron hooks, a boar-sized roasting spit, angle irons and four separate side ovens. As she ran a hand over the embossed lions on one of the cast iron doors, she could almost smell fresh bread baking. Her stomach growled.

Given Beth's inexperience with operating a boat, Mr. Silverstein had thoughtfully arranged for a week's worth of fresh food to be laid in. She examined the unfamiliar labels on the canned goods and sniffed the fruit and breads on the table before opening the squat refrigerator to find a quart of fresh milk—its thick cream filling the top two inches of the bottle, a half dozen brown eggs, two chops and butter. Too tired to make anything elaborate, she snatched two eggs from their cardboard container.

She scrambled the eggs then noticed a five-gallon glass container of yellow liquid fueled the stove. Shrugging at the oddity, she turned a porcelain knob and waited for a familiar click-click-click. When nothing happen she immediately flipped off the knob and stared at the white enameled, cast iron contraption. Even her fifth floor walkup's stove had an electric ignition. Now what?

Matches. After a three-minute hunt, she struck one and held it near a burner as she turned the appropriate knob. Nothing happened. She tried three more times before huffing in exasperation and dumping her eggs down the drain.

Toast and an apple, then.

She found an ancient toaster, but it took awhile before she could get its sides to flop open. "I could starve to death at this rate," she muttered, dropping two slices of bread into it and shoving the toaster's odd shaped plug into the wall outlet.

"*Oh, shit!*"

She jumped back as a shower of fluorescent sparks spewed from the wall socket. The fireworks continued as ribbons of acrid smoke oozed out of the toaster.

"God damn it!" She yanked the toaster's cord from the wall. When the sparks abruptly ceased, she heaved a sigh and heard a masculine chuckle. Startled, she spun around.

Seeing no one, she lowered her hands and released her breath. "Next, you'll be seeing ghosts," she chided, feeling foolish.

She was, after all, a city chick, well used to the wail of sirens, screeching tires, and things that go bump in the night. She shouldn't be jumping, heart in her throat, because sparks flew and an errant wind whipping around outside decided to come down the roasting pit's flue.

She turned her attention back to the toaster. It felt cool. Gingerly, she touched the socket. Finding no heat, she thanked God for small favors, grabbed two apples from the table and shut off the light. Whatever caused the problem could wait for daylight.

Chapter 2

Totally incredulous, Beth stared at the electrician Tom Silverstein had sent to solve her kitchen's wiring problem.

"Am I understanding you correctly, Mr. MacBride? All the wiring is made of *aluminum?*"

The electrician nodded. "Aye, all of it. 'Twas commonly used at the turn of the century. The twentieth, I'm meanin'. 'Tis all gonna have to be replaced. 'Tis dangerous, ye ken?"

She *kenned* all right, feeling lucky she still had eyebrows.

She'd already discovered the plumbing in the keep was shaky at best, knocking and banging as she tried to purge the rarely used pipes. She'd concluded from the amount of rust and the thick scum lining the east wing's claw footed tub, her predecessor had only bathed when the seasons changed.

She heaved a resigned sigh. "How much will it cost to replace the wiring in just the main living areas?" She didn't want to know or even speculate on how much fixing *all* the wiring would cost. She'd have to take care of the rest the same way she paid off her credit cards. A bit at a time. Right now, she simply wanted to use a hair dryer, leave a hall light on at night, and make toast without burning the place to the ground.

She took comfort where she could. The electrician wouldn't be knocking any holes in her newly acquired walls. The wiring ran in tubing along the stone floors, walls, and plaster ceilings.

"Dinna worry about the cost, my lady. I'll work up an estimate and send it to Mr. Silverstein in a day or two. I'm sure we men can come to a meeting of the minds."

After a broken night's sleep and a hard morning of cleaning, Beth had little patience for a patronizing pat on the head.

She'd already found water-damaged paneling, six windows with broken panes, more that wouldn't open, and she'd only examined half the keep. She shuddered to think what else lay in wait. She'd be dead broke in a month at the rate things were going, "maintenance" or no.

And this was *her* keep, damn it. Not Tom Silverstein's.

"Mr. MacBride, I'll be the one to approve or reject your estimate, so please send it to me. Meanwhile, is there anything I should do to keep from setting this place ablaze?"

He made a thick "*humphing*" sound at the back of his throat and puffed out his chest. "Aye. Dinna plug anything else in. And dinna leave any lamps on when ye go to sleep. Wouldna do to have ye wake and find yerself and the castle afire, now would it?"

"Ah." She wanted to cuff his surly ears.

When Silverstein returned for her boating lesson,

she'd request a different electrician. The job would take weeks—if not months—to complete, and she couldn't hold her tongue around this man for that long.

She walked down the stairs and into the bailey with him. Waving goodbye, she smiled benignly and warned, "Do be quick as you pass under the portcullis, Mr. MacBride...wouldn't do to wake and find you skewered to the ground, now would it?"

~#~

Duncan had never heard a woman curse so much in his life—or death, come to think on it.

He'd followed Beth for most of the morning as she tore through his keep with the speed of a waterspout, tearing down window covers and poking into corners and cupboards like some crazed ferret. He paid close attention to what she found fascinating and to what offended her thin, aquiline nose. He had to concede she recognized craftsmanship when she found it. But the more dust, decay, and fractured furniture she found, the more colorful her language became.

Still rattled by her presence, he retreated to his solar and flopped down on his side—the left side—of his great bed. In the wee hours of the night he'd come into his room and been relieved to discover she'd chosen the right side.

He'd settled next to her. Fingering a silky strand of her hair as she slept, he thought about the curse that had sent him into this place of neither life nor death. He again pondered the curse—the prophecy—etched into his grave marker by that witch, the mother of his third wife. He'd been so relieved to find the carved words—to learn there was hope—he'd memorized every letter.

Only by ain token trice blessed...had to mean his

wedding ring...*would one come to change ye fate.*

Could this mouse, this new heir, be *the one* spoken of? Was she strong enough? Had he simply made a dreadful mistake by trusting the last unattached woman? At least the titian had taught him a valued lesson; he'd never again let his weakness for flame-colored hair lead him by the balls. He still couldn't believe he'd thought himself in love with the witch.

Well, he harbored no fear of repeating his mistake with this one. Miss Pudding was as plain as porridge. But she did have good skin. And a nice mouth.

She slept so soundly; with such stillness, in fact, he'd been forced to touch her twice during the night to be sure she still breathed. She'd grumbled briefly, but soon settled back into the deepest slumber he'd ever witnessed. Odd.

And *odd* didn't begin to describe her morning ablutions.

He studied the parade of bottles and glossy black cases on the dresser a past descendant had added to the room. Never in his wildest dreams could he imagine going through all that Beth did of a morning.

He should have felt guilty watching her, but once she'd begun, he'd not been able to pull his disbelieving gaze away. No whole man could have.

She had bounced out of the bed with a smile and immediately stripped to her skin—nice, smooth, milky white skin; so pale it made the rosy nipples of her small, high breasts and the chestnut thatch between her legs stand out in delightful contrast.

She then proceeded to use two of the bottles from her collection to wash her hair, another to wash her face, and yet another to clean her long limbs and lithe body. All in tepid water since she'd not taken the time last night to light the fires below. She then did the most amazing thing.

She ran a sharp, blue handled blade under her arms, over her smooth muscled legs and ever so carefully about the edges of her downy thatch. It had nearly been his undoing.

By the time he caught his breath, she had dried herself, and started to ever so slowly cover herself in a rich, vanilla- scented cream. Watching the seductive display *had* been his undoing. He'd forced himself from the room.

When curiosity again took the upper hand, he returned to find her standing before the mirror dressed in purple leggings and a thick matching sweater. Her wet, shoulder length hair had been pulled back into a loose knot at her nape. He'd crossed his arms and leaned on the doorframe wondering what she would do now.

For a brief moment she appeared a wee bit sad as she stared at her reflection, then she reached for yet another bottle. She went through four before she picked up one of the glossy black cases. Then the morning's most bizarre event occurred. She began painting a portrait.

Like an artist, she wielded first broad brushes then fine, and using pigments—both solid and liquid—she re-created herself.

Having turned her ordinary gray eyes into rather appealing smoky pools, she surprised him by suddenly gasping. The tool that had made her lashes sooty hit the floor as she spun around facing him.

Startled, he watched as her gaze darted around the room. He, too, began looking about, expecting to find something sinister. Seeing nothing, he moved to her right and waited.

She shuddered for a brief moment, huffed, and faced the mirror once again. Her gaze continued to dart about the room on occasion as she painted her full lips a soft rose, but nothing further disturbed her.

She then left the solar to tear his home asunder.

~#~

Standing in the bailey, a hand shielding her eyes, Beth asked, "What do you think, Tom?"

She grinned at the glare bouncing off the first and second story windows. Her castle would definitely make an awesome bed and breakfast.

"Lovely. Ye'll be blinding every seaman from here to the Isle of Mull by week's end. Are ye sure, lass, ye dinna want any help? There are day workers aplenty. I could send one out to do this for ye."

"Oh, I'm sure." She didn't want to be tripping over any more people than was absolutely necessary after making her monumental discovery this morning.

Her castle was haunted.

Her new and decidedly friendlier electricians, Bart and Will Fraiser, would start work tomorrow morning and that would be disturbing enough.

She smiled at Tom. By mid-morning she knew, without a doubt, they were in need of a frank discussion if her living at Blackstone was to have any chance of success. "Why did you lie to me?"

Tom's face flushed. "I'll never lie to you, lass!"

"Ah, but you have—when I asked if Blackstone was haunted."

"Nay. You asked if I'd *seen* a ghost and I answered truthfully. I've never."

"I've seen him, Tom."

At first, she'd only catch startling glimpses of him, like a mote floating in the corner of her eye. Heart thudding, she'd spin around...and find nothing. Finally realizing she only saw the tall, translucent creature if she happened to be looking in a mirror, she started watching for him in anything reflective. And did. She'd become quite good at focusing in on the specter as he hovered behind her, becoming more fascinated with his blue-black hair and beard, steel blue eyes, and heavily muscled physique with each consecutive sighting; hence, all her shiny windows. On those rare occasions when he stood very close, she'd also catch a whiff of cold, fetid air.

"Who is he?"

A concerned scowl suddenly replaced the flush of embarrassment on Tom's face. "Has he done or said anything to frighten you, lass?"

"No. He's only startled me a few times." She wasn't about to tell Tom she was quite certain her decidedly masculine ghost had watched her bathe yesterday. She felt embarrassed enough.

"Good." Tom placed a hand at her waist and directed her to the patch of lawn surrounding Blackstone's ancient well at the center of the bailey. "Come, have a seat in the sun. The telling of Duncan Angus MacDougall's tale and mine will take some time."

~#~

Duncan put down his heir's peculiar lists—things she wanted to repair and purchase—and scowled out the great hall's window to where his solicitor and Beth sat.

"What on earth can they be talking about for this long?"

They had nothing in common and certainly couldn't

be discussing him. 'Twas forbidden until he'd made himself known to the heir, and he certainly wasn't ready to do that. Not yet, anyway.

Being aware of his presence would, no doubt, send Miss Beth screaming back to America, which wouldn't do, not at all. He had yet to test her mettle, didna know if she was *the one*. If he found her wanting—and he suspected he might for she was so...*odd*, then she could stay or go as she pleased.

He again scanned the list entitled Order From Home. Murphy's Oil Soap was self-explanatory, but what is Soft Scrub? Ah! That must be the cleanser she uses when bathing. He smiled, his mornings looking decidedly brighter. She wanted a case of it.

Reading the second sheet—B and B Provisions, his frown returned. She wanted ten sets of Egyptian cotton sheets and triple the number of towels, all in white. Seemed excessive, even for a woman who bathed daily. And why would she want one hundred bees' wax candles, twenty down pillows, and five down comforters? They had electricity and used only one bed.

The woman was decidedly odd or a spendthrift, but he could depend on his solicitor. Silverstein would rein her in. Tommy had kept that fop, the previous heir, on a tight purse, allowing him only a minimal draw each month. What the man did with the money, Duncan never knew. Probably drank it away. The fop certainly hadn't spent it on maintaining the keep.

Duncan looked out the window. Beth and Tom were finally standing. Thank God. She'd be coming in.

With no small measure of shock he realized his current agitation stemmed not from her lists but from feeling lonely. How odd.

~#~

"So you see, since 1395 when Duncan rescued my forbearers Isaac and Rachael from the villagers intent on torching them at the stake, we Silversteins have felt a moral obligation to serve Duncan, even in his ghostly form.

"Each generation has provided an executor, who functions exactly as Isaac did, to serve as a financial advisor to subsequent heirs, overseeing the estate's limited assets so Blackstone won't fall to complete ruin as so many castles about Scotland have. So long as there are Silversteins, the ghost will have his home. Our debt to him is enormous. Our line wouldn't exist today—I'd not have been born—had Duncan MacDougall not had a strong arm and the moral courage to save Isaac and Rachael." His lips quirked to formed a lopsided grin. "And each generation has kept a journal of their trials in meeting that obligation."

Beth sighed. "It's hard to imagine sane, God-fearing villagers blaming a simple man and his pregnant wife for the plague."

Tom shrugged. "They were strangers, Beth, Parisian Jews who spoke only broken English and no Gael. Isaac and Rachael couldn't make themselves understood to the villagers. At the time, French was the language of the court, of the educated wealthy. And keep in mind, just fifty years earlier Europe's population had been decimated; literally half the population had died from plague. Religious zealots abound. The Flagellants were walking about beating themselves with whips in the belief that if they punished themselves, God would spare them. Others blamed the Jews. When Isaac and Rachael's arrival happened to coincided with what was thought to be another outbreak..." He raised his hands in a hopeless gesture.

"Well, I, for one, am very glad the MacDougall brought Rachael and Isaac to Drasmoor. I couldn't manage without you."

"Thank you, my lady."

"I'm the one who should be thanking you."

Dying to know more about her ghost, she asked, "Is there a chance I might read some of your journals?"

Tom grinned, but he shook his head. "Only a Silverstein may read them."

Masking her disappointment, Beth said, "Speaking of Silversteins, how is your lovely wife?"

"Her back aches, her feet look like pillows, and she canna get out of bed without help. She's not a happy woman."

Beth laughed. "Well, give her my best."

"Aye." He buttoned his coat, readying to take his leave. "I'll be bringing the ledger and checkbook to you on my next visit."

She tried to hide her surprise at this major concession. Tom had been opposed to her handling anything but her maintenance funds—a meager six hundred pounds per month—just a few days ago.

She grinned. "What changed your mind?"

"The windows, lass." He chuckled. "And the fact that you're not packed and on your way to the airport after seeing his querulous lordship."

"Ah." Pleased, she ducked her chin to hide the blush she felt creeping up her neck.

Tom didn't need to know it would have taken a team of horses to drag her out of the keep now that she'd seen her frequently scowling but handsome specter.

Would it be possible for her to establish a companionship of sorts with her ghost? Duncan was, after all, dead, so she wouldn't really be exposing her heart to another rejection if she tried to garner his attention and failed. Was it possible or just a flight of fancy? Could her ghost speak to her? Keep her company during long winter nights? And if so, what would it take to prompt him into it?

Chapter 3

Duncan found Beth in the kitchen, chattering like a squirrel into her telephone. Frowning, he rested an elbow on the roasting pit mantle.

"It'll cost how much?" Beth asked the phone, heaving an exasperated sigh. "Then send only the catalogs by air. Ya. I'd kill to be on-line." She rearranged the spice jars on the table. "Right now? What I miss most are you, Junior's Cheesecake, and West Wing."

He scowled in confusion. He could understand her missing a friend or cake, but how could she miss the west wing? 'Twas one hundred feet long, three stories high and attached to the left side of the keep.

"Silverstein didn't have a problem with my starting a B and B, but asked that I wait until after my six-month probation. Then I can do as I like."

Duncan wondered once again what the two B's stood for. As long as it didn't stand for *bingeing* and *buggery* and made her happy, he supposed it didn't matter. This would be her home after all. His and hers to share. Alone. Until—or rather, unless—he decided to take her.

She giggled. "Of course you're invited. Do you think you can get time off at Christmas?" She listened, looking pensive. "Oh. Then I'll look forward to seeing you in June." As she said goodbye, her eyes grew glassy, reflecting the lamp's light like liquid pewter.

Humph! She shouldn't use the bloody telephone if it made her forlorn. If it continued to cause her distress, he'd do them both a favor and misplace the damn thing. The piping tune it played whenever it wanted her attention was annoying as hell, anyway.

She brushed at a tear and pocketed the telephone.

"Onward and upward," Beth muttered.

He eyed her warily.

~#~

In a dusty storage room, Beth smiled as she ran a careful hand over the small icon-like portrait she'd unearthed. "It's about time."

Centuries of grime and mildew coated the painted wood in her hands, but she felt sure she'd found what she'd been looking for, her ghost's portrait.

Clutching it to her chest, she pushed back through the mountain of antique furnishings she'd piled behind her in her quest to find his likeness. Outside the storage room, she reexamined the other canvases she'd set aside, beautiful portraits and landscapes that would add interest to the keep's great hall. After a bath, she'd research their dates against the forty-odd journals she'd found in the library. It would be fun discovering who the individuals were. Hopefully, she could learn enough in the next six months to dazzle her guests with stories seeped in love, gallantry, and mayhem.

Sighing, she held her specter's portrait at arm's length to study the deep blue eyes and heavy beard. "Is your chin square, dear ghost, under all the black fuzz?" She hoped so.

Because he always appeared dressed in a swatch of tartan, a sleeveless furred tunic and a wide leather belt whenever she spied him hovering behind her, she knew Duncan had shoulders and arms that could make any woman swoon. Her ghost's legs were equally attractive if one was into heavily muscled thighs and long powerful calves. She sighed, an unprotected corner of her heart wishing he were flesh and blood.

~ # ~

"Good riddance," Duncan grumbled as the electricians scrambled into their launch and headed for Drasmoor. To escape their clamoring, he'd spent the better part of the day bored out of his mind on the keep's parapet.

Beth had evidently found the men equally disturbing since she'd spent the afternoon churning earth along the bailey's east wall. Wondering what she was up to now, he entered the keep.

"Where in hell did she find *that?*" He frowned at the small portrait leaning against the solar's hearth. He had ordered the ugly rendering burned before its pigments had dried.

Beth had any number of better paintings to choose from if she wanted to brighten the room. Why on earth had she chosen his portrait?

As artists went, his cousin would have made a fine butcher. The portrait only proved what Duncan had known all along. The youth's only talent lay in wielding a sword. Yet, here the ugly portrait was again after six hundred years. His ferret heir would be the death of him, if he weren't already dead.

And where was she?

He prowled the upper floors looking for her without

success, and then descended to the hall. He didn't find her in the great room, but saw that two of his favorite chairs were suddenly there. Apparently, she'd found the fop's reclining throne as offensive as he had and banished it. He caressed the recently oiled rosewood falcons at rest on the chairs' high backs.

He'd brought the chairs to Blackstone from Normandy; one of the few prizes he'd been able to salvage after the battle of Rouin. The leather seats were now cracked and brittle, but 'twas good to see them again in the great hall, nonetheless.

Minutes later, he found Beth sitting before the cistern-fed water heater, filthy and looking dejected, a pile of spent matches at her side.

He examined the firebox. She'd put in enough kindling, but she'd stacked the bricks of coal like a meticulous mason, eliminating any chance for a draft. She was down to her last match and muttering.

She struck the match, watched the kindling flare, and then just as quickly snuff out. She kicked the firebox door closed.

Tears welling in her eyes, she shouted, "I can't live like this!" She stalked away. "I don't care if I starve, I'm ordering a real water heater tomorrow."

Her kick caused her carefully laid coal to shift, and Duncan quickly fanned the dying embers. When the kindling ignited with a whoosh, he thumped the tank and caught her attention.

Beth bent and examined the scarlet glow. She then straightened and looked about. Brushing way her tears, she tipped her chin and twitched her nose like a fox on the hunt. When she muttered, "Thank you. That was very nice of you," his knees buckled.

Waiting for her bathwater to heat, Beth curled in one of the deep falcon chairs and opened her greatest find of the day, the third volume of the Blackstone Diaries.

The original diary, bound in wood and written on the frailest parchment she'd ever seen, had been written in Latin and in her ghost's own hand. Had she been able to translate the fading broad script, she still would have hesitated, fearing she'd destroy the volume by simply turning the pages.

The second volume, a translation written in 1640, was nearly as delicate. Scanning the first page she'd cursed. Only someone comfortable with Shakespeare could have readily understood it.

She smiled opening the third volume. In legible English she read, *The Diary of Duncan Angus MacDougall, translation by Miles Bolton MacDougall, 1860.*

She carefully opened this volume to the twelfth page. So far she'd learned Duncan, a knight who'd earned his spurs at the age of fourteen, had returned to Drasmoor after fighting in France to find his father and brothers dead along with half the clan, and himself now laird. He was awaiting the birth of his first child, angry about a neighboring clan's recent raid on his kine—which she took to mean cattle—and worried about another outbreak of the Black Death recently reported in Edinburgh.

The mason guides, cajoles, and shouts. All, hands bleeding, labor day and night, yet I fear 'tis not fast enough. Surely, if Pope Clement the V could survive the ravages of the ungodly plague by walling his portly self into his chambers as all around him perished, then so shall we on this isle. I pray Blackstone's walls complete before the scourge finds us again.

Quarantine. That's why he built this massive structure out here in the middle of the harbor instead of on the high hills surrounding Drasmoor. My word. She turned the page.

'Tis laid, the walls' last stone. Work on the keep continues as women hoard food and water. My Mary's birthing time draws near, yet she falters not. I have pleaded, begged her return to her father's stronghold, but to no avail. She loathes his second wife and will not leave. The reeving has subsided after we repossessed our ten kine and six of the Bruce's as payment for the aggravation he caused me. Death continues its march toward us.

For ten consecutive pages Duncan detailed their progress, his worries shifting like flotsam from men's injuries to the weather, to his dwindling coffers, to his wife. Daily notations soon changed to weekly, each more worrisome than the last.

On the twenty-second page she read, *God has turned his face from me. Three days past, I dug into the frozen earth to lay Mary to rest, our babe in her arms. Like her name namesake, she bore our son in a manger for we have little else for shelter since the keep is only four walls and the Black Death has taken up refuge in the village just south of us. I weep for the lass for she was brave, uttering nary a word. I have yet to inform the Campbell. He will not take well the death of his beloved daughter and with her, the bairn. Well he should blame me. For had I not listened to her pleadings, had I sent her to him (to Dunstaffnage Castle) she and our son might be alive today. Come spring, I will build Blackstone's chapel above her. It grieves me I have not the means to ease her way to heaven with a Papal Bull, but when able I will praise her selfless devotion as wife with a bronze effigy. I loved her not, nor her I, but I grieve. For the babe and her good soul.*

Beth's cell phone rang, startling her. She fumbled in her pocket for it and snapped it open. "Hello?"

"Tom here, my lady. Are you all right? You sound...hoarse."

She cleared the thickness in her throat. "I'm fine. I was just reading." The picture of Mary MacDougall, lying half-frozen, laboring in a bed of straw prompted her to ask after Margaret.

"She's eating us out of hearth and home." He chuckled. "I called to let you know you've two packages here from New York. May I bring them by tomorrow?"

"Thank you, but I'll come to you. I've let the launch intimidate me for long enough. I need to just do it and get it over with."

"The telly forecasts a bonnie day. You should be fine. Call me just before you leave, and I'll keep watch from the quay."

"Thank you. You'll be pleased to know that miserable excuse for a water heater is finally working."

He chuckled. "Just remember to add more fuel every so often and you'll have warm water come mornin', as well."

"God, I hate that tank. And the kerosene stove stinks. Literally."

"I know. Hopefully, the markets will improve and you'll have more coins to work with in the coming months."

"From your lips to God's ears."

He laughed. "Give me a ring when you set out

tomorrow."

"I will. Give Margaret a kiss for me."

She snapped her lifeline to the outside world closed. Here she was complaining about cold water and a smelly stove with the tale of the MacDougall's bride still spread on her lap. How self-absorbed could a body be? Had she been born in the early fifteenth century, could she have survived what this woman had not? She shuddered and thanked God for placing her in this century where—should she ever give birth—there were hospitals and epidurals.

She'd never have made it in the fourteenth century. First, she couldn't imagine living under the thumb of ancient Catholicism. The tithes Duncan paid were crippling. The period's mandatory daily worship services made her cringe. And the needless guilt Duncan carried because he couldn't afford a Papal Bull—a coin, according to the footnote, one could purchase from the Pope to ensured the deceased would bypass purgatory and go straight to heaven—only re-enforced her distrust of organized religions. Yup, she much preferred her one-on-one relationship with God, whereby she thanked and complained on a regular basis, and He, on rare occasions, acquiesced and answered a prayer.

She sighed and turned the page. "What's this?" Before her disbelieving eyes was written a decidedly clever but cold-blooded plot for murder.

~#~

Duncan squinted against the blinding sunlight bouncing off the sea as he paced the parapet.

Since muttering "thank you" yesterday, Beth thrice spun around and looked him in the eye. Once, she'd even had the audacity to wave and wink! He shuddered.

Had she the *sight*? Nay. Surely. To aggravate him further, the wee ferret had found his diaries. He would now have to keep an even closer eye on her.

He raised his gaze and saw Beth standing on Drasmoor's quay, dressed in a bright yellow slicker and rubber boots. "Finally."

His agitation grew as she made her way across the bay to the castle. She maneuvered the launch, which sat gunwale deep in the water and was nigh on to overflowing with packages, like a drunkard, weaving right then left, and on more than one occasion completely broadside to on-coming breakers. His heart was in his throat by the time she docked.

"The daft woman should be kept under lock and key for her own good."

He took the spiraling stairs two at a time to the great hall, his determination to call her to task for risking her life growing with each step. Her knowing of his existence and grinning about it was one thing. Suffering the fury of his wrath in the next few minutes would be another, entirely. "And obey me she will, by God! For she be woman, and I, her laird, be *man*!"

He charged into the great hall just as Beth, looking disgustingly pleased with herself, with her arms loaded with packages, came in from the opposite doorway. Before he could roar his displeasure, Will Frasier dropped the wires he held for his father and yelled, "My lady! Let me help ye with those."

A piercing scream then rocked the chandeliers.

They spun and found the elder Bart Frasier—caught in a web of arcing wires—vibrating like a crazed puppet, his face contorted into a ghastly mask of agony. Acrid smoke filled the air.

"*Da!*" Will bellowed.

Beth, screaming, opened her arms. Her packages toppled as her booted foot slammed into the old man's chest. Freed from the killing current, Bart dropped like a felled tree to the floor.

Dodging the dangling, still sparking wires, Beth crouched at the old man's side. "Oh, God. Please, God," she pleaded, while running trembling fingers along Fraser's neck. She listened to the man's chest, and then threw her cell phone at Frasier's son. "Call for help!"

To Duncan's shock, Beth next tipped back the electrician's head, swiped the foamy spittle from his lips, and started blowing into the dead man's blue mouth. Not once, but repeatedly. To Duncan's utter amazement, Frasier's mottled skin began to pink.

Beth stopped breathing into Bart's mouth and again ran her fingers along his neck.

Will collapsed to his knees beside her. "The police are coming."

Beth nodded and breathed again into the old man.

"Is he alive?" Will asked. "Will he be all right? Ack! 'Tis all my fault."

Beth, looking no less terrified than the son, didn't answer but pressed her ear to the elder Fraiser's chest. When she lifted her head a quivering smile took shape. "He's breathing on his own now."

Duncan rocked back in surprise. 'Twas a bloody miracle!

Young Frasier's tears started falling in earnest as he caressed his father's brow. "Da, I'm so sorry." To Beth he said, "Thank you."

Within minutes the police launch arrived. They

secured the still unconscious Fraser onto a board and shuttled him out.

On the quay, Duncan stood at Beth's side as she waved the men off. He then followed her hunched-shouldered progress into the keep, up and out on to the parapet.

As she watched the police launch cross the bay—her face now a horrid mess of black streaks—she whispered, "Go with God."

His odd but brave wee heir then began to quake and sob in heartbreaking earnest.

Deciding she should not, he murmured at a volume she might hear, "There's no need for tears, lass, for ye did well. Verra well, indeed."

Heart once again bounding, Beth jerked. Did Duncan Angus MacDougall, her resident voyeur, just speak to her? She held her breath while every nerve in her body focused on hearing.

She turned, hoping. Her gaze shifted from one corner of the high parapet to the next. Nothing.

"Ah," murmured her ghost. "Why is it, lass, that ye canna see me now, yet on occasion, ye can?"

Her heart slammed into her ribs. His voice rumbled from only two feet away. She reached out a tentative hand.

He chuckled, "Ye canna touch me in my present state, lass. Oh, that I wish you could, but 'tis not time."

"Why...?" She didn't know where to begin her inquisition, her nerves still rattled by all that had just happened.

"Because, I'm dead, lass."

"No...I understand that you're dead." She grinned as

she dashed away tears. "I meant to ask, why have you finally decided to speak to me?"

"Ye appear to be in need of someone at the moment."

"Ah." Her handsome specter was compassionate. "I'm Beth."

"Aye, I know that. I'm Duncan Angus MacDougall, also called The Black, the MacDougall, or laird."

"Do you have a preference?"

"Hmm."

She waited, focusing on the dense cold hovering before her.

"From what little I know of ye, I'd be pleased ta have ye address me as Duncan."

Oh, my. He wanted to be on a first name basis with her. Her excitement multiplied at the prospect. She wanted to ask if he felt cold, if he ate, slept, or why he'd chosen to speak to her when he hadn't talked to Tom. For some inexplicable reason she asked, "Are you ever lonely?"

"Aye, at times."

"Me, too." Burning started at the back of her throat again, a familiar sting at the back of her eyes. A dead man was making her life palatable and she was happy about it. *What's wrong with this picture, Beth?*

"Duncan, do you mind my being here?"

"Nay, lass. I'm quite pleased you've come. 'Tis a big place for one wee man."

She grinned, sniffing back tears. "From what I hear, there's nothing *wee* about you."

His laughter rumbled like wooden barrels rolling down a long hall. "To be sure, lass, there is naught on this body that's wee."

She felt a blush creep up her neck, turned from the

mass of cold air and studied the harbor. Did ghosts miss making—

Good gravy. She was definitely in worse shape than she'd thought.

Beth watched the police launch dock at Drasmoor and men scramble out of the waiting ambulance. As soon as the elder Frasier was loaded into the ambulance, it took off, lights flashing and sirens woo, woo, wooing, which to Beth's ears didn't sound near as serious—as urgent—as its high-pitched, screaming New York City's counterparts.

"As I said, lass, ye did verra well."

"I pray he recovers consciousness soon."

"God's hand was on ye shoulder. Fraser will be fine."

When the ambulance disappeared from view she turned to watch the sun set, something she hadn't been able to enjoy very often in a city filled with skyscrapers.

Looking like a giant orange, the sun slowly slid behind a distant line of molten silver. Wide swatches of orchid, flame, and daffodil surrounded the spectacle. She thought it a fitting close to her first week as owner of Castle Blackstone.

"Do you sleep?" she asked her specter.

"Of course."

"Where?"

"Where I choose."

Of course he did. "Do you eat?"

"Nay, and I do miss that verra much. The taste of roasted venison I sorely crave."

"What else do you miss?"

"The men who stood at my side, the sounds of babes at play, the feel of a woman's skin under my hand." He chuckled. "The taste of fine whisky, and of course, reeving. Ack, 'tis nothing finer on a fair night than racing the wind for home on a sturdy mount with yer enemy braying at yer back."

Whoa! She'd been under the impression he'd done it simply to get his cattle back. Apparently not.

The sun slipped away for the night and she shivered.

"'Tis time to go below, lass, before ye catch yer death."

She nodded. As she headed for the stairs, she asked, "Will I ever see you clearly?"

Silence answered back.

~#~

Beth, exhausted but still awake, reached for the ringing phone. "Hello?"

"Tom here, my lady. Just thought you'll like to know Bart Frasier has awakened in hospital. He's a bit befuddled and missing a good bit of hair, but the doctor says he'll recover."

"Thank God. Is his son okay?"

"Aye. Young Will finally settled once his Da was alert and talking. How are you?"

"I'm...can you hold on a moment?" She reached for her compact and scanned the solar. Finding herself alone, she whispered, "Tom, he spoke to me. Up on the parapet."

"Who?"

"*The ghost...Duncan!*"

"Are ye sure ye're not imagining things, lass, after the shock—"

"We had a *conversation*, Tom."

"My word. Did he materialize?"

"No. He said it wasn't time."

Tom muttered, "I must tell Margaret at once," then

said, "Lass, do be careful. Ye understand he has a mighty temper when provoked."

"I will. Margaret told me what he did after Sheffield died, and about the night he nearly destroyed the hall. Did they really find his claymore stuck in the ceiling?"

"Aye. Our laird dinna take well that lad's death. According to my grandfather, the MacDougall had been verra fond of Kyle, had made himself known to lad from the cradle." Tom fell silent for a moment, and then said, "If ye can, get some rest."

"I'll try. Do keep me abreast of Mr. Fraser's progress and don't forget to call as soon as the roses arrive."

"Will do. Goodnight, Beth."

She snapped the phone closed and scanned the room once again with the mirror. Her ghost had apparently retired, which was just as well. She wasn't sure she could handle anymore tonight.

~#~

"*Ha!*" It had taken a week but he finally had her cell phone.

Contemplating the joy he'd take in pitching the noisy thing into the sea, Duncan cautiously lifted the cover. As he examined the lighted screen and buttons, it shrilled out to her. Startled, he dropped it.

"God's breathe!" Did the thing have eyes? He then heard Beth's quick footsteps on the stairs. He scooped up the phone and placed it on the dresser where he'd found it. "Later," he hissed, retreating to a corner.

Panting, Beth ran into the room and flipped open her phone. "Hello?" After a pause she said, "I'm fine, Margaret. Thank you for asking." She listened for a moment. "Terrific. Did they deliver all four varieties? Ah huh. No problem. I'll come right over. No need. I'm turning into quite the sailor." She started straightening the bed with her free hand. "I'll see you soon. Bye."

Duncan cursed as Beth dropped her phone onto the dresser and walked into the bath chamber. In the confusion following Bart's accident, he'd forgotten to ban her from using the bloody launch.

He looked out the window. Cloudless cobalt blue hung over Drasmoor and its flat-as-glass harbor. He could see no evidence of wind and see no clouds on the horizon. Should he deny her a few hours reprieve when all looked calm and safe? Nay. Had he the opportunity to leave the isle, he would. He heaved a resigned sigh. Some did say "practice makes perfect."

Hearing water running into the tub lifted his mood only marginally. He walked to the bath chamber.

"You'd better leave," Beth muttered as she poured her rose and lily crystals into the water. "You're not the only one around here who can pitch a fit when provoked."

Cursing and not yet kenning how she sensed his presence, he backed into the solar.

He looked at the cell phone. He could dispose of the piping box later. 'Twas more important he check the launch; to be sure there were no leaks, enough petrol, and that the oars were in place should the damn engine fail.

Rocked by a sudden gust of cold wind, Beth looked up from her task of securing her rosebushes in the boat's bow to see ominous, lead-bellied thunderheads gathering on the horizon. Frowning, she looked beyond the quay and found Drasmoor's once glass-smooth harbor churning with whitecaps. "Not good."

She'd dallied longer than intended, enjoying her visit

with Margaret—who'd filled Beth with tea, scones, and gossip—and the infamous gardener Ms. Crombie, but now she had to hurry.

Untying the rope that secured her launch to the dock, Beth said, "I'm must apologize, Mrs. Crombie, but I'm afraid we'll have to continue my lesson another time." She pointed to the sky. "I need to start back before that storm hits."

"Ack! And here I am prattling on." The old woman clasped Beth's hand with fragile, gnarled fingers. "Please come often, my lady. I'd love to spend more time with ye, if ye're of a mind."

"Thank you. I'd love to."

Beth settled at the rear of the boat. With an eye on the sky, she yanked on the starter cord and the engine coughed to life. *Please, God, get me home safely.*

Apprehension mounting, she waved a final time to Mrs. Crombie and headed out into the choppy water.

~#~

On Blackstone's parapet, Duncan's gut churned as he strained to see Beth through the sheeting torrent. Cursing himself for allowing her to go, he caught sight of her—stark white in a heaving world of gray—just before the wind shifted and drove the rain sideways yet again, obliterating his view.

He raced to another break in the parapet's battlement hoping for a clearer line of sight to no avail. His futile efforts were wasting precious time. He had to shift, to materialize. He was useless to Beth in his present state.

Against every instinct that clamored to keep her in view, he closed his eyes. He suppressed the vision of Beth's terrified expression and focused on becoming one with the elements, focus on all things solid and whole, his only hope to help her.

Seconds felt like hours as he concentrated on simply being.

When he suddenly felt rain for the first time in centuries and cold for the first time in decades, he gasped, threw back his head and threw wide his arms. He roared as he opened his eyes to the brutal assault of the sheeting rain. He'd done it.

Relieved to his marrow, he resumed his search. On the next flash of lightening he caught sight of Beth, eyes wide in terror, just as she and the boat, now sideways, disappeared beneath a crushing wave.

"*Nayyy!*" ripped from his throat as he dove over the parapet.

~#~

Duncan, clutching Beth's unconscious half-frozen body tight to his heaving chest, raced up Blackstone's stairs to the solar.

Fearing he'd found her too late, he laid her on the bed and ran a shaking hand along her throat. Though her skin wore a worrisome blue cast and felt like ice, to his monumental relief he felt a strong pulse throb beneath his fingertips. He threw the bed covering across her and frantically rubbed her near frozen limbs.

"Can ye hear me, lass?" Getting no response, he shook her. "Lass! Do ye hear me? Ye canna die. Nay, ye be *The One*."

He blinked back tears as he blew on her hands. "Please, God, after bringin' her to me, ye canna be thinking of takin' her back." He'd not—would not—lose this lass. Nay, not after waiting so many lifetimes for her. She had the mettle, the fortitude, to break the curse.

Heart pounding, he scrambled over her and stood

before the carved headboard. He reached above his head and turned the woodcock's head until it came loose in his hand.

Reaching into the four-inch thick wood, he extracted a brittle leather pouch. He tore it open and dropped the Brooch of Lorne—Robert the Bruce's ornate clasp—onto the bed. He stared at what remained in his hand, at the gold and pigeon-blood ruby ring he'd not seen in centuries. His breath caught as the key to his redemption glittered in his palm.

Beth had yet to finish the diary, dinna know all that had gone before, but he had no choice. Before she was lost to him, he had to take her.

He dropped to his knees, cradled her in his arms, and kissed her cold forehead. "Wee ferret, I pray ye can forgive me for what I'm about to do."

He tightened his hold on her. As he kissed her dusky lips, he slipped his wedding ring onto the middle finger of her left hand and the world turned lightening blue.

Chapter 4

Beth awoke in the dark, drenched and chilled to the bone. She winced against the roaring cacophony assaulting her ears from above. Covering them with shaking hands, she briefly looked around the dismal, unfamiliar space. She had no idea where she lay and didn't care. Her head hurt unmercifully, more so when she coughed up a mouthful of salt water. *Think, Beth, think!*

The last thing she could recall was hanging onto her capsized boat for dear life as wave after unrelenting wave tried to push her under.

She winced as lightening cracked again. Hearing what sounded like horses and men screaming, she pictured her beautiful mullioned windows slamming on frail hinges against the keep's walls. She tried to sit. Wondering how she was still alive could wait until she secured the keep. She didn't need—nor could she afford—another broken window.

A heavy weight held her lower torso and legs pinned. She craned her neck to see why and found two lifeless women, their faces dark and bloody—their mouths open like effigy masks, holding her down. Bile rose in her throat. She screamed.

The roof of her prison sprang open before her scream's echo stopped. A heavily muscled arm reached for her. Grasping the man's hand, Beth stared, mouth agape, into the steel blue eyes of her rescuer.

"Duncan?"

The Laird of Blackstone looked about the confines of the fractured coach. Seeing only one woman alive, one who looked nothing like the bride he'd been told to expect, he cursed. He shoved the dead women aside and pulled up on the crying woman's hand. The Bruce would pay with his life for this.

As he lifted her through the door, lightening flashed. Its light bounced off the rubies in the ring she wore on her left hand. Sudden, overwhelming relief flooded him. It was his betrothal ring. Thank God! 'Twas of no account that the abbess had gilded the lily—hell, the woman was apparently blind—for his bride lived.

Before he could set her on the ground, her hands flew to his face. Her cold fingers fluttered across his cheeks for an instant before her arms wrapped tightly around his neck.

"Oh, Duncan! I've never..." She stopped and he followed her gaze. Her eyes grew wide as they took in the carnage he and his men had wrought.

"Duncan...?"

What followed, he could only guess at. Before he could ask her to repeat herself, she turned ashen and promptly fainted.

"Well, ye did it again. Will ye never learn?" Angus, his second in command, asked as he peered over his shoulder. "One look at ye and yer softer-than-puddin' bride faints." His best friend's gaze shifted, as did his own, from the woman's face to her outlandish clothing. "And what on earth is she wearing?"

Duncan had no idea, but she'd been living on the continent and their ways were strange. Perhaps his intended had dressed as a man thinking it safer. Her odd leggings would make for an easier, faster ride home, in any event. She could ride astride on the way to their wedding.

~#~

Beth opened her eyes, this time in Blackstone's great hall, standing in Duncan's fierce embrace. Without a word, he spun her toward the small man with his back to the fire. Fire? Why was there a fire? She'd yet to have the flues cleaned.

She blinked, trying to understand why the fat little man in brown was in her home and what he now mumbled about. He said something to Duncan in Gael, and her ghost growled something in return. Head still spinning, she pushed on Duncan's arm, but his grip only tightened.

She ran a dry tongue over her chapped lips and again tasted salt. "Please let go."

Duncan responded by issuing another order to the concerned looking man before her. The room continued to list so she tried focusing on the large wooden crucifix on the little man's chest.

What in hell is going on?

Frowning, the brown-cloaked man continued mumbling and Duncan answered. Pity clouded the little man's eyes when he placed her hand in Duncan's. He finally addressed her. When he asked, "Doth thou pledge thy troth?" Beth's heart tripped with understanding.

Stunned, she tried to pull her hand from her ghost's

grasp. She slurred, "I can't think, let alone..." and the world went black.

"She has swooned," Father Given sputtered as if everyone in the hall were blind. "We must stop the ceremony."

Duncan, his right arm fully occupied with his faint bride, reached out with his left arm and grabbed the priest's frock. He hissed feeling the stitches in his wounded shoulder tear open. "Priest, we will continue. She consented, said 'Aye Katherine LeBeau' before swooning and I've witnesses aplenty who'll willingly attest to it." He glanced over his shoulder to his clansmen standing around the room. To the man they all nodded. Duncan again faced the priest. "I dinna rescue her just an hour ago—killing seven men in the doing—to have ye now deny her wish to wed. 'Tis not her fault the poor wee lass was attacked by the Bruce's men." He leveled a glare at the priest then shook him for good measure. "Continue!"

Duncan had to make Katherine LeBeau Demont his bride before sunset. He had no choice.

Their regent, the Duke of Albany, was determined to control Katherine's dowered lands through Duncan's loyalty. The man had made it abundantly clear this distant niece of his was to be Duncan's bride by this date or Duncan would lose all his holdings, no doubt, to the Bruce.

Just the *thought* of his clan—ever loyal to him— being turned out upon this brutal land without food or shelter, without his strong arm to protect them, was intolerable. He shook the priest again. "Do we ken one another?"

The priest reluctantly nodded and raced through the

remainder of the ceremony. When the priest finally mumbled "Amen", Duncan uttered a satisfied grunt.

At his side, Angus slapped him on the back in congratulations causing Duncan to growl, "Damn, man!"

"Augh, Duncan, I'm sorry. I forgot."

"If 'twas yer bloody back, I doubt ye would."

His last wife Eleanor had done her evil well. She'd been dead a fortnight and his shoulder was still a ragged, inflamed mess after her assault. Had he not been made wary by finding her traitorous missive to her lover, she might well have succeeded in killing him. When she fell on her own blade during their struggle and died, she'd done him a favor. He'd never liked her, but having to kill her—a woman—wouldn't have set well on his conscience.

He'd sworn then never to marry again. Having pledged his fidelity thrice to keep his clan secure and suffered the consequences, one would have thought thrice enough to please God and king. But nay. Before Eleanor's grave had had a chance to sprout grass or his shoulder to heal, Albany's edict—King's seal and all—had arrived.

He looked down at the drenched bride in his arms. Her eyes were ringed with soot and her cheeks streaked black and bloody. A mottled bruise the size of a goose egg marred her high forehead. No wonder the woman had fainted.

He looked at his friend. "While I carry her to the solar, order the food served."

"I'll take her," Angus offered.

"Nay. She's mine now, for better or worse."

~#~

Beth opened her eyes to find familiar bedposts and an

equally familiar board and beamed ceiling. She was in her bed, in Blackstone's solar. She sighed. It had all been a dreadful dream. Thank heaven.

She stretched and nearly screamed. Good Lord, what had happened to her legs and back?

The storm. She remembered struggling to get onto the capsized boat. She must have wrenched a muscle or three. Cautiously, she rolled onto her side and saw heavy drapes hanging where only her sparkling mullion windows should be. Her brain then filled with flashes of being trapped in a box with two dead women, of Duncan, of severed limbs and bleeding men, and then the priest.

Her gaze flew around the room. Oh, God! The tapestries, the gilt mirror, the brass and-irons in the fireplace were all gone. Seeing that the dresser with her prized make-up collection had also disappeared while she slept brought her straight to her feet. The room spun and she reached for a bed poster. She was still trapped in her nightmare. She took several deep breaths and pinched her wrist. Hard. Nothing changed.

"Just calm down, Beth. This is only a dream. A bad dream, but nothing more. Just wash your face and you'll see." Head aching and heart pounding, she walked into the bathroom.

She stifled a scream with her hands.

Where her tub should have been hung odd, long-sleeved gowns. Where her sink should have been sat large chests. Where the toilet should have been sat nothing. She felt an overwhelming urge to scream yet again.

"This can't be happening." She spun and raced to the east facing windows and threw back a covering. Her beautiful mullion windows were gone. Only soft lavender light and a gentle sea breeze greeted her.

It was dawn; the sun was just starting to gild the hills across the bay. She couldn't have lost a whole day, could she? Panicked, she searched the shore for the familiar, white stucco buildings of Drasmoor, for the church steeple and flower-lined streets. She found only fine spirals of smoke rising from a myriad of squat thatched buildings scattered near the beach and into the hills. The boats lining the beach were small with reefed sails. There wasn't an outboard motor in sight.

"Where the hell am I?" She pushed an agitated hand through her hair, winced then tentatively explored the lump on her forehead.

Had she washed-up on some distant beach where there just happened to be another castle? Given the ferocity of the storm, it was altogether possible. Yes, that's what happened. She hadn't lost her mind. The rest was simply a nightmare.

She heaved a sigh and wondered where her rescuer hid. Probably still asleep given the hour. When her stomach growled, she muttered, "No wonder you have a headache." She'd missed two meals on top of being knocked unconscious. But more pressing than hunger was her need to find a bathroom.

Since she couldn't wander the halls in the tissue thin nightgown someone—she hoped it had been a woman—put on her, she looked for her clothes. Not finding her jeans or sweater, she donned a green silk sleeveless cloak.

She peeked into the hall and heard someone stirring below.

Her unease only grew as she reached the third level. The floor plan of this keep was identical to hers, but the décor wasn't.

This castle hadn't been modernized. Oil sconces lined the walls and brittle rushes crunched under foot. The owner had to be a purest. Wondering if the owner had opened his home to tourists—which would explain why the place looked like an armory—she turned a corner and collided with a small, dark-haired woman of about thirty years dressed in a period costume.

"I'm so sorry." Beth steadied the startled woman carrying a mountain of cloth. "I was just looking for the bathroom."

"Um..., " The woman, her dark eyes growing round, looked about helplessly.

Beth, deciding the woman had to be new here as well, gave the petite woman's arm a pat. "Never mind. I'll find it myself." As she turned to go, the woman tugged Beth's sleeve and pointed in the direction she'd just come from. Great. She'd managed to pass the bathroom.

Following the woman, Beth wondered how far from home she'd landed. Would someone be available to give her a lift back to Drasmoor right away? The Silversteins were probably having a fit thinking she'd drowned. She needed to call them. Surely her host had a phone for emergencies, if nothing else.

Arriving back in the solar, Beth groaned. If she didn't find the bathroom soon, she'd explode.

The woman, murmuring in French, held out the bundle of clothing. Beth smiled as best she could. "Miss, I need to find a bathroom. Now." She placed a hand on her lower belly and started to jig. The woman's face lit with understanding.

The lady laughed. "*Ah, oui, oui, madame.*"

"Yes, I have to wee wee, as soon as humanely possible, if you don't mind."

To Beth's astonishment, the woman reached under the bed and pulled out a chamber pot.

"Ah." Apparently, her host not only turned his back on electricity but on indoor plumbing, as well. Perhaps this castle was a museum. There were a plethora of them listed on maps and in tourist guidebooks. She took the crazed pot from her hostess's hand. When in Rome...

~#~

Duncan, having no appetite, pushed his still full trencher away. He'd not slept, being sore and fevered, and now felt far worse. Adding to his misery, he'd peaked into the solar late last night to be sure his bride still breathed and been shocked by her state. Not only was the woman bruised and battered, she was as plain as porridge. How he would garner the enthusiasm to bed the woman was beyond knowing. But it had to be done—and soon—if he wanted to keep all he'd slaved over.

"Duncan, why so glum?"

He looked up to find Flora Campbell, his first wife's sister, at his elbow. As usual she looked the vision of womanhood draped in a vivid blue damask cotehardie that enhanced the tone of her milk white skin. Her deep chestnut eyes laughed at him—danced above a perfectly bowed grin. "Where is thy fair new lady?"

Flora had no doubt heard all that had transpired last night, right down to the finest details about his new wife's appearance. Having little patience for Flora's taunting humor on the best of days, he felt the sudden urge to wipe the smug expression from her face with the back of his hand. "Good morn, Flora."

"Can I offer ye something else?" She leaned

forward—giving him a clear view down her décolleté—and tipped his trencher. "Ye apparently have no appetite for what ye've been given."

As always, Flora wielded her tongue like a double-edged claymore. If ye took offense, she'd claim ye'd misconstrued her meaning. And if a willing man waylaid her after she'd flirted outrageously, she acted the wounded party. Lord knew he'd broken up many a fight after a night's mead had loosened his men's inhibitions—and her tongue—to pay any heed to her beauty. Which, according to Angus, was reason enough for her taunting him.

Duncan had put forth five good men—not close friends—in the hopes of marrying her off, but to no avail. Regrettably, Flora was not a *domina*—a wealthy widow entitled to one third of her husband's estate, so he'd not been able tempt a greedy man with land. Nor was she religious enough to become a voweress, one of those mature women who chose to devote their lives to God in some distant nunnery. Flora was only a beautiful, poorly dowered woman who chose remain unmarried just to annoy him.

About to tell her to leave him in peace, a murmur rose in the hall. He looked up to find his bruised bride standing in the doorway beside his advisor's wife, Rachael. Studying his ladywife, he couldn't help but wonder what he'd done that she should be foisted upon him. He shrugged. It didn't matter at present, for his new ladywife appeared more than a wee bit frightened as her gaze swept the crowded hall.

He made his way toward her. When her gaze made contact with his, she blanched then swayed. He was nay the bonniest of men to be sure, but that was ridiculous, definitely not a good sign that she was again ready to faint at the mere sight of him before one and all.

"My lady." He took her cold hand in his to steady her.

Beth's breath caught. Duncan's calloused hands felt not warm but hot as they swallowed hers.

And it was true.

Her ghost was now flesh and blood, tall and gloriously handsome despite his high flush. But how could this be? And who were all these people staring at her? She knew she looked frightful without make-up, but staring bordered on rude. And why were they all dressed for a costume party at dawn?

With a hand at her waist, Duncan guided her through the throng to the opposite end of the hall. He pulled out a chair and motioned for her to take a seat. With effort, she tore her gaze from the women in their odd headdresses and the bearded men wearing broadswords only to see the very falcon chairs she'd retrieved from the storeroom. Her heart slammed into her ribs.

She grasped Duncan's hot hands with her now frigid ones. Shaking, fearing the answer, she asked, "Where the hell am I?"

Chapter 5

Anger roiled in Duncan's belly. He'd suffered through three loveless political marriages and now the house of Stewart had foisted a raving lunatic on him.

Mutely, he watched as his new wife, muttering and wringing her hands, pace the solar. He understood only a scattering of words, for she spoke her English quickly and with an unfamiliar accent. His efforts to calm her using French and Gael had been for naught. She only shook her head as she continued her frantic muttering and pacing.

Feeling a strong kinship with the biblical Job and annoyed beyond endurance, he finally bellowed, "Katherine, sit ye!"

She jumped, blanched, and with mouth agape stared at him. She then took a deep breath and glared back. "I'm Beth." She tapped her chest. "Beth."

"Beth?"

"Aye." She crossed the room and tapped his chest. "Duncan." She tapped her own. "Beth."

Ah, she wanted him to call her Beth. Fine, he'd call her rhubarb if would stop her damn muttering and pacing. "Beth."

She waved her hands about asking another rapid question, and he shook his head in confusion. Sighing in apparent exasperation, she took his hand and pulled him to the window.

"Where am I?" She asked the question very slowly—as if she spoke to a bairn—and pointed to the village.

"Drasmoor."

"And this?" She waved a fluttering hand around the room and to the floor.

They were finally making progress. Perhaps she was not wode—mad—but merely simple. He could only pray. "Blackstone. I am the MacDougall, yer laird and husband."

When her eyes grew huge, he stood straighter. She was obviously impressed, as well she should be. She then mewed, "*ooh*," in what could only be described as agony and crossed the room. She sat on the bed and buried her face in her hands. Confused, he went to her side and lifted her chin to find a disturbing flood of tears. "What ails ye, lass?"

"What year is this?"

"Doth not ye ken?" When she shook her head, he sighed. Slowly he told her, "'Tis the year of our Lord one thousand, four hundred and eight."

"How?"

Aye, how indeed, had life passed so quickly? Not knowing the answer himself, he merely opened his hands and shrugged.

The simple gesture nearly brought him to his knees. He grabbed the bedpost for support as beads of sweat erupted across his face and icy chills swept his limbs. His innards started to churn. *Damn Eleanor and her blade.*

"Duncan?" His new bride's shaking hand flew to his

forehead. "My Lord! What's wrong?"

He pushed her hand away and straightened. "Naught is wrong. Rest ye now. Rachael will come for ye at sup."

She tried to press her hand to his forehead again.

"*Nay.*" He dodged to her right. He just needed to rest, to shake off the lassitude and fever that continued to confound him but he was not ill. He forced a smile. His confused bride could probably do with a little rest, as well. The bruising on her forehead had deepened in hue. Only heaven and Rachael knew what other damage hid beneath his bride's borrowed gown.

Standing in the solar doorway, looking at his befuddle wife, he silently cursed. Once he felt more himself, the Bruce would pay dearly for this insult. Albany's insult couldn't be dealt with swiftly or as obviously, but in due course he, too, would feel the wrath of the MacDougall. He studied the confusion and hurt in Beth's eyes. God's teeth! His revenge would suit the crime.

He was being deprived of the possibility for having a healthy and competent heir.

~#~

Beth, standing before the solar window, pinched her arm one more time. "Ouch!"

Spending the day in hiding, telling herself she was caught in some macabre dream had accomplished nothing. The sun had risen to its zenith and the village of Drasmoor had remained as she'd found it at dawn, just a scattering of little thatched huts. Many of the boats had returned with the day's catch and at least fifty people now milled around the shoreline.

How on earth had this happened? Had she brought it on herself?

She'd been a secret Anglophile for years. She consumed historical romances—particularly those with a swatch of tartan or thistle on their covers—like they were made of air. She'd frequently wished she could live in the past with a dark, handsome hero, but good Lord, she'd never expected it to happen!

Or had her wishing for Duncan to be flesh and blood been the cause? Whoever said, "Be careful what you wish for," hadn't known the half of it. And here she was in the early fifteenth century—the age of chivalry and romance with a Highland hunk having claimed her—without so much as a mascara wand. How cruel can life get? She heaved a sigh.

"Wishful thinking has never gotten you anywhere but here, Beth, so you'd best <u>do</u> something or you'll never get back to your own world."

Her stomach growled in earnest making her decision on where to start simple. After eating, she would search out her husband.

Husband.

She looked down at the gold and ruby ring she now wore. She didn't remember Duncan placing it on her finger, but then she couldn't remember much more than leaning into his side as she wavered before the priest. Apparently, in this day and age, brides needn't consent—let alone be lucid—to wed. But why had he agreed to their marriage? They'd only shared a week together, and had only spoken once. She shook her head and spun the ring on her finger.

Years ago she'd reconciled herself to the fact that she'd never wear such a ring, that love wasn't something she would ever experience. Had he fallen in love with her? Was that why she'd shifted in time? More importantly, was she capable of falling in love in return?

She grunted, unable to lie to herself. Her simple fascination with her handsome spirit had converted to something more meaningful, deeper, days ago. Hadn't she dreamt of him? Hadn't she pictured him sitting across from her chatting the nights away? Of course she'd pictured them together in the twenty first century...

Her stomach growled again. Out of habit she looked for a mirror to check her make-up. "Oh, God." The thought of mingling with the people downstairs with her face as bare as a baby's bottom twice in one day made her hands shake.

She'd been too confused and upset when Rachael had helped her dress this morning to worry, but not now.

Her hands traveled from her lips to the beautiful brocade gown she wore, across the rich peacock colors to the thick pearl beading on the bodice. The gown's beauty had distracted her this morning. That, and battling Rachael's attempts to beautify her. The Frenchwoman, to Beth's horror, wanted to pluck Beth's eyebrows off and raise her forehead by plucking out her natural hairline to create the same high-domed look Rachael, herself, sported. Rachael, having lost that battle, decreed Beth *would* wear a headdress, the woman's personal favorite being an over-sized, over-starched nun-like affair of white linen. After another half hour argument filled with hand gestures and wretched eye rolling, Beth reluctantly consented to having her hair braided and tucked into two golden snoods that covered her ears and was secured to her head by a smooth brass ringlet.

Her hands shifted to the narrow, jeweled belt at her waist. She fingered one of the smooth purple stones and sighed. She only had two choices, starve to death in her room or face her demons sans make-up but in a beautiful dress. Neither held any appeal, but her head ached and her gut burned. Resigned to the inevitable, she pinched her cheeks, licked her lips and headed for the door.

In the great hall she found a half dozen men sitting at long tables. Some nodded as they stood. When Rachael entered, Beth hurried over to her.

"Where is Duncan?" Hoping to ease the pounding in her head, she reached for an untouched loaf of dark bread on the table. She broke off a piece and found it dry and gritty. Hoping to soften it enough to swallow, she peeked into a nearby pitcher and sniffed. Ale. Yuk!

"The MacDougall 'tis with my husband, *tres honoree dame.*"

"Where?"

"In yon bailey." Rachael waved toward the east facing windows.

Beth smiled. She'd not had to repeat her words to be understood. *Keep it short and sweet, Beth, and you might just survive until you can find your way out of this nightmare.*

"May I have some water, please?"

"Of course, *madame.*" Rachael scanned the room and muttered, "Zee lazy lass. 'Twill be brought to yer solar forthwith."

"Thank you, but I'll just have a glass here."

Rachael frowned at her for a moment, shrugged, then turned away.

Beth nibbled on her bread and studied her fellow diners and the room's decor. Most of the men, huddled in groups, and the women, shuffling past with arms full of ale tankards, were fair and blue eyed. They ranged in age but not one—save the priest— carried any spare fat, which she found surprising, given the volume of food they were consuming. After watching several men pitch bones to the floor, she cautiously peeked under her chair and immediately raised her feet.

An enterprising student could have re-created a dinosaur from the waste in the rushes. No wonder the room smelled rank. And all this time she'd been blaming the occupants' lack of deodorant.

The bread continued to roll like pebbles in Beth's mouth and she looked about for Rachael. Wondering what could be keeping her, Beth noticed a beautiful familiar looking woman studying her from a shadowed corner of the hall. Beth smiled tentatively. The woman rose. As she approached, Beth realized why the woman looked so familiar. The woman's flawless skin, chocolate doe eyes, and mahogany hair made her the spitting image of Winona Ryder. *Oh, lordy, just what I need. Another naturally beautiful woman in my life.*

"*Bon jour, tres honoree dame.*" The lovely woman curtsied. "*Je m'appelle Flora Campbell.*"

"Good morning." Beth's smile faltered. "I'm afraid I don't speak French."

"Nay? But 'tis the tongue of all *gentils hommes*. Ye must speak."

"No. I'm sorry."

Her confusion evident, *Miss I'm Too Lovely for My Clothes* tried again. "I be Flora Campbell. I bid ye welcome." To Beth, the woman didn't look so much welcoming—weelcooming, as she pronounced it—as curious.

"Thank you." Beth waved toward the empty place next to her. "Please sit." As Flora made herself comfortable Beth assessed the lady with an expert eye.

Yup, the woman's full lips, kangaroo-long lashes, and flawless skin with its dusting of rose at the cheeks were all products of Mother Nature. Even her choice of a magenta gown was perfect. It enhanced her coloring and accentuated her perfect figure. Beth took a deep breath and swallowed her envy. Unfortunately, swallowing it couldn't keep her from feeling like a warthog under the woman's scrutiny.

"Ye spake oddly," Flora told her. "Where from cometh ye?"

"America." When her companion's brow furrowed, Beth added, "From across the sea, far away."

"Ah, and your dower?"

"Dower?"

"Ye hostile and lands."

Ah, she means dowery. Why else would a handsome man like Duncan MacDougall choose someone like her, huh? "I have a castle on an isle."

"'Tis as grand?" Flora's wave encompassed the room.

"Absolutely identical."

Apparently not pleased, Flora cast a critical eye over Beth's costume. "If thou art well-dowered, why doth ye wear the gowns of the laird's third wife?"

Did she just say third wife? The wad of bread Beth had been chewing suddenly clotted her throat. How the hell many wives has Duncan had? She'd read about only one. Is this woman—now looking down her perfect little nose at her—implying she was number four? And where the hell is Rachael and the water? A body could die of thirst around here.

"Ye must ken ye uncle, the Duke of Albany well."

"No...nay, I've never met him." Beth missed

whatever the woman said next as she continued to ruminate over Duncan's other wives. Did they divorce during this time? She didn't think so.

Flora tapped Beth's arm to get her attention. "Why, then, dost Albany find ye digne to wed The MacDougall?"

Beth shrugged. "You'll have to ask him, Flora. I haven't a clue."

"Clue?"

Beth didn't get a chance to explain her American slang. Rachael, looking quite pleased, had arrived with a large pan of hot water, toweling, and a small mirror.

"Ye water and glass, *madame*."

As the fourth Lady MacDougall groaned, Flora curtsied and backed away. She wove her way back through the cluttered hall and resumed her place in the far corner. She picked up her needlework and pretended to embroider as she studied Blackstone's newest mistress through lowered lashes.

So this is the next wife Duncan the Black gets to torment. The new Lady MacDougall was certainly nothing to look at and as addled, poor thing, as rumor accounts. So how will he dispose of this one? Twill, no doubt, be the easiest to eliminate yet. For kill her he will, just as he killed her beloved sister. And if he dinna, she'd tend to it herself.

~#~

Duncan ran an agitated hand through his hair as he stood in the bailey and studied the shafts of papers Isaac Silverstein had compiled.

"Have we enough to finish the kirk *and* get through the winter?"

Isaac rolled a shoulder, "*Oui*, but only if ye dinna

have the brass effigy made. Simply carve Mary's name into the stone, and forego the elaborate woodwork."

No effigy. As he buried her, he'd *promised* Mary she'd be memorialized in bronze. His second and third wives he'd made no such promise to, but Mary had been a good woman and deserved the honor. Too, her sister Flora and her father, the Campbell, would expect it.

He looked about the bailey, his gaze settling on the blacksmith pounding out hinges for doors he'd yet to find enough wood to make. Perhaps he'd been foolish in not taking up the Duke of Albany's offer. 'Twas not too late. He could don his armor and once again sell his soul and arm, becoming a mercenary fighting in Normandy for the French King against Henry IV of England. The thought of maiming and killing men he held no personal grudge against yet again he found distressing. As much as leaving Blackstone unfinished and in the hands of untried warriors, for he knew Angus and Douglas would insist on following him. But if it has to be done. . .

Damn his hapless sire.

"Halt fashing, Duncan," Isaac murmured. 'Tis making ye ill. We must simply be prudent. All will be well."

"We lost half of our wee kine in that late snowstorm, Isaac. Ye ken we must now barter or buy meat if we don't want to butcher our breeders."

"True, but the fishing is going well, *non*? The women are drying flakes in salt as we speak, and the crops look promising, so we willna starve."

"Looking promising and being harvested are not the same thing."

"Duncan, do ye not trust me?"

He looked at his advisor, the man who not ten years

ago had been sentenced by the villagers of Ballimoor to cumburenda—burning at the stake—and sighed. "Aye, I trust ye. Ye've kept me afloat with ye wee trading all these years with naught but a few marks of silver."

"And will continue to do so. Here." He handed Duncan an invitation bearing the King's seal. "The tournament is to be held in honor of His Majesty's birthday in two months time. No man can beat ye at the lists or at jousting, so yer fears are for naught, *mon ami*." Isaac gave him a slap on the shoulder as he walked away.

Duncan hissed as his back muscles knotted like the tarred shrouds on a ship. Pain radiated down his spine and left arm. "Merciful mother of God, why will I not heal?"

He felt a tap on his good arm.

"We need to talk." His wode new ladywife stood at his side with her hands on her hips.

He frowned seeing her for the first time in the harsh light of day. God's Breath! Save for the bruising and the silver flashing from her gray eyes, she had to be the plainest female he'd ever beheld. His gaze instinctively traveled downward. A good foot taller than she, he had no difficulty looking into the gaping bodice of her gown. He seriously doubted she could nourish a babe with what little she had to offer, let alone keep a man like himself— one with a preference for heavy-breasted women— satisfied. The thought of breeding prompted him to ask, "How many years be ye?"

She clutched the top of her gown and frowned at him. "Twenty-four. Why?"

The answer surprised him. He'd been told she was just sixteen. Did Albany think he'd not ask, or had His Conniving Highness merely assumed she'd have a strong enough sense of self-preservation to lie? And what other lies has Albany foisted upon him?

"Duncan, we need to talk. I need to know how I came to be here, and I *really* need to go back. And why did you marry me? We certainly don't know each other well enough." She heaved an exasperated sigh as he stared at her. "I know. I probably brought this about with my foolish daydreams, but all this..." Her arms waved about. "In truth, this is nothing like I imagined. Not with men urinating off the battlements into the ocean, food being thrown to the floor, my being dressed in wife number three's clothes—which don't fit as you've already noticed—and my not being able to drink the damn water."

What the hell was she ranting about in her odd English? Why would she want to drink water? And what gave her the impression he'd tolerate that tone of voice from her? "Wife, I dinna like ye speech nor ken yer aggravations." Seeing the men stopping their work to stare, he grabbed her arm.

Hauling his agitated bride toward the keep, he whispered through clenched teeth, "Were ye not at meat, wife? Were ye not clothed? What do ye find so grievous?"

"Stop manhandling me!" She tried to pull from his grasp.

"Nay, not 'til ye be calm and respond with thought."

"Fine." She sounded more dejected than angry as she tripped over her gown on the stairs to the solar. "I'll answer anything you like, so long as you help me get back to where I belong."

"Ye belong here and ye belong to me, woman." He walked her across solar and pushed her into a chair before the cold fireplace. In the process, he felt another stitch tear in his shoulder. When the pain eased—when he opened his eyes, he groaned seeing her expression.

"Bloody hell, woman, dinna start to greet." He couldna abide a woman's tears. They made him feel guilty, made something inside him want to run and hide. Or smash something.

She wiped the wetness from her cheeks and straightened. "I'm not *greeting*. I just want to go home; to my coffee, to my mullioned windows, to my make-up, and God help me, to my fu—screwed-up plumbing and kerosene stove." Seeing his shock, she blanched white and fresh tears coursed down her cheeks. "I'm sorry, I didn't mean to swear." She turned her face to the window and whispered. "It's just that I don't understand any of this, and I'm frightened." She took a deep shuddering breath and murmured, "So very frightened."

He had no idea what *caw fee* or *o seen stove* meant, but he did understand her terror.

He took a seat across from her and reached for her hands. "Lass, were ye a voweress?"

She'd come to him from a French nunnery where she'd been living since her husband's death. Since only the most pious—the religiously zealous—did this, her cursing not only came as a shock, it underscored the level of her distress.

He wanted to strangle Albany.

His second wife, unbeknownst to him, had been a religious fanatic and look how that ended? 'Twas sad, that this woman should also be land rich and coin poor. Otherwise, she might have had the hundred pounds sterling per year needed to keep Albany from marrying her off, and they would have both been spared.

"Tis sorry I be, lass, but ye be my bride and here ye must remain."

"*No*. I could lose my *home*." She wrung her hands. "I need to get back to the twenty-first century where I belong."

He blinked. He couldna possibly have heard her correctly. If he had, she was truly brain-coddled. But no matter, she had to remain at Blackstone if he and his clan were to keep *their* home.

They spoke *at* each other rather than *with* each other, for what felt like hours.

Beth finally gave up.

Now, she simply wanted to hide from his furious perusal. Her eyes felt blood-shot and her nose...she didn't want to think about. It had the nasty habit of turning scarlet from bridge to tip whenever tears threatened and they'd done more than threaten in the last half-hour. She suspected she looked like a baboon's ass, which, no doubt, did little to enhance her credibility.

She stood and walked to the window while Duncan, an obviously unhappy man, tried to digest what she'd told him.

"Ye be wode, woman, if ye truly believe yerself a spirit."

Great. Not only did he have no memory of her, he still didn't understand. To make matters worse, he had called her *wode* frequently enough for her to understand he thought her insane. "No, Duncan, I'm not a spirit. I do know—ken—I'm flesh and blood."

She twisted the ring on her hand. Was she the first wife to wear it or the fourth? Thank heaven she'd found Duncan's diary and had spoken to him before this nightmare began. If she hadn't, she'd likely be jumping out the window after enduring his ceaseless ranting and glaring.

"Duncan, stop." She held up her hands in defeat. "We're not getting anywhere. You can't or won't help me, and I'm too tired right now to care." The dull throb at her temples had converted to stabbing needles of pain behind her eyes. Her teeth were even beginning to ache. "I need something to eat."

Obviously exasperated, Duncan threw up his hands. When he resumed his thick burred grumbling and huffing at a staccato pace before the fireplace, she walked out the door.

~#~

"She then turned her back to me and walked out! *On me, her laird!*" Parched, Duncan reached for the tankard on the hall table and took a deep swallow of ale. "I tell ye, Angus, this woman isna long for the grave. Had I not already lost three wives, I swear I would have smote her then and there, putting us both out of our miseries." The utter gall of the wench!

"My lord?"

He turned to find Flora at his elbow, grinning like a cat with a mouth full of feathers. "*What?*"

"Yer lady, sire. She's not at Vespers. The priest is most anxious. He canna start without her and she canna be found."

Duncan clamped down on an oath. "Start without her."

"But—"

"Do as I say!" He waved her away. When she curtsied and slid away looking none to pleased, Duncan cursed.

Angus grinned. "Now what?"

72

Duncan took another swallow and came to his feet. "We find her, then haul her to the chapel, trussed if need be."

~#~

When Beth's capsized launch was discovered bobbing in the harbor, a hue and cry raced through Drasmoor. Women, keening, raced along the beaches and headlands in search of Beth. Men, swearing and praying, ran for their boats and grappling hooks. Tom Silverstein raced to his launch and headed for Blackstone.

The ride across the harbor felt like the longest of his life though he pushed the throttle to maximum speed. With his gaze raking the boulders at Blackstone's base for Beth, he nearly collided with Blackstone's quay. He threw the engine into reverse. As the engine choked and the sea churned, nearly swamping the stern, he threw a line around a cast iron pole and jumped.

Yelling Beth's name at the top of his lungs, he tore through the bailey and into the keep. Heart pounding, palms sweating, he ran up the stairs and into the solar. The room stood empty. He sniffed the still air. Something had caught fire, but what? He bellowed for her again. Silence answered.

Shaken, fearing Beth had truly drowned and been washed out to sea, he walked to the rumpled bed and spied a bit of torn leather and a wink of gold. He moved the covers and couldn't believe his eyes. He was staring at the famed Broach of Lorne—the only tangible proof the MacDougall clan had defeated Robert the Bruce in battle—rested among the coverlet's folds. His heart nearly stopped. No one had seen the Bruce's bejeweled ornament in six centuries. He'd come to believe it a legend, just as his treacherous heart had begun to suspect the coming of *the one* had to be. He reached out a tentative hand to pick it up and realized the bedding was wet. He brought the damask to his nose and sniffed. There was no mistaking the clammy scent. Seawater.

His heart stuttered with understanding. "She hasna drowned." His laird had somehow rescued her. Tom fingered the broach with shaking fingers. He listened. Hearing nothing, feeling nothing but a heavy stillness in the room, he took a shuddering breath. "It has begun."

Now, all he could do was he pray for Beth. His infant son's future depended on it.

Chapter 6

Disappointed by Duncan's anger and his resistance to helping her, Beth roamed from room to room thumping on panels, spying behind wall hangings, and looking under beds and rugs in the hopes of finding a secret passage that could take her back to her world. When none materialized, she, desperate, sought out mirrors thinking she might be able to pass through one like *Alice in the Looking Glass*. After hours of searching through the dusty keep and storage rooms, nothing had changed but the condition of her clothing.

Her only consolation...her head felt better. Whatever Rachael had put in her tea had certainly taken care of her headache. Knowing such medicinal cures existed in this day and time improved her mood marginally.

Bone weary, she sought refuge from the curious in an out-of-the way sitting room. She ran her fingers over the spines of the books on various tables around the room. Chartier's *Le Belle Dame sans Merci*. "Humph, French."

Books had become an important part of her life over the years. They were her comfort and respite in an often cold and uncaring world. She desperately needed her copy of Lorraine Heath's *Parting Gifts*. She reread the novel during bleak periods when she needed an excuse for a good cathartic cry and the reassurance that good times regularly followed times like these. Or Diana Gabaldon's Highlander series. She sighed at the irony. Here she had her own flesh and blood Highland hunk— more glorious than she even imagined Gabaldon's Jamie Frasier to be—and she was hiding, because she refused to deal with the pain.

During their *discussion* it become painfully apparent Duncan couldn't abide the sight of her.

She heaved a sigh and opened the elaborately decorated *Abby of the Holy Grail* and discovered—after much effort—the author wanted to teach her how to build a nunnery in her heart. She snorted. "Not likely."

She opened the little *The Book of Hours*, only to find awkward sounding prayers the author expected the reader to recite eight times a day. Like anyone in their right mind had that kind of time on their hands.

She examined *A Calendar of Saints*, innumerable prayer sheets, lyrics sheets, poems, a volume containing recipes for curing bizarre sounding medical conditions, a volume of veterinary recommendations, and saints' legends. The number of religious texts surprised her. Though Catholic, Duncan didn't strike her as a particularly religious man, so why did he have so many? After a long hunt she finally found what she was hoping to find. With all the wives coming and going around Blackstone, she knew there had to be a few romances somewhere in the mix.

"Let's see. *Lancelot*, *Tristen*, *Merlin*, *Sir Degrevant*, whoever he is, and the *Quest for the Holy Grail*. I may not lose my mind after all."

She carried her prizes to a high, window seat and made herself comfortable. She open *Lancelot* and was disappointed to find it written in French, as were *Tristen* and *Sir Degrevant*. She opened *Quest for the Holy Grail* and sighed. It was written in English. Not hers, but close enough.

Within minutes her gaze drifted from the awkward text to the widow, her thoughts again on escaping her nightmare. She studied the water lapping the rocks below. A black churning sea had been her last real memory. She'd tasted it even as she awoke trapped in the carriage. Her eyes widened, her heart thudded. That's *it!*

She had to get into the water to escape this time and re-enter her own.

"Pardon, *tres honoree dame*, I did not mean to disturb ye."

She started and turned to find Rachael's husband, Isaac Silverstein, standing in the doorway with his arms full of scrolls. She waved him in. "Please come. I didn't know—ken— this room was being used." Heart thudding, she started to rise.

"Nay, please sit. Ye'll not *incomoder* me."

Beth grinned at his mix of French and English, so like his wife's. Her awe at meeting people she'd come to know only as historical figures through Tom's stories and Duncan's diary had yet to wane.

Isaac, tall and thin, like his multi-great grandson Tom, walked toward her. "Why be ye not at Vespers?"

"Vespers?"

"Prayers."

"Ah. I'm not Catholic."

He frowned then tipped up the book in her hands to read the cover. "A good tale."

"I hope so."

"Ye dinna choose a religious tomb?"

She wrinkled her nose. "I prefer escapism." When his

frown deepened, she clarified, "I like legends and tales. Love stories with happy endings."

"Ah. And yer first husband, dame? His passion?"

She felt a blush rise. "I've never been married." Seeing his eyes widen, she added, "Until now...to Duncan."

"But *non, madame*. You were married in France, *oui*?"

"No. I've never been to France, and I've certainly never been married before." She spun the gold band on her finger. How could something so beautiful—that should hold such promise—make her feel so empty? "This is the very first time."

Scowling, he studied her for a moment then asked, "*Madame*, may I ask ye full Christian name?"

"Katherine Elizabeth MacDougall Pudding...ah, MacDougall." She grinned. "Hmmm, I have two MacDougall's now."

"Hmm, indeed." He chewed his lower lip for a moment. "*Excusez moi, madame*, I have something I must attend."

She stood. "It was a pleasure speaking with you. Rachael has been such ..."

Isaac raced out the door like the hounds of hell were on his tail, which left her saying, "...a big help," to an empty room.

~#~

"Dearest, we must talk." Isaac put his hand on Rachael's bottom and pushed her into the distillery and closed the door.

"Husband, as much as I'd like to play, I'm much too busy for nonsense right now."

"Hush!" He quickly scanned the small room to be

78

sure a lad wasn't napping beneath a bench. "I just had a most distressing conversation with the MacDougall's new wife."

"And?"

"I can not take the time to explain now, but trust I'm asking this boon with purpose. I need you to find out all you can about our new lady's past."

"Ask her yourself. I have wool to dye, clothing to mend—"

"Rachael, I fear our Duncan has married an imposter."

She blanched. "But this can not be! If this is so, we loose everything."

Isaac, sweating profusely, nodded.

~#~

Duncan glanced over the parapet to see Beth, her skirts tucked up between her exposed legs, crawling in crab fashion across the boulders at the keep's footing. "What in the name of all 'tis holy is she doing now?"

Angus looked down. "I hazard to guess, my friend, but we'd best capture her before she slides into the sea."

Duncan tore down the stairs. "She's daft, I tell ye." He shouldered his way past two men entering the keep's doorway. 'Twas a damn shame, too. She had lovely legs. "I would most willingly let her drown but for fashing over Albany's retribution should she, too, die under my protection."

"Aye," Angus agreed, "there is that." They jogged across the bailey and through the arched portcullis. "Think drowning be her intent?"

"I neither ken nor care, just so long as she doesna succeed."

They raced around the castle's rocky face, repeatedly

slipping on the jagged boulders, only to find the area they had last spotted Lady Beth now empty of all but lichen and barnacles.

"Do ye think she fell?" Angus scanned the water for her body.

"Nay. Look." Duncan jumped a puddle and pointed to wet footprints just above the waterline heading toward the opposite side of the keep. Heart bounding with relief, he said, "Come."

They circumnavigated the entire keep without catching site of his wode wife. Going through the portcullis, Duncan growled to the guard, "Have ye seen Lady Beth?"

"Aye, my lord. She just entered the keep looking like a drown cat whilst carrying kelp."

"Kelp?" He stormed across the bailey, rubbing blood from the stinging cuts on his palms. "I tell ye, Angus, the woman will be the death of me."

He strode into the great hall, ready to breathe fire. "Where is she?" he demanded of everyone in the room.

Flora cocked her head to the side. "By she, do ye mean your bonnie wife, my lord?"

Only haste kept a civil tongue in his head. "Aye."

Flora's pouty lips curled at the corners as she pointed to the stairs. "She passed just a moment ago."

He stomped across the hall.

At his heels, Angus asked, "What will ye do when ye find her?"

"I'm trussing her for now, and then—as soon as I am able—I am placing her under lock and key in the west wing."

After his and his ladywife's wee talk in the solar, he had ordered the mason to break through two of the storage room walls to make a reasonably spacious prison apartment for her. He wasn't, after all, an uncaring man. She would live in relative comfort until she or he passed to their heavenly reward. The last one to survive would be declared the winner.

~#~

Beth heaved a sigh staring at the wilting kelp she'd wrapped in bits of twine and hung from the east wing's storage room rafters. Her foray into the sea—her hope of escaping this archaic world—had been a freezing disaster. Nothing had changed except her body temperature and the condition of her gown. She *had* to escape. Her ego couldn't take much more.

Unlike the compassionate tease Duncan had been in her time, the real Duncan remained distant, as if she were unfit for decent company. Nor could she take much more of Miss "I'm Too Sexy for My Clothes" Flora Campbell hovering about. It hurt for some inexplicable reason seeing Duncan's gaze rake over the pretty woman. Beth stared again at her kelp.

Once dried and ground into a fine powder, the kelp—with the aid of oatmeal and a few egg whites—should make a passable face wash. She hoped. She couldn't continue using the butter and rose petal concoction Rachael had loaned her much longer. Her face would turn into zit-central by week's end and without make-up...

She shuddered and headed toward the great hall in search of Rachael.

Isaac's petite wife had offered to help her alter the third wife's gowns. The project held little appeal—no one in their right mind wanted to wear a dead madwoman's castoffs, but she needed clothing and wife number three's gowns were the only ones that came close to fitting.

Beth found the hall crowded with anxious, milling clansmen. Finally finding Rachael among the throng, she asked, "What's wrong?"

"Tis the Laird. He collapsed in the bailey."

Fear churned in Beth's belly as she glanced at the clansmen, from one concerned expression to another. "Where is he? I want to see him."

Rachael patted Beth's arm. "Nay to fash, *madame*."

"I want to see Duncan, *now*."

Rachael heaved a sigh. "As ye luste."

On the third floor, Rachael led Beth to a familiar looking, barrel-chested man standing before a closed door. He'd been introduced to her as Duncan's second in command. Rachael whispered to him and he shook his head.

He bowed toward Beth. "My lady."

"Good day. I would like to see my husband."

He crossed his arms. "Nay, my lady, ye canna." What followed she could only guess at, but his meaning was clear; he wasn't about to move aside.

She'd dealt with his kind in the past at the St. Regis and assumed a haughty stance and tone. "What is your name?"

His face flushed and his scowled deepened. The first time she'd seen him—the night Duncan had pulled her from the coach—his hands and clothing had been covered in blood. It was painfully apparent the man was not used to being challenged. Particularly, by a woman.

"Angus MacDougall, my lady."

"Step aside, Mr. MacDougall. I will see my husband. *Now*."

"Nay. Ye are not welcome, so sayith yer husband and yon doctor."

Doctor? Beth's heart tripped with foreboding. Men of Duncan's ilk only resorted to doctors when facing death's door. She glared at Angus and reached for the door latch.

His bulk shifted to block her way and his right hand settled on the hilt of his dirk. "*Nay*, lady. I luste ye take leave with Rachael. The MacDougall will spake with ye when he is wont."

So, the man wanted her gone. Rachael apparently did, too. She kept tugging at Beth's arm. Well, she had news for both of them. She was going in. The man lying on the other side of the door Angus so effectively blocked was *her damn husband*!

Beth jerked her arm free of Rachael and stared at the burly Scot. Since anger and haughtiness hadn't worked, she had to change tactics.

She stepped closer and patted the Angus's massive chest. "We both want what is best for Duncan, don't we?" She spoke slowly, enunciating each word. He nodded. "Good. I'm Duncan's wife and I'm worried. In order to help him, I must know what ails him. And I can't do that from this side of the door." She absently brushed a few crumbs from his tunic. "Do you understand?" He nodded. "Grand, then please step aside."

He grinned without humor, displaying square, even teeth beneath a red mustache. Just as Angus again shook his head, a gut-wrenching moan—sufficient to raise the hairs on Beth's arms —emanated through the thick door at his back.

Without giving it a second thought, Beth slammed

her knee into the towering Scot's groin.

"*Merde!*" Rachael squealed as Angus, ashen faced, dropped to his knees, his hands cradling his testicles.

As he rolled onto his side groaning, Beth hiked her skirts and stepped over him. "Sorry, Angus, but you gave me no choice." She reached for the door latch. "Rachael, be a dear, and take care of Angus, *si vous plait*." As the door swung open, Beth exhausted her limited high school French by adding, "*Merci*."

Beth found Duncan, ghost white, on a small cot, his left arm dangling over the edge. The old man at Duncan's side scowled at her then turned his attention back to Duncan's forearm where blood poured from a four-inch gash.

She raced to Duncan's side and asked, "What the hell do you think you're doing?"

The old man ignored her as he scrambled to collect Duncan's blood in a wooden bowl.

Beth knocked the bowl from the man's dirty hands and pushed him aside. She pressed on the wound to stem the flow and felt heat radiating off Duncan's body. "My God, he's burning up."

"*Nay*, my lady!" The doctor tried to push her away. "Ye must let the foul humors drain. 'Tis the only way."

"Take your filthy hands off him!" She slammed an elbow into the old man's ribs. The man's body odor alone nearly took her breath away.

She applied firm pressure to her husband's wound and bellowed, "RACHAEL!"

When the Frenchwoman poked her head through the doorway, Beth said, "Get this idiot out of here and find something to bind Duncan's wound."

"Pardon, *madame*?"

Beth took a deep breath, and tried again, this time at a much slower pace. "Please take the doctor away and find a dressing for this." She moved her hand so Rachael could see the wound the fool had inflicted.

"Oh! *Oui, madame*." Rachael waved toward the door. "Doctor', *si vous plait*."

"Rampe woman!" the doctor growled as he collected his questionable medical kit.

Beth returned his glare. "What did you just say?"

Rachael bit her lower lip. "He thinks ye rude, *madame*."

"I don't care what he thinks so long as he gets the hell out of here." Beth placed her free hand on Duncan's forehead. Her husband's fever had to be one hundred and four degrees, at the very least. Did they have aspirin in the fifteenth century? And what on earth could cause such a fever?

She bent over him. "Duncan? Can you hear me?" He hadn't so much as blinked during her altercation with the doctor. "Can you open your eyes?" He didn't respond and her worry escalated.

She needed to undress him and needed two hands to do it. She looked about the monastic room for something to bind his wound. Finding nothing, she pulled at the left sleeve of her gown. It was fairly clean, unlike her skirt, which had been dragging over dusty stairwells and filthy rushes. Wrenching the sleeve free, she wrapped it around Duncan's heavily muscled forearm. Having successfully stemmed the bleeding, she turned her attention to the difficulty of undressing her unconscious husband.

Beth had managed to free one of Duncan's arms from his jacket when Angus lunged through the doorway. He face was a mask of rage as he held himself upright on the door.

"My lady," he growled, "ye'd best—"

"Stop threatening, Angus, and get over here." She pushed hair off her face with a shaking hand. Her throat burned, felt raw. She started wrestling Duncan's left arm out of his shirt. "He's burning up—fevered. Help me get him undressed."

Angus staggered toward the bed. "Move." He pushed her aside. Not trusting him, Beth scooted to the opposite side of the bed.

"Oh my God!" Her hand flew to her mouth as Angus rolled her husband and she could see the jagged wound stretching across Duncan's left shoulder. Eight inches in length, it was a nauseating mass of mustard yellow, purple, and scarlet. Inflammation in the surrounding tissue looked like rays radiating off a setting sun. The few stitches that held it all together strained over the wound's bulging, purulent core.

Angus looked over his liege lord's shoulder to see what she gaped over and moaned. "Ack, man! Why had ye not said somethin'?"

Beth dashed away her tears. "Hurry. We need to get his clothes off."

Angus grunted and yanked off Duncan's shirt. He had Duncan balanced on his side when Rachael raced into the room with a bowl of water, a small dressing, and a needle and thread.

Beth grabbed the bowl from her hands. "I need more water—hot, boiling water—and more dressings." When Rachael frowned at her, Beth showed her Duncan's shoulder.

Rachael immediately blanched.

"*Now*, Rachael." Beth waved the small pile of white

linen at the woman. "I need *more.*" The woman nodded and raced out the door.

Beth bit into her bottom lip and tentatively prodded around her husband's shoulder. When puss oozed through his gaping stitches her stomach recoiled. Voice shaking, she said, "Angus, you have no reason to trust me, but *please,* I beg you, just do as I ask." Her tears started falling in earnest as she scrubbed her hands in the water bowl. "I need to clean the cut on his arm before it, too, becomes infected."

The damn fool doctor hadn't bothered to wash his hands before slicing into Duncan. Beth seriously doubted he'd bothered to clean the blade he probably used to eat and clean his nails with. God only knew what added bacteria he'd introduced into Duncan's system.

While Angus rotated Duncan onto his back, Beth stared at the supplies Rachael had deposited on the side table. Her stomach quivered. She'd never stuck a needle into anyone in her life, but she had sewn enough Cornish hens closed to feed an army. Surely, she could handle the needle and thread with some competence. She certainly couldn't do worse than those around her. She, at the very least, understood sterility.

As she exposed the wound on Duncan's arm, Rachael raced in with a pot of steaming water and Isaac followed with soap and enough sheeting to wrap a mummy.

She tore the fabric into strips then plunged a hand full into the scalding water.

"*Nay, madame!*" Rachael squealed.

It took everything Beth had not to scream herself. Her hands scarlet, she wrung out the fabric and started cleaning Duncan's wounded arm.

Once satisfied the cut was as clean as possible given

the circumstances, Beth picked up the needle and silk thread. Angus immediately stayed her hand and muttered something to Isaac. Beth waited. Isaac apparently took her side because Angus released her arm.

"Please, God," Beth whispered, as she pierced Duncan's skin, "keep my hands and my stomach steady."

Thankful her husband didn't flinch and grateful she'd not passed out nor tossed her breakfast with the first thrust, Beth gathered her wits and continued, placing ten consecutive stitches deep and tight in Duncan's forearm under everyone's watchful gaze.

She looked up to find Rachael at her elbow holding a crock of suave reeking of medicinal herbs and grease. She shook her head but Rachael kept saying, "*Oui, madame*, 'tis best."

Reluctantly, Beth picked up another piece of fabric and plunged her hands back into the water. Confident she'd killed most of the germs and all of the skin on her hands, she wrapped the swatch of fabric around her finger, scooped out some poultice and applied it sparingly to Duncan's arm.

Once his arm was dressed, she straightened and wiped the sweat and tears from her eyes. She found Angus staring at her. She told him, "It's time to clean his shoulder wound."

Wordlessly, Angus rolled Duncan onto his side as the others stared.

Knowing she needed to open the wound to drain the puss, she held out her hand. "Your blade...dirk."

He stared at her through narrowed eyes and murmured something to Isaac. Isaac murmured something back, and Angus reluctantly handed her the blade, hilt first. She dropped the blade into the deep pot of water. After a moment she bit her lip and retrieved it, this time suffering pain clear to her elbow.

She looked Angus in the eye and nodded. When the burly man tightened his grip on Duncan, she took a deep breath and sliced through the few knots holding Duncan's shoulder together. A cupful of purulent fluid flowed like hot honey down Duncan's back. Bile raced to her mouth. Even Angus gagged with the stench.

Forced to mouth breath, she murmured, "Rachael, more hot water."

Rachael, still bug-eyed, whispered, "*Oui, madame*," and flew from the room.

Beth poked and prodded to extract the puss hidden in pockets beneath Duncan's inflamed skin. As she worked, she fervently wished her husband would open his eyes or, at the very least, groan. When he didn't do either, panic ate at her limited composure and her hands began to shake. Were her efforts too little, too late?

She wasn't a doctor; she had no antibiotics, no IV fluids, no way of even knowing what his temperature was.

As her eyes began to tear-up yet again, Rachael arrived with fresh hot water. Beth again plunged her hands into the scalding heat. She would do all she could with her limited knowledge—all garnered from the Discovery Channel and friends, and then place her trust—Duncan's life—in God's hands.

With the wound clean, Beth agonized over whether or not she should stitch it closed. From her limited experience rushing kitchen staff to emergency rooms, she knew stitches had to be placed within twelve hours. According to those surrounding her, Duncan's wound was weeks—not hours—old. Hearing loud murmurs, she looked up and found the doorway filled with anxious faces.

Think, Beth, think. Hadn't the doctors told Linda they couldn't close her son's wound after operating on his ruptured appendix? Yes. They had to pack the wound with saline-soaked gauze and let it heal on its own, from the bottom up. Linda said the method left a dreadful scar, but the boy lived. "Rachael, I need salt."

Beth had no idea what proportion of salt to water would be best to make a saline solution, but decided too little might be better for healing than too much.

"Salt, *madam*?'

"Aye, salt, and make those people go away." As soon as she finished tending his wound, she'd need privacy to sponge Duncan down with cold water, to reduce his fever. That's what Tammy did every time her baby developed a high fever thanks to innumerable ear infections. Of course, she also gave the baby Tylenol and antibiotics...

~#~

Watching the quiet rise and fall of Duncan's chest, Beth's breathing synchronized with his. With each intake of air her hope rose, with each fall of his chest she worried it might be his last. He hadn't regained consciousness, hadn't moved a voluntary muscle once during her long vigil. Her beautiful ghost, now flesh and blood, bulging muscles and broad brow, was trying his damnedest to die on her. And it hurt. Hurt so, she thought she, too, might die.

It made no sense. He didn't care for her. Thought her insane. And still she thought him more man than she had ever imagined existing. He had only to speak, roll those delicious r's, and her knees turned to jelly.

To make matters more untenable, unlike their time on the parapet when he was ghost and she a badly shaken woman, when he'd been compassionate and funny, now he only railed at her. She suspected, given the clan's worried faces and tears, he was compassionate by nature. Just not with her.

Rachael tapped her shoulder, startling her.

"*Madame*, please go to sleep. I will watch the MacDougall."

Beth straightened, wiping welled tears with the heels of her hands. "Thank you, Rachael, but no. I'll stay." She laid a tentative hand on Duncan's forehead and her fear re-ignited. His fever was raging again.

She took a deep breath. She didn't understand how the fates had brought her back in time, but suspected it was because Duncan had died too soon. She wasn't about to let him make the same mistake twice. "I need more cold water."

Rachael clucked. "Ye also need take meat, if not sleep."

"No...nay." Food was the last thing she needed with her stomach still in knots and the close room still reeking of infection. "Just bring the water."

No sooner had Rachael left, than Angus returned. "How fares my lord?" He placed a hand on Duncan's brow.

"It's still too soon to know."

"He *willna* die."

"I hope not, but that's in God's hands."

Angus resumed his station, one he'd held since their ordeal began. Leaning against the wall with one leg cocked and his arms crossed, he looked like a petulant teen on a street corner. "Why care thee?"

Why, indeed, did she care about a man who'd only shouted at her since she'd arrived? "He's my husband."

"Ye love him not." Angus's scowl deepened. "Ye have yet to tup, so should he die, ye'll not inherit."

"Tup?"

"Ye have yet to consummate yer vows."

How in hell did Angus know this? Only she, plain-as-pudding Pudding, could be married three—no, four days—to the dreamiest hunk this side of a romance novel and still be a virgin, but that wasn't the point. Ire rising, she stood and glared at her husband's guard. "Whether or not we've *tupped* is none of your damn business." She would have banished Angus from the room had he not made it abundantly clear he wasn't about to leave her alone with Duncan. "And another thing. I have a castle of my own—far nicer than this, I might add—so don't you dare suggest I'd do away with Duncan to take what is rightfully his." Through grit teeth she asked, "Do I make myself clear?"

He glared back. "Verra."

"So long as we understand each other." She huffed and sat back down on the high-backed chair Rachael had provided when she realized Beth wasn't about to leave Duncan's side.

She looked at her hands and arms. They hurt despite Rachael's ointment. Tiny blisters lined her fingers like corn on a cob. Tears came unbidden as she looked at the only part of her person she thought pretty. They'd be scarred.

Chapter 7

Duncan felt fluid pass his lips and gagged. What ever it was tasted like low tide, salty and rank.

"Shh, Duncan." A cool hand touched his brow. "You must drink this."

Ack! He recognized the voice. Why would the woman not leave him in peace? He rolled away from his ladywife and white-hot pain shot down his left arm and spine. He flopped onto his back and struggled to open his eyes. His voice cracked as he managed, "Leave."

"No. You need to drink this if you're to heal."

Heal? From what? His lashes finally untangled. Beth, his termagant wife, hovered over him with tears in her eyes and a hollow reed in her hand. Why?

He turned his head and saw he wasn't in the solar but in one of the smaller third floor rooms. Ah. He'd relinquished the solar to his ladywife until her apartment could be completed. Soon she'd be locked away. Verra good.

"Duncan, open your mouth." He turned his attention back to her and saw she now held a spoon.

"Leave."

She shook her head and pinched his nose. When he

opened his mouth to yell, it filled with broth. He choked as he swatted aimlessly. Dear God, what ailed him? His strength had evaporated.

Beth held out another spoonful. "You *are* going to drink this. We can do it the easy way or the hard, but one way or the other, it's going in." He shook his head and she reached for his nose again. Rather than drown he opened his mouth.

"Thank you. I'll not have you dying of malnutrition after all you've put me through these last five days."

He scowled. What five days?

She heaved a sigh as she approached with another spoonful of broth. He recognized the taste. It was one of Rachael's noxious remedies. For what, he could not recall.

"You scared the stuffing out of me," Beth mumbled. He scowled at her as he opened his mouth for another spoonful of broth.

"I swear I've never been so frightened in my life as I was that first night. You were so hot I honestly thought you'd have a seizure." He opened his mouth again like a wee bird. She shoveled more broth in.

"It didn't help having Angus hovering over my shoulder for the first three days looking like he wanted to slit my throat, either." She shuddered. "I really thought he might the first time I removed your dressings." She ladled more soup into him. "I couldn't blame him, though. Your wound looked ghastly, and he didn't know me from a hole in the ground and here I was, taking over, issuing orders. Thank God, he listened. Truth be told, your man-at-arms would have had his hands full had he done otherwise. And don't get me started on that ass of a doctor. It's no small wonder you didn't die."

What the hell is she rattling on about?

"Your shoulder still looks bad, but it's a far sight better now, so..." She gave him another mouthful of broth.

Ah, his shoulder wound. He flexed his left shoulder. It still hurt but not nearly as much as it had just...

"Where—" He cleared the thickness in his throat. "Where is Angus?"

"In the hall. Would you like me to call him?"

"Aye."

She put down the bowl, ran a tentative hand down his cheek and grinned. "You need a shave, but I guess that can wait."

Shave? He touched his face and felt stubble. His beard was gone! *What the bloody hell is going on here?* He struggled to sit, only to find himself too weak to lift more than his head and his good shoulder. *God's teeth!* "Angus. Now."

She smiled. "As you wish, sire." Too his utter surprise, she placed a kiss on his forehead before leaving.

~#~

"Finally, ye wake." Angus clasped Duncan's hand. "Ye know ye verra nearly shent my week by almost dying?"

"Dying?"

"Aye." Angus dropped his voice to a whisper. "Had it not been for yonder wife, ye well may have. She's not left yer side but to relieve herself in the garderobe. And why on earth did ye not say yer shoulder was a pestilence?"

Duncan shrugged his good shoulder. "I thought it healing." Angus raised a disbelieving brow and grunted before glancing at Beth who now stood straight backed and staring out the room's small window.

"Yer yon ladywife threatened all manner of mayhem when I suggested we bring back the doctor. Said she'd smote the man and then my bonnie self if '*the raunchy bastard so much as crossed the threshold!*' Aye, those were her exact words."

"I donna understand *raunchy*." Bastard, he understood just fine.

"Nor I, but her meaning sat clear as well water." Angus chuckled. "And here I thought ye'd wed a pious woman."

He had. Hadn't he? She certainly wasn't reticent about threatening, but swearing in Angus's presence? No lady born would hazard such.

"Aye, and how she keened over ye, too, in the wee hours when she thought me asleep at the watch." Angus shook his head, looking as bemused as Duncan felt. "She didna keen aloud, but silently, tears flowing like a burn, stroking yer brow. And she crooned when she thought herself alone with ye. I didna know her songs, but they were as soft as any lullaby."

How odd. Not a moment ago Lady Beth had nearly suffocated him by holding his nose.

"And my beard?"

Angus shrugged. "She said ye needed stripping to break yer fever and strip ye, we did, down to the flesh, face and all."

Was naught sacred to the woman? With trepidation, Duncan raised a shaking hand to his head and found his hair still attached but braided. Praise the saints.

Angus chuckled, "She appeared quite satisfied with uncovering ye face and left it at that."

"Help me up."

Angus rested a hand on Duncan's good shoulder. "Nay. Yon doctor wife would have my sweeties in her fist within a heartbeat. Ye are fevered still, though not as before. I've seen yer back, man. 'Tis still a long way from healed."

Duncan heaved an exasperated sigh. He had a hundred things he needed to attend to if he'd truly been out like a doused fire for five days. "As yer liege lord, I order ye to help me up."

"Nay. I'd rather face yer fury on yer next good day, than deal with yon lady's ire on this one." He patted Duncan's hand. "Oblige me by staying put, do as she asks, and mend."

Angus raised his voice and addressed Beth. "My lady, I take my leave, entrusting my lord into yer capable hands."

Beth blinked in surprise. Her husband's second in command was leaving his post? "As you wish—luste, Sir Angus." His surprise at her deference registered before he could mask it. "Have a good day, Angus, and thank you for all your help."

Looking bemused, he bowed.

Beth returned to Duncan's side. "So, now it's just you and me against the world, huh? Are you hungry?" When his brow remained furrowed she made eating motions with her hands.

"Aye."

"I'll see what the kitchen has to offer. Hopefully it's not that dreadful haggis again." She shuddered, picturing the sheep gut stuffed with oats and Lord knew what all else. She wouldn't have been the least surprised to learn they packed a pig's squeak in with its blood.

A few minutes later she returned with a trencher of

diced lamb and porridge. When she finished shoveling the contents of the bread bowl into him, she gently dabbed the corners of his mouth.

Glory, you're a handsome man.

She'd been so pleased to discover a beautifully crafted mouth and square jaw under all the hair. And his lashes were to die for, so long and thick they tangled as he slept. She sighed, reluctant to admit she hovered precariously close to a precipice, one she couldn't risk falling over, of falling head over heels.

You'd better stop mooning and start focusing on the hard truth, Beth. Duncan might eventually feel gratitude, but he'll never feel love. Besides, you're going to find your way back to coffee, toilet paper—she still couldn't get over using Lamb's Ear leaves—and your little black cases of much-needed Chanel.

"What ails ye?"

She cleared her throat. "Nothing." She checked his temperature with her palm. "It's time to sponge you down again." He said nothing, which she took as consent and readied the bed.

As she placed sheeting under each of his limbs he started to scowl. When she soaked a cloth in cool water and wiped his face, his gaze never wavered from hers. What was he thinking?

She bathed his neck then his arms. Still he remained mute.

Realizing she'd put off the inevitable for as long as she dared, she lowered the sheet to his hips. Feeling a blush creep up her neck, she glanced away.

She'd thought nothing of touching his body intimately while he lay unconscious—it simply had to be done—but now her handsome husband-in-name-only stared at her, quite aware of where her hands and gaze traveled. She took a deep breath. *Get a grip, Beth, and just do it.*

If he has a problem with her bathing him, he'll let you know in short order. Then you can get huffy and tell him it's for his own good and to just shut up.

He said not a word as she sponged the broad, muscular planes of his chest and arms. As she readied another cloth to wipe down his well-delineated stomach she dared to glance up and found him staring at her through hooded eyes. She caught a slight twitch of his lips. Suspecting he was near to grinning, she cleared her throat and put on a stern face. Better he think her annoyed by having to do this, than suspect the depth of her embarrassment. Unfortunately, touching him while he was fully aware was a decidedly new experience. Totally unnerving, in fact, since his body was the first adult male's she'd ever touched, seen naked outside of a movie. And he was breathtaking.

He murmured, "Dosth ye approve?"

Her face suddenly felt like a blast furnace.

She chewed her lower lip. What the heck should she say? *If you were healthy, I'd kill to spend one night in your arms?* Not likely. "Aye, you're being very good, staying so still."

This time his lips did curl into a grin.

Duncan, she wished, *why don't you just close your eyes and let me finish with this before I expire. Good gravy.*

Her hands shook as she wrung cool water from the cloth. She grabbed a lung full of air and placed the cloth on his muscular abdomen. Her fragile confidence wavered when glorious muscle rippled under her hands.

You can do this, she silently chided. Hell, she'd done it for five days. Today should be no different.

Right.

Her hand grazed the fine, curly hairs on his lower abdomen, and a steeple appeared within the sheeting covering his privates. She nearly swallowed her tongue.

Oh, good Lord. Now, what? She couldn't just stop. He had a fever. Was this...reaction...simply a biological thing that happened whenever cold water came too close to a man's plumbing? Probably. Yes. It certainly couldn't be a response to her.

Though the tenting was surely a temperature issue, she retreated, wash basin in hand, to the end of the bed. She lifted his left foot. As her hands rose along his leg, she kept her gaze locked on the cloth in her hand. Minutes later Beth accidentally glanced up to find the steeple decidedly taller.

To her horror, hot blood flair in her cheeks.

God, if you get me through this, I swear I'll never curse again in my life.

Chapter 8

To Duncan's amusement, his ladywife's complexion bore a strong resemblance to a freshly cut beet. As he watched her labor over his body he dared not laugh for fear she'd expire on the spot or run from the room screaming.

And her hands felt wonderful, as did the cool water she kept applying so carefully. She had a gentle touch. A good trait in a wife.

Wife. Something he'd not wanted but now had, nonetheless.

He felt relief knowing there was a possibility he could bed her, in knowing his cock hadn't been adversely effected like the rest of his body by the ravishes of Eleanor's blade.

When Beth's hands fluttered against the inside of his left thigh, he closed his eyes and nearly groaned. Had he the strength, he would have reached out, pulled her on top of him and gladly tupped her, greasy hair and all, just to relieve the pressure she'd created in his groin. Had he tupped her the night they wed, he might even suggest she use those incredible hands to relieve his anguish, but that, unfortunately, was currently out of the question. Served him right for delaying the inevitable.

"Duncan, please roll onto your good side."

He opened his eyes. Her color hadn't faded and she had chewed her lower lip berry red. The color was attractive beneath her slate gray eyes. He grinned. "Ye have good hands, wife."

He hadn't thought it possible, but she turned an even brighter shade of red.

"Thank you." She ran a nervous hand to her neck and rubbed. "Would you mind?" She waved in a circle.

Rolling onto his right shoulder took his breath away. Had Eleanor not been already been dead, he'd have found a way to kill her. God's Teeth!

"*Shh*, just relax."

He hadn't realized he'd groaned. With the sheeting tucked under his back from shoulders to hip, he again felt her soft hands. She caressed his back with cool water. After a few ragged breaths he finally relaxed under her touch. As her hands crept lower—massaging the taut muscles of his lower back in slow steady circles—his manhood stained at attention. When she ran her hands around the cheeks of his buttocks, he groaned again.

She leaned over. "Did I hurt you?"

"Nay." She might yet be the death of him, but certainly not from pain. "Have ye a tale, lass?" Trying to fathom her odd manner of speech might prove distracting enough to ease the pressure in his groin.

"A tail?"

"Aye, a ballad."

"Ah. That kind of tale." Her hands slid slowly down his legs. To his consternation, it took several agonizing minutes before she took a deep breath and started.

"Once upon a time a wee lass named Kathy found

herself all alone. She didn't understand—ken—why her parents had died or why a lady took her from home and told her she needed to find a new mother and father. Kathy didn't want new parents, she wanted *her* parents, but she was brave. She didn't cry when the lady placed her in an orphanage—a house for lost children. She was told new parents would come and so she waited.

"Many times over the next few years she was paraded before people, but never chosen. Years passed and many adults came and took other children home, but no one ever came for Kathy."

Hearing her voice crack, Duncan craned his neck to look at his ladywife's face. She blinked and motioned for him to turn around.

"Kathy eventually became sullen in her resignation." This time when his wife hesitated, her hands also stilled. True, her tale was sad, but why did she take the child's tale so personally?

"One day the orphanage closed and Kathy was placed in foster care. She didn't mind, believing she'd now have a mother and father of her own once again.

"But Kathy soon realized she had only been placed in her new home to help take care of babies. Try as she might, her new parents never offered affection, never hugged or kissed her. She went to school and then came home to care for the babies, day after day. Eventually, her foster parents tired. No new babies came and they sent Kathy to another family."

Duncan had been fostered to the Campbell as a lad of ten to earn his spurs. He, too, had been lonely on occasion. What affection he did receive came only in the way of backslapping and goodhearted teasing. He'd not been hugged or kissed either. So why was his wife sounding so forlorn for Kathy? As he pondered, her hands began massaging his calves with cool water.

"In her new home," his ladywife continued, "Mrs. Proctor was kind, but Mr. Proctor tried to corner Kathy whenever he found opportunity. At twelve years, her figure—body—had started to curve, to look womanly. One day, she came home to find herself alone with Mr. Proctor. He tried to bed her. Terrified, she fought. She got sick on him, bloodied his nose with a lamp, and then escaped. That's the first time I...Kathy ran away."

Ah! He now understood the cause of his ladywife's angst. He hoped the man had been caught and hung; him and any dog, horse or falcon found with him, which 'tis the law of the land.

Beth sighed as she began removing the dressing around his shoulder. "Having no money—marks—Kathy didn't get far. She was caught and given to a lady named Mrs. Wade, a very odd woman."

His ladywife stopped her tale. He looked over his shoulder to see her holding a cup of the water over his wound.

"Duncan, this might sting."

He might have shamed himself by yelling had she not warned him in advance. To his consternation she had the nerve to pour more into his wound. She then murmured, "This will hurt a wee bit more," and jerked the dressing from his back. He grit his teeth against the agony and wondered what the hell she considered truly painful.

Duncan praised the saints that he was abed. He knew to his marrow his legs wouldn't have held him had he been standing, so great were his back spasms.

"Are you okay?"

When he didn't respond, for he couldn't just yet, she

asked, "Did I cause you much pain?"

He blinked the tears away, thankful his back was to her. "Nay." He took a deep shuddering breath and managed, "About the odd woman."

"Ah, yes, the odd woman. Mrs. Wade took great pains to find fault with Kathy from her hair roots to the soles of her feet. Between the woman's constant badgering and Kathy's inability to read like her peers, Kathy had many headaches." Beth stopped to dry his back. "One day when Kathy complained about another headache Mrs. Wade snuck up behind Kathy, lifted Kathy's pony tail—her long hair had been tied with a band at the top of her head—and cut it off. At the scalp."

"Ack, the poor lass had lice."

"No. Just headaches and now no hair."

"Humph." Many a lass's only beauty lay in her hair. No wonder Lady Beth's voice cracked.

A moment later Beth warned, "I'm sorry, but this will sting."

His ladywife did not lie. The salt-infused packing stung, but not nearly as horribly as the removal of the first. After a moment he felt compelled to ask, "Why doth the odd woman bear such ill will toward Kathy?"

"I don't know. In any event, she told Kathy, 'Now, you'll have no more headaches.'"

"Do the headaches vanish?"

"Eventually, but not until Kathy turns eighteen and escapes the woman."

Silent now, Beth wrapped a fresh strip of sheeting around his shoulder with gentle hands. As he lifted his left arm to accommodate her, he murmured, "Ye tell a sad tale, wife."

"Not so sad. Kathy grew into womanhood, tougher

than most. She worked hard and became a respected lady."

He frowned as Beth helped him roll onto his back. "Doth ye knowest this Lady Kathy?"

She nibbled at her bottom lip. "I'm afraid so."

Before he could ask if Lady Kathy married and lived happily ever after, someone knocked.

Seeing his solicitor, Duncan smiled. "Ah, Isaac. Come in."

Chapter 9

After Beth excused herself, Isaac asked, "How fare ye, *mon ami*?"

"I live. Something I hear 'twas in serious question not long past."

"Aye. Ye look better. Have ye much pain?"

"Nay, though I feel as brawn a newborn bairn."

"'Tis good to hear for I bring troubling news."

"The Bruce?"

"Mayhap. 'Tis regarding yer good ladywife."

Brow furrowing, Duncan growled, "Out with it, man."

"I'm verra sorry to say this, but I believe ye wife isna the woman sent by Albany."

Duncan guffawed. "Ye're as wode as I first thought Lady Beth, Isaac."

"Nay, something is verra wrong. I questioned the lass myself, as has Rachael. Lady Beth claims never to have lived in France and never to have married. Her tale remains unchanged with each telling."

"But she wears my ring."

"Aye, but Lady Beth has no memory of how it came into her possession. She claims you must have placed it on her hand after she fainted."

Duncan looked incredulous. "Nay! She had it on when I lifted her from the carriage. She must be the one."

"*Mon ami*, I'm just relaying my concerns. Ye are married to a woman we know little or nothing about, who claims her Christian name to be Katherine Elizabeth MacDougall Pudding. 'Tis not the name of the woman ye contracted to marry. Lady Beth may well be the right bride, but is so delus...*insense'* she does not know who she is. Or she could be another, entirely."

Isaac started to pace. Lady Beth had not hesitated to answer when asked about her past. Only one truly crazed—or intent on appearing so—would respond in such a manner. More troubling was her denying being Catholic. "We must discover the truth before Albany hears of this. If he believes you deliberately defied him by marrying a woman not of his choosing, or worse, if she is his niece and he hears ye refused to consummate because she's crazed, he'll not hesitate to strip ye of all ye have."

"Aye." Duncan scowled out the window in thought. "Lady Beth must be Albany's niece. Why else would the Bruce have tried to kill her? 'Tis no other possibility."

Isaac wasn't so sure. They had a boy king, James I, trapped in the Tower of London and the lad's ambitious regent uncle held sway over all in Scotland. While Albany—in no hurry to pay Henry IV the lad's ransom— played God, half of Scotland's chieftains were either plotting, raiding, or at each other's throats.

Isaac ran a hand through his thinning hair. He'd be bald before this ended. "Wode or sane, if ye believe Lady Beth be the one sent, ye canna give the Bruce reason to cry foul to Albany."

"'Tis decided," Duncan grumbled. "Sane or wode, I will tup the woman as soon as I am able. Consummation binds the marriage. Since the woman is a widow and willna bleed, ye must act as witness."

Isaac shuddered at the prospect. "Ask the priest. He has no love for ye. And John the Bruce will not be able to claim that we—being friends—ye lied about bedding the lady and I swore to it in an effort to defeat him. The priest bearing witness would be safer."

After a moment's thought Duncan nodded. "Aye, then should I learn Lady Beth deliberately deceived me, I'll deal with her."

It was the sanest plan given the circumstances and Isaac nodded. "Shall I send her to ye?"

Trepidation climbed Isaac's spine as Duncan growled, "Oh, aye, Isaac, send my lady in."

~#~

"Ah, she returns." Duncan's gaze traveled down the length of his wife's lithe form. "Wife, come ye closer."

At his side, she asked, "Are you in pain? Did Isaac say something to upset you?"

"Nay." He pointed to her feet. "What, pray tell, are those ye wear?"

She looked down and waggled a foot. "Sneakers." She smiled as if they were the most natural things in the world for a ladywife to don. "I can run three miles in thirty minutes and not feel a thing in these."

"You lie, lass." He waved toward the small window and the mountains beyond. "My horse can barely run that distance in that time."

She grinned. "Where I live the ground is flat. I run along the paths in Central Park." When he continued to just scowl she added, "In New York, where I once worked. Remember? I told you about it when I arrived."

She'd said much—most of it confusing babble—that first day. Now, being more accustomed to her speech, he prayed he'd have less trouble garnering the truth. His future depended on it. As she started to unbraid his hair, he said, "Tell me of this new York."

"New York has very tall buildings, some with over one hundred floors, levels. We call them skyscrapers."

He craned his neck to stare at her in disbelief.

She nodded and turned his head back around. "As I was saying, New York is our financial capital and has the best food in the world. You should taste Junior's cheesecake."

She sighed a bit too wistfully for his liking and he wondered what this junior meant to her.

"We have theaters and universities—you might call them colleges."

"And your home in the new York?"

"My home was nothing special, a small apartment. Before I got transported here, I had been thinking about staying at my castle permanently."

Ah huh! Now he was getting somewhere. "Tell me of this castle."

"I recently inherited it from my mother's people. It looks exactly like this one. But I have indoor plumbing, cranky as it is."

"Plum ink?" He kenned this not but heard the note of pride in her voice.

"Plum-ming. Running water inside the keep. I even have a contraption to heat the water. Just turn a faucet—tap—and voila, hot water any time you want it." She ran her fingers through his hair then picked up the brush. "Most of the time, anyway."

Her imagination had to be the grandest he'd ever witnessed for her world to be filled with *sky scrapes* and *plum minks*.

"I want to turn the castle into a bed and breakfast—a place for travelers to stay overnight—but I guess that will be delayed."

"How many be in yer hostiel?"

"I live alone."

He knew her to be a widow, so she must have misunderstood his question. "Aye, but how many suggits, guards?"

"None. As I said, I live alone. That's one of the reasons I wanted to convert the castle into a bed and breakfast. So I'd have company, occasionally."

God's teeth! He spun and found her smiling like a bairn on Michaelmas Eve. 'Twas no wonder Albany wanted her wed.

No woman in her right mind would invite strangers to her hearth without armed protection. She would have endangered herself and the holding. Dumbfounded, he shook his head in utter disbelief.

Before he could ask another question, a scullery lass arrived with fresh water. "Out!" He wasna allowing his softheaded wife to change his dressing again quite yet. His stomach still shook from the last change.

"Duncan, your hair needs to be washed." Beth wrinkled her nose.

"Oh." He nodded to the girl. "My apologies, lass. Do as my lady wife lustes."

Beth ordered him flat on his back. After the girl left, Beth tapped the container in her hands. "What do you call this?

"A posnet."

"I call it a pan." She positioned it under his neck then scooped warm water over his head, carefully shielding his eyes as she did it. "Do you understand—ken—most of what I say?"

"Not all, but most." He relaxed as her hands gently massaged soap into his hair and scalp. He'd been a wee bairn the last time anyone other than he had washed his hair. How odd—and kind—that she should think to do this.

"Duncan, I'm confused by how I got here." She paused. "Do you know?"

He looked up into her glossy, clear gray eyes, her confusion and distress were quite evident as she bit her bottom lip and blinked away threatening tears.

Taken together—her question, odd ways, and her plans for her castle—he decided his wife was merely addled. If Isaac is correct, if there was a plot afoot, she had to be only a pawn in a game in which she had no knowledge.

He would bed her as soon as possible, yet he still couldn't spill his seed within her. He had to discover—for his heir's sake—if her coddled brain resulted from heredity or from being coshed on the head. Given her odd turn of mind, the task wouldn't be an easy one.

"Doth it matter how ye came to be here, lass? Ye be here, we be legally wed, and I shall protect ye."

She snorted as her hands continued their lulling magic on his scalp. "Duncan, it's not that simple. Doesn't it bother you that we're married but have no love for each other? That we don't even know each other?"

"Nay, 'tis the way of marriage. We shall grow accustomed to one another in time."

"I doubt I'll ever grow accustomed to anything in this

time. I don't even know what's expected of me."

He grinned, "Practice patience." He then had a brilliant thought. "Can ye read, lass?"

"Yes." She sounded affronted. "I can also calculate percentages in my head, but that's not going to help." She started rinsing his hair. "It's upsetting having someone like Flora looking askance at me because I can't speak French, and having Rachael dress me. I feel like an idiot here. I want to go home."

Her voice sounded so plaintive, so bairn-like, he almost smiled. How had this poor addled woman, living in France since her husband's death, survived? "Wife, I ken the solution to yer woes."

"You do?" To his disappointment her hands began making quick work of drying his hair. "Truly?"

"Truly. On the morrow, ye shall have the answers ye seek."

"Bless you, Duncan Angus MacDougall!" To his utter surprise, she gave him a resounding kiss on the lips. And she tasted of mint.

~#~

Beth's euphoria dissolved like cotton candy in her mouth, gone before she had a chance to fully enjoy it. She didn't know whether to laugh or cry as she stared at Duncan's solution to all her problems—a book entitled *What The Goodwife Taught Her Daughter*. Knowing she'd likely be reduced to hysterics, she did neither, and opened the leather bound volume under his watchful gaze. She slowly scanned the pages. The author had fixated on table manners, but the book's main emphasis stressed piety, deference, and of all things, restraint. Just what she needed—more restraints, as if donning headgear, mountains of velvet, and curtsying constantly weren't restrictive enough.

She closed the book and turned the ring on her still sensitive fingers. Funny, she'd always thought that if she ever wore such a band it would represent love, commitment, and the promise of common goals. When an annoying burn started at the back of her throat she sniffed and smoothed down the pleats of her bodice.

She had no right to complain. Despite her looks and lack of education, she now owned a castle and had a husband, abrasive and annoying as they both managed to be at times. She should be thanking God for his largess, not wishing for things that apparently weren't meant to be. She should be content with knowing Duncan would survive. Glancing up and finding her hubby looking inordinately pleased, she murmured, "Thank you."

"Ye are most welcome. 'Tis a helpful tome, I'm told."

"I'm sure it is." She placed it on the foot of his bed. "I'll begin reading today." If nothing else, perhaps she could garner some insight into the elaborate finger movements Rachel, Isaac and Flora employed as they ate. She still couldn't believe the clan didn't used forks. "We need to change your dressing now."

Duncan's good humor immediately evaporated, leaving him looking like a petulant four-year-old who'd just been told he was getting a haircut. "Ack! Can it not wait?"

"Nay, my lord. If you have any intention of getting out of bed any time soon, we need to change the dressing twice a day, so roll over."

He huffed but did as she asked. "Finish yer tale."

She sprinkled salt into the warm water at his bedside. "Which tale?"

"The tale of Lady Kathy."

"Ah." She stripped off the linen holding his dressing in place. "Kathy found work serving food."

"Where?"

"In New York at a hotel—a very big house where travelers spend the night. She worked very hard and one day she received a promotion—a higher rank. She now had full charge of all the people serving food. Three years passed and she had an opportunity to rise again." Beth smiled, recalling how excited she'd been the day the general manager of the St. Regis had called and offered her the job. "Now she worked at the most elegant hotel in the city, arranging parties."

"I ken not *par tees*."

Beth slowly poured her warm saline solution over the dried packing in his shoulder. He hissed as it soaked in.

"Sorry." She winced for him as she poured more, to be sure the dressings edges would loosen. "Parties are banquets where people gather to celebrate."

"Ah."

"All was going well until a man arrived at her door saying she'd inherited a castle on an isle."

He asked through gritted teeth, "Where is this castle?"

"Here in Scotland, near Oban." She gingerly picked up one corner of the dressing. "This is going to hurt." She held her breath as she peeled away the old packing. Her prayers had been answered. She found only bright red healthy tissue beneath. There was no evidence of infection. The gash was now only a half-inch deep. Duncan would have a scar eight inches in length and nearly three inches in width, but who cared? He lived. She again thanked God the man had the constitution of an ox.

When she blotted the wound, Duncan shuddered and his heavy muscles contracted under her hands. He hissed, "The castle, lass."

She patted his shoulder. "Yes, the castle. It's smaller than many, but lovely to Kathy. This is the first real home she's ever had." Ready to place a fresh saline dressing into the wound, she whispered, "Kathy's castle is haunted."

"Ack!" He took a deep breath as the packing hit his wound. "*A ghost?*"

She smiled, quite pleased her announcement had the desired effect of distracting him. "Aye, a big, handsome, decidedly masculine ghost haunts her castle. He follows her constantly, upstairs and down." Beth wrapped fresh linen around his shoulder then lowered her voice to a conspirator's whisper. "She even caught him spying on her as she bathed."

"Nay! And where is her cur of a husband whilst all this chasing and spying goes on?"

Beth suppressed the urge to laugh. Duncan, her resident voyeur, was incensed by the prospect of a man spying on a woman at this stage in his life. "Kathy has no husband. Where she comes from men choose their ladies by fairness of face and by the size of their breasts. The bigger the breasts, the better. Unfortunately, Kathy is thin and plain."

"'Tis madness. Fair fades, breasts droop, but not so *stones*. The woman is worth her weight in *or* to a landless Knight of Girt and Sword."

"Is *or* gold?" She tried rolling her r's as he had. "The yellow metal?"

"Aye, 'tis." He frowned. "Lady Kathy's clan hath

verra strange ways, Beth. Verra strange."

She patted his good arm. "We're done."

"Help me sit, lass."

"It's too soon."

"Nay, 'tis past time." He held out his good arm. Seeing this wasn't a battle she could win, she reluctantly grasped his good arm. Her hands didn't come close to circumnavigating his right, heavily-muscled bicep as she levered him upright. Once vertical, Duncan immediately blanched and wavered. Angus walked in just as she caught Duncan's lolling head against her chest.

"My Lady!" Angus strode forward and took Duncan's weight from her arms. "Ack, man, ye need to rest awhile longer."

"Nay." Duncan shook his head. "How can I stand if I canna garner the strength to sit? The dizziness will pass in a wee bit."

When Angus gave Beth one of those *can't you control him* looks that strangers give parents when their toddlers throw fits in supermarkets, she held up her hands. "Angus, according to *What The Goodwife Taught Her Daughter* I'm to acquiesce to his every wish with a smile on my face, so don't start with me." She placed a cool, wet cloth on her husband's forehead. "Take slow deep breaths, hon. Are you still dizzy?"

"A wee bit."

Angus steadied Duncan before asking her, "What means *hon*?"

Beth felt a blush race from her chest to her hair roots. "It...means 'honey.' It's a casual term like 'you there', nothing more."

To her relief Angus only raised a thick, auburn eyebrow and made a thick *humphing* sound, but said no more.

"Wife, I need speak with Angus. Could ye return in an hour's time, lass? We can finish the tale then."

She nodded, glad for the excuse to escape. Later, she would have ample time to finish her tale as he called it. The sooner he understood her plight, the sooner they could find a way out for her.

Soon she she'd be back to her ghost, coffee and make-up. Pondering why the thought should cause a weird sinking feeling in her stomach, she closed the door.

"Ye should not be sitting up, friend."

Duncan shook his head. "I must." He looked at the closed door. "What do you know of Lady Beth?"

Angus grinned. "She may be plain and too wee for yer robust tastes, but she does have a warrior's heart. Ye'd be dead now, if not for her wee hands. My shock was extreme when she plunged them into scalding water—not once but many times—to keep the bad humors at bay."

"Ye speak of witchcraft?" The notion of his bride practicing the evil craft nearly unseated him.

"Nay. She spoke of cleanliness and Godliness." Angus shrugged. "I understood naught of these evil humors—*germs* as she named them—but Rachael and Isaac knew them well. Her way—of absolute cleanliness—'tis, apparently, also in Isaac's bible. Knowing him to be Godly in his own odd way and to be yer trusted friend, I did not interfere with her ritual." He grinned as he wiped the sweat from Duncan's brow. "In truth I had nay choice. Ye were closing fast on death, so I gave her sway."

Duncan nodded. "Since I still draw breath, I cannot fault yer logic, Angus." It did not sit well hearing he owed his life to Beth while still questioning whether she was or was not sane...or whether she was or was not the woman he'd contracted to marry. He had to get to the bottom of the quandary soon.

"Angus, ye need not be standing here bracing me like a buttress. Help me to that chair."

Instead of helping him stand, Angus pulled the chair to the side of the bed and slid his arms under Duncan's legs.

When Duncan started to protest, Angus grumbled, "I'll not be the cause of ye falling on yer daft head. But should ye be so stupid as to stand, now I'll not have to drag yer blasted overgrown self so far to the bed."

Settled into the high-backed chair, his good shoulder supporting his back, Duncan mumbled, "Thank ye."

"Ye're most welcome."

"Has the Bruce moved on our kine or any of the outlying crofts?" Since Duncan had killed seven of John's men, it wouldn't have surprised him had John set fire to all their outlying homes.

"Nay. All is quiet, but 'tis only a matter of time before he seeks revenge."

Duncan nodded. The Bruce wouldn't be alone in seeking retribution. He, Duncan the Black, still had a serious score to settle.

"Have ye discovered who the two dead women were in the carriage with my lady?" Not knowing but assuming the best, he'd ordered them buried in consecrated ground.

Angus shook his head as he started to clean his nails with his dirk. "'Tis unlikely their Mother Superior has received yer missive yet."

Duncan had assumed the women accompanying Beth

had come from the French nunnery with her, which brought another question to mind. Why hadn't Beth mentioned the ladies? True, she'd been too overwrought initially, but not now. Mayhap, she could furnish their names. If she still found their passing too painful to discuss, he would let the matter pass. They were, after all, dead, and 'twas naught he could do to rectify that. "How goes the labor in the chapel and fields?"

"In the chapel, slow but steady. The guards report all's quiet about the oat and rye." Angus cleared his throat. "I need bring another matter to your attention."

"Aye?"

"Eleanor's mother is dead."

"Dead?" Kenning the old hag hadn't a clan to run to after he'd banished her from Blackstone, Duncan hadn't the heart to drive her off his lands entirely. She was often seen lurking along the border of his and the Bruce's lands. He now hoped she hadn't been murdered. "How?"

"According to Betty, the woman who sheltered her, on the same night Lady Beth arrived, the old crone grew highly agitated. Thinking the cause the storm, Betty tried to calm her, but she only grew more crazed. After two days of constant keening and senseless raving, she simply died." Angus shrugged. "Thinking ye'd not object, I ordered her buried quickly and without ceremony up yon."

Duncan blew out a breath, relieved to his marrow that he wouldn't have to seek revenge for a dead woman he'd despised. "Verra good."

Angus sheathed his dirk and finally grinned. "And ye will, no doubt, be pleased to hear the bloody bush ye've been coddling these past two years has finally bloomed."

Duncan laughed. "'Tis not a brush, ye heathen, 'tis a

tree. A lemon tree."

Duncan had fallen in love with its fragrant blossoms and fruit while on his way to the Holy Land. Two years ago he had asked a friend in Italia to ship one to him. He'd potted the wee scrawny branch the moment it arrived and had nursed it through two winters in his solar. He grinned. In the span of a few more full moons he would once again hold the beautiful, golden fruit in his hands.

Angus grinned. "Need ye anything else?"

"Aye. The next time ye come this way please bring my diary and writing tools." He wiggled a brow. "I must record this momentous occasion."

Angus bowed with his right hand over his heart. "As my liege lord commands."

Duncan laughed. They'd grown up together, played and fought like brothers. "Out with ye, fool, and send in my wife."

Aye, this time God had dealt fairly with him. He had provided the prized fruit as compensation for giving him an addled wife.

Chapter 10

Two days later Beth poked at the cold, overcooked joints of lamb and questionable blood pudding—their cook's fifteenth century version of lunch—and wanted to pull her hair out.

Bad food aside, every time she had Duncan alone and tried to restart her story, something or someone had interrupted them.

This morning it had been Miss I'm Too Sexy for My Clothes, Flora Campbell. The woman had rushed in whining about some dispute she was having with another woman over drying cloth or dying wool—Beth still wasn't sure which. Duncan then had to hear the other woman's version of events. As far as Beth could tell, given their rapid and odd phrasing, the altercation had started over rights to a favorite work area.

It took an hour for Duncan to sort out the truth. All the ladies' hair snatching and swatting stemmed from jealousy. The older woman had apparently caught Flora flirting with her man. Duncan had sternly admonished them both and set them to working on alternate days. Neither looked too pleased as they left. Then Angus arrived and on it went.

Beth looked about. Most in the castle were eating.

She decided now was as good a time as any to try seeing Duncan again. She stood and quickly turned.

Her nose collided with her husband's chest.

He grabbed her shoulders to keep her from toppling. "Be ye all right, my lady? I didna mean to startle ye."

She cradled her poor nose with her fingers and tried to blink the sting away. "What are you doing downstairs? You should be resting."

He made one of his thick *humphing* sounds at the back of his throat in answer and scanned the room. Beth glared at Angus, now standing behind her husband's shoulder. He just shrugged.

Seeing she'd get no help from that quarter, she said, "Duncan, you could relapse if you overtire."

"Relapse?"

She wanted to cuff his ears. By now he understood her well enough. "Yes, husband, your fever and weakness could return."

He cocked an eyebrow, "Cease fashing, woman. I am mended enough." She opened her mouth to protest again, and he placed a firm finger to her lips. "I am sorely tired of rest and coddling. 'Tis much I need attend to, so say no more or leave."

He was dismissing her! Why the arrogant...

She spun on her heel, embarrassed to her hair roots. How dare he chastise her before an audience?

Before she could take a step, his hand clasped her arm. She instinctively pulled back. He hauled her into his side with little or no effort. Through clenched teeth, she hissed, "Let go."

He leaned down and whispered directly into her ear, "My dear lady, I canna be seen being ordered about like yer lap dog. I command yon men with the mere lift of my hand, only because they respect my past valor and fear my reprisal should they not obey." He squeezed her arm just a bit. "Ye ken?"

Fear and embarrassment made blood pound in her ears. Determined not to show it, she hissed, "Aye, my lord."

Please, God, get me out of here!

He surveyed her face for a moment, then whispered. "Fash not, goodwife. Ye may always say what ye must to me in private."

Ya, right. *And what happens "in private" if what I have to say isn't to your liking?* She shuddered.

While vulnerable and dependent, her husband had been as docile and compliant as a trained bear. On the mend now and feeling more himself, was he finally showing his true colors?

She looked at the hand that held her captive, then into the depths of his steel blue eyes. Masking her anger behind a patently false smile, she asked, "Is there anything else, my lord?"

He huffed. Why he sounded exasperated she couldn't imagine. She was the injured party here.

He released his grip on her arm. "Nay, my lady, not at this time."

Head high, she stalked away.

Duncan frowned watching Beth's straight-backed progress through the hall. She was still obviously furious with him and he hadn't a thought as to why. He had apologized, no?

"Ack, ye're a brave man, Duncan," Angus muttered, as he pulled out Duncan's chair. "The last time I nay-said the wench, I found my balls in my throat."

Duncan grimaced as he settled at the table. "Not so

brave, friend. Having heard what happened to ye, I made damn sure I kept my hip to her." He shook his head. "She is a confusion, Angus. As gentle as the mist at gloaming one moment, a flame-eyed termagant the next. And her tales...augh, you've not heard the like. I swear I could live one hundred years and understand her not."

"Understand her or not, ye must consummate this marriage soon."

"So ye heard?"

"Who hasn't?"

"Tonight 'twill be done." When Angus's ale suddenly spewed across the table, Duncan cast a scathing glance at him. "Think me not man enough?"

Angus stopped wiping the ale from his beard and held up his hands. "'Twas not my meaning." He finished cleaning his face. "Ye merely surprised me by choosing *this* night. Yer wee wife left me with the distinct impression she'd sooner geld ye as look at ye. 'Tis all."

Humph! His friend did have a point. What to do? He couldn't take time to woo his lady into a favorable frame of mind, having been locked away from his duties for nigh onto a week. He'd have to ponder the problem further. He did, after all, have six hours before dark.

As he finished his meat, the solution to his dilemma dawned. It lay just above his head in the library. Beth had been most impressed with *What the Goodwife Taught Her Daughter*. She could only be doubly pleased and placed in a perfect set of mind with his next surprise.

Chapter 11

I'm going to kill him.

Beth reread the title just to be sure she hadn't misunderstood. Yup, that's the title. *One Hundred Ways For A Goodwife To Please Her Husband.*

Stabbing would be too good for the man. Poisoning would be better...a long, slow, painful poisoning she could watch and gloat over. Yes, that was the way to go.

She tossed the book onto the solar's high poster bed and picked up the heavy granite pestle and mortar she'd appropriated from the castle's distillery.

As she wrenched dried kelp leaves from their rubbery stalks, Rachael tapped her hunched shoulder.

"Doth not my lord's gift please thee, *madame?*"

"I appreciate the value of the book, Rachael. I just don't appreciate the theme."

"I dinna ken *la raison.* 'Tis *tresbonne*—very well illustrated, *non?*"

Beth took her frustration out on the kelp, grinding furiously. "Aye, Rachael, it is. Unfortunately, I have no interest in learning how to kowtow any more than I do now." The depictions of preferred sexual positions had been the final straw.

"Cow tow, *madame*?"

Beth dumped the powdered kelp into a bowl and reached for the oats. "It means 'to bow and scrape,' to do my master's bidding without so much as a by-your-leave." She slammed the pestle into the oats and began separating hull from nut. "How I ever imagined myself attracted to that man is beyond comprehension."

"Surely, ye ken the ways of men, *madame*? They huff and puff, but are mere *petit garcon*—laddies—in here." She tapped her heart. "In truth, they fear us."

Beth's hands stilled. "Fear us? What do you mean?"

Rachael smiled. "Ah, *madame*, 'tis kenned by all *Francaise*—

—women of my country. Did your mater not teach ye this as an *enfant*?"

"If by mater you mean my mother, she died when I was a babe."

"Ah! 'Tis no wonder, then." Rachael sat on the bed and patted the place at her side. "Come, we must talk before 'tis too late."

"Too late for what?"

Rachael sighed. "Ye shall learn."

An hour later Beth could only gape at the woman who—not ten years earlier—had nearly burned at the stake.

According to Rachael, Duncan had to bed Beth as soon as humanly possible to keep his fiefdom and—unless Beth ran for her life—there would be no nay-saying him, as Rachael so tactlessly put it. Good God Almighty!

Beth started pacing. "Rachael, are you absolutely certain he means to do this tonight?"

"Aye, *madame*."

Having already ripped her headdress off, Beth ran an agitated hand through her hair. "Please, Rachael, no more 'madames' or 'dames.' Call me Beth."

"As ye luste, but only in private, mad...Beth. 'Twould not be *s'approprier*—uhmm, appropriate—in the public, *non*?"

Beth waved a distracted hand. "Whatever."

She still couldn't believe Duncan—her ghost, the hulking man of her dreams, the man she still contemplated slaying—actually thought he could just walk through the solar door and jump her bones. Tonight! How could he even think it after he'd acted the Neanderthal in the hall, embarrassing her before everyone? What madness was this?

"Rachael, there's got to be a way I can get out of this."

Now well aware that Beth was still a virgin, her French friend pushed out her lower lip in thought, "There may be, but 'twould only be *l' ajournement temporaire*."

As she had for the last hour, Beth mentally rearranged Rachael's words and shifted the accent on syllables, and suddenly hope bloomed. "You're saying there *is* a way to postpone this?"

"*Oui*, but 'tis only—"

"A temporary adjournment, I understand, but what?"

"Claim yer flowers."

Beth shook her head. How the hell could flowers possibly save her?

"Yer bloody flow, *mad*—Beth."

"Aaah!"

"*Oui*, Beth, ah!"

~#~

Duncan ran a shaking hand over his bristle-coated

jaw. There was no help for it. He had to shave or rub his ladywife's face raw when he bedded her. Hopefully, he could accomplish the task without slitting his throat.

He balanced his dirk in his hand. How would this first tupping go? He'd had little problem bedding his first wife. She'd not enthused, but she'd not wailed either. As time passed, he'd been disappointed knowing she'd not seek his attention, would not return his kisses, but then she hadn't turned from him, either. The same, unfortunately, could *not* be said for his second and third wives.

He'd taken inordinate time with his second wife, having no knowledge nor love of her, and her being only fifteen years, but she'd still cried, lying like a slab of granite beneath him as he claimed his rights. She'd not said a word as he'd gently cleansed her. Only after he'd finished tending her, did she start praying—hands clutched between her perfect breasts—for his immortal soul in endless, fractious whispers. To his horror, he awoke the next morning to Angus's frantic shaking and the news that his lady had jumped from the parapet and lay broken on the rocky headland below.

His third wife had apparently been better schooled in the ways of men and women for she'd not keened, yet still she remained remote each time they tupped despite his best efforts. At the time he had no way of knowing that she loved another and thought him a heathen. 'Twas only when she buried her blade in his back did he come to understand her full loathing for him. And by then 'twas too late.

Praise the saints, this new wife is a widow. He'd had his fill of virgins.

Surely, Isaac had misunderstood Beth's responses to

his questions. Had she not caressed Duncan with gentle hands and cool water whilst he lay fevered and naked as a wee bird? Certainly no virgin would ever do such. And she had shaved him without so much as a nick, which only proved she'd done so in the past for her first husband. That thought—that she'd gently ministered to another—caused a sudden, inexplicable tightening in his gut. Odd.

He wet his face and reluctantly pressed the blade to his cheek. Since Beth obviously preferred a babe-like visage over a manly beard, he supposed shaving 'twas the least he could do for the poor addled lass. She had brought him back from the brink of death, after all.

As he scraped over his jaw he heaved a sigh.

He'd never been comfortable, as some men were, enjoying the occasional prime flesh of loose women. Tupping with their ilk 'twas something he'd done as a lad to gain skill but not since.

A mature man should, he believed, save his seed for his ladywife, the vessel of a legitimate and fertile womb. But would Lady Beth graciously accept his attention? Or would she, like his last two wives, grit her teeth and pray for the act to be over?

If he learned her colorful, chaotic thoughts stemmed only from an injury, would she be joyful when she carried his seed, his heir?

So many questions with no answers.

Smooth cheeked, he donned the collarless jerkin he'd chosen for this special occasion. Flora had once told him the deep blue brocade enhanced the color of his eyes. He didn't know whether it did or not, but she'd smiled so perhaps Beth would find it pleasing, as well. And he would have preferred to be physically stronger for this night, but...

He squared his shoulders and heaved a sigh of resignation. He'd delayed as long as he dared. The deed must now be done.

~#~

Finished with shaving her legs, Beth put away the short blade Rachael had loaned her, and started smearing her homemade kelp cleanser on her face. "I hope this works better than it smells."

She grinned, her thoughts on Rachael. The poor woman had been wide-eyed thinking the worst when Beth had asked for the knife. It had taken forever to convince her new friend she only wanted to shave, that she felt dirty with a week's worth of stubble on her body. Rachael, still not sure what Beth was about, had insisted on watching. Her exclamations had almost—but not quite—put Duncan's plans for the upcoming night out of mind.

Beth prayed Rachael's "flower" plan would work, but what if it didn't? She had heard some men didn't mind having sex during a woman's period, though for the life of her she couldn't image a woman agreeing to it.

In his current physical condition, there was the possibility she could out run him. But what if he bellowed for help? Angus and half the world would come running. And if she did manage to elude his men, where would she go? Blackstone was already locked down for the night. From earlier observation she knew Duncan's nightly precautions would have impressed a state pen warden. She grimaced, and her kelp mask tugged.

She had no choice but to hope Rachael's plan would hold Duncan at bay. Ignoring the small voice in her head that screamed, "Run while you still can", she closed her eyes and splashed water on her face.

Feeling a tap her on the shoulder, she jumped.

"God's teeth, woman! What have ye on yer visage?"

Beth looked like a startled frog. Duncan's shock dissolved into laughter when his green-as-grass wife began to blush. God, she had to be the oddest, funniest thing he'd ever seen.

He gasped for air when she stomped a bare foot at him and pointed to the door. "Out, you great lummox!"

"Beth, my dear..." He took a deep breath and tried to look contrite, but laughter started bubbling out of his chest again.

If he didn't get control, all would be lost, but saints above, what had ever possessed her? He cleared his throat to smother the chuckle hovering behind his tongue.

Finished with her scrubbing and blotting, she again faced him, this time with a look of righteous indignation. "Are you quite through?" she asked.

He nodded, still not trusting his voice.

"Good," she huffed. "We should go down stairs and have something to eat. I'm hungry."

While she rooted under the bed like a ferret for something, he struggled with his demons and finally managed, "Beth, 'twill be brought in forthwith."

"Oh?" She appeared more startled than pleased. "But...I need to see Rachael."

"Ye may speak with her come morn', lass. She isna goin' away." He grinned when she blanched, and her shoes dropped to the floor with a thud.

"Oh."

Why did she suddenly look like he was about to consume her for sup? Had she been told? He approached her and she warily backed away.

132

When he had her cornered between the bed and the wall, he slowly reached for the pins holding her hair atop her head. He preferred her hair loose, softly framing her face.

As her braids fell into his hands she stuttered, "Are you sure...sure you don't want to go downstairs?" She placed a hand on his chest. "We really should. The food will be warmer."

"The food will be warm enough here." He ran his fingers through her thick braids, loosening her silken hair until it fell into soft waves. "Your hair is a bonnie shade, like chestnuts."

She swallowed, eyes locked on his face.

He ran a finger down her cheek, remaining silent as her color began to rise. When it settled on a sunset vermilion, he whispered, "Yer skin is soft, lady, like a lamb's ear or a rose petal."

She ducked her chin and looked away, exposing her neck to his perusal. Not bad, sleek and long. He brushed his lips against her golden skin just as a knock came to the door.

She immediately squeaked, "I'll get that!"

He stayed her with a hand. "No need." As her eyes grew wide, he called, "Enter."

He kept an arm around her waist and guided her toward the table the two serving lasses loaded with every delicacy his pantry had to offer. When the lasses began to leave, his wife's hungry gaze followed them to the door.

Oh, aye, she knew only too well what was afoot.

When the door closed, he motioned toward one of the chairs before the fireplace. "Please sit."

She settled, looking more than a wee bit pensive. Thinking it would calm her, he served, depositing moderate portions of everything into her trencher before loading his own. He then poured generous amounts of his finest wine in both their goblets.

She sniffed the goblet. "I didn't know you had wine."

"'Tis saved for special occasions." He'd been told she would not consume ale. Wanting her a bit tipsy, he was not about to serve her the boiled water she preferred. He spoke amiably about his day as he ate, and she downed half a horn of wine and poked at her food.

"I thought ye hungry, lass."

"Huh?" She looked up from her trencher and mustered a wee smile. "Oh. I guess my hunger passed."

No doubt, when ye realized I wasna about to let ye escape.

He refilled her elk horn goblet. "Do ye find the solar to yer liking?"

She nodded. "But it must be cold in winter. Have you thought of putting in glass?"

"Aye, someday all will be glazed, but fear not the winter cold." He grinned. "I am a warm soul."

"Ah." She licked her lips and fiddled with her food again.

After a moment she said, "Where I come from couples—men and women—date, get to know each other before they..." She bit into her bottom lip and chewed.

"Tup," he offered, trying to suppress a grin. For a widow she was verra shy.

"Ya, 'tup' is a good word." She took another healthy swallow of wine. "You see, my people like to feel comfortable with one another. People don't just jump into bed together...immediately." When he raised a disbelieving brow, she amended, "Well, okay, some do, but it's not the right way. Do you see—ken—what I mean?"

"Aye."

"Thank heaven we got that straightened out." She expelled a great whoosh of air and picked up her knife. "I knew, if given an explanation, you'd understand."

He waited until she'd eaten a couple of mouthfuls before saying, "Tell me yer way, my lady."

"My way?"

"Aye, yer way of a man kenning a woman." He had to find out quickly. The priest would be entering the secret passage and have his eye pressed to the spy hole as soon as he called for the food to be taken away.

"Well, I'd like a man to give me flowers and take me to dinner. To talk as we walk or sit together, that sort of thing. We call it dating."

He grinned. So far he hadn't done too badly. He'd fed her and they were talking. "About the tupping."

"You're back to that again, are you?" She heaved a sigh. "Well, I'm not speaking from experience you understand—ken—but I always thought it would be nice to have a man with slow hands." She grinned self-consciously and trilled the words of her favorite country song, *Slow Hands*, about a man who understood he needed to take his time making love to his lady, and not come and go in a heated rush. She blushed anew and ducked her chin. "It's a popular song where I come from by a man named Conway Twitty. I've always thought it romantic."

He found her voice lilting and her wine-induced behavior endearing. Such an odd creature, his wife. And what kind of an oaf had she married that she dreamed of a balladeer with slow hands and an odd surname? He huffed at her first husband's stupidity. Well, he, for one, could be as slow and gentle as she wanted. With that thought in mind, he asked, "What think ye of yer new book?"

"Ah, the new book." She fiddled with her knife and sucked in her cheeks. "Duncan, it's very pretty, but a little too...condescending to women for my taste." Seeing he did not comprehend, she added, "Where I come from women are treated as equals."

"'Tis so here." The Magna Carta had made it so, particularly for those poor wee souls who happened to marry or be promised to brutish men. He didn't like the skeptical look in her eye, but left the argument for another day. His objective at the moment was not, after all, to prove his rightness in such matters, but to spread her thighs and consummate this forced marriage—or all would be lost.

Hoping to lower her guard, he reached for her hand. He turned it palm up in his.

Some claim eyes were the window into one's soul but her delicate, decidedly feminine hands had already illuminated her soul to his perusal. With them, she had brought him back from the brink of death. And—if Angus was to be believed—she had cried over him in the process. That alone warranted his best efforts as he consummated their vows. He ran his thumb gently across her palm, noting new flesh were the water had burned. He was taken aback by her skin's softness. A softness now mirrored in her eyes. "Have ye a passion in life, lass?"

She blushed. "I love to cook and to read. And you?"

He grinned. Dare he tell her? She hadn't pulled her hand away. Nay, not yet. "Being laird is enough."

"All work and no play will make you a dull lad,

Duncan."

He grinned and lifted a brow. When he murmured, "My thoughts, exactly," she choked on her wine.

He pounded her gently on the back. When she finally turned a natural pink he asked, "Are ye finished, lass?" When she nodded, he went to the door.

Within moments the room had been cleared, the door locked, and his lady had backed herself into a corner again.

He stood at the foot of his large bed and held out his hand. He whispered, "Lass, come here."

She shook her head, and he shrugged. He could give her more time. He had to undress anyway and snuff out all but one candle. He saw no point in giving the blasted priest more than a glimpse of this coupling. No more than need be to insure his holdings were safe.

He tended to the candles first, suspecting his size might put his shy lady off should she get too clear a view of things. He then tried to shrug out of his coat and immediately groaned.

To his surprise Beth ran to his side. "Duncan, you're going to tear yourself open again. Let me."

She carefully eased his jerkin off. As she started to walk away with it folded over her arm, he caught her wrist and pulled her into his embrace.

"Nay, my lady, 'tis time." He lifted her chin with a finger and placed a gentle kiss on her forehead. "I promise this eve will be as slow as ye luste." He placed a hand on her neck and felt her pulse bounding under his fingers. He smiled when fabric slip past his legs, surprised that just his touch had been enough to cause her to lose her grip of his jerkin. He kicked it under the bed.

She pressed both palms to his chest. "Duncan, I really

don't want..."

"Sssh, lass, ye have nay reason to fash." He gently brushed his lips against her forehead. He heard her little intake of breath when he drifted lower to kiss her eyelids. When his lips slid over her soft cheeks to hover over her lips, the pressure she applied to his chest eased.

Ah. Apparently, she didn't mind being kissed, perhaps was even curious. He'd not argue with that. He'd been staring at her lush, full lips for days wondering how they'd feel.

He ran his tongue along the crease of her trembling lips then nibbled on her plump lower one. Plain though she be, his lady did have a nicely shaped mouth, full and nearly liquid under his. He licked and she gasped, opening for him.

Never one to miss an opportunity, he delved into her. Ah. To his delight she tasted of wine and mint, her tongue felt like velvet as it slid slowly against his. He deepened the kiss, languishing in the silken interior of her mouth as her warm feminine scent filled his chest. When he changed angles to plunge deeper still, she moaned. Her velvet growl set his heart racing. He could not remember when that had happened last. Mayhap, never.

His blood heating, he ran a gentle hand up from her waist to caress the sweet fullness of her breast, only to have her stiffen in his arms. Ah. She did mean *slow*. No matter. 'Twas all the better for his purposes.

With any luck the priest hidden behind the wall was already in his cups and half way to sleep. Since noon, Angus had been pouring as much mead as possible down the damn man's gullet. Hopefully, he'd be out cold when they joined or near enough that he'd not dare naysay their coupling done.

Duncan refocused on the task at hand—his assault against his bride's shy nature. Since she'd not pushed his hand from her breast, he gently swirled his thumb along the side of the decidedly firm globe. He could have hoped for more to hold, but what he stroked felt deliciously female and his manhood rose.

He cradled her to his hips. As his fingers captured her nipple, to stroke it firm, she gasped and he deepened his kiss. To his delight her breath heated, as did her skin. Her hands began inching up his chest to his shoulders, traveled as if by their own accord. When they slid around his neck, fingers burrowing deep into his hair, he groaned into her mouth and slid a hand to her buttocks. Delighted with her unexpected response, with the taste and feel of her, he gently drew her against his throbbing need and slowly backed her toward the bed.

His height, while a good thing in battle, made aligning inflamed body parts while standing with a woman nigh onto impossible. He needed her on her back, and he needed it now.

He deepened his kiss before lifting her with his good arm. She mewed into his mouth as he slowly lowered her onto the bed. He settled as best he could—given her blasted skirt—between her warm thighs. Her tongue caressed his. Ah, yes, this is what a man lives for. A woman not afraid to show pleasure, a woman willing to give as well as receive.

He cradled her left breast in his palm, his thumb finding joy as it traced the firm nub of her nipple. Would they be pink or a deep caramel, he wondered, sliding his lips along her jaw and settling on her shoulder. He needed to taste her, needed to suckle her nipples like a hungry babe. Needed to rock into her hips, to feel the heat and moisture that hid beneath the layers of fabric keeping him at bay.

He shifted his weight to his left arm, much to his shoulder's dismay, and slid his free hand down her leg.

Her hands suddenly slammed into his chest.

"No!" She pushed again at his chest. "Duncan, please, we can't."

He blinked. "Huh?" What in God's name had taken her out of her warm lassitude so suddenly? He rocked up onto his elbows, his hands now on either side of her face. "What's wrong, lass?" He studied her anxious expression and silently cursed. Had he been moving too quickly? Had he been too rough? What?

"I..." Her pupils were still dilated with lust as her gaze darted from his face to the door. She nibbled on her lower lip, her breath still hot and fast from their kissing. Nothing made sense to him.

She swallowed hard. "I...I have my flowers."

Her flowers? Nay. This couldna be. He'd have noticed her waddling like a babe with a load in its nappy. At the least, she would have occasionally cradled her belly.

He inhaled, his nares flaring slightly as he sampled the heated air between his face and hers. *Nay, 'tis nothing here to indicate flowers.*

As he studied her features more closely, she blushed and turned her face away.

Ah huh! The wench lies.

"Humph!" He ran a gentle finger along her lower lip. When he did it again, her gaze locked on his lips and took on the decidedly unfocused look of passion. He watched, bemused, as her tongue tentatively slid along the path his finger had taken. Aye, she's lying, but why?

"Ye flowers, lass?"

Her gaze shifted to his chest as she nodded like a sandpiper. She started worrying her lovely lower lip near to death with her upper teeth. "Uh-huh."

He brushed a loose strand from her forehead and fingered its silky texture. "Ye'd not be telling a fib out of fear or mayhap shyness, now would ye?"

"Oh, no! No, no, no. I have my flowers." She had yet to look him in the eye. "Definitely."

"I see." He kissed her brow, and was pleased to see her gaze found his lips once again as he pulled away. "Well, my ladywife, then I fear I canna go on...." She sighed, visibly more relaxed. She patted his chest.

He rocked up onto his knees, his hands coming to rest on either side of her hips. He smiled. When she offered him a tentative smile of her own, he added, "...until I check."

He buried his face between her skirted thighs and heard a squeal loud enough to wake the dead.

Chapter 12

*P*lease, God, take me now!

Beth squealed louder and longer as Duncan noisily snuffled and sniffed at her crotch again. This time she tugged on his ears for all she was worth. "Duncan! Stop! What hell are you doing?"

If a body could die of mortification, she wanted to be on the short list. Had to be on it. She struggled to sit, and finding she couldn't, she swatted his head. "Damn it, Duncan!"

He finally came up for air, laughing to kill himself. "Ah, lass, ye are a wondrously poor liar."

In less than a heartbeat he rocked forward and settled on top of her, as he had before, his knee gently wedging her legs apart. Her treacherous thighs instinctively separated to accommodate his weight before she'd realized what they had done, so she again found herself pinned under more than two hundred pounds of solid muscle, and if her loins were correct, nearly as much bulging manhood.

He captured her hands in each of his own and settled them above her head. She stared wide-eyed at his suddenly inscrutable features. Then slowly, one corner of his mouth curled and a wicked gleam took shape in his eyes.

Uh-oh!

He started to slowly rock against her hips as his grin widened.

Now, God. Now would be a good time to take me!

She turned her face as his mouth drew near. She'd play no part in this...this seduction. He'd not said, "I'm fond of you," much less said "I love you." The fact that she'd mooned over him, cried over him, and was totally confused by her body's response to him didn't matter one wit. She couldn't make love to him. She just couldn't.

His lips grazed along her neck. "Ah, lass, ye are a wonder." When he sucked gently where her neck and shoulder met, she gasped as unexpected tingles raced down her spine. *Oh my word.*

No, she just couldn't open her heart to the pain again, could not allow herself to become vulnerable.

He licked the spot and she moaned. He then moved his lips only an inch further down and did it again.

When his lips stopped to nibble again, she did manage to whisper, "Duncan, husband, I really don't think..."

His pelvis, gently rocking between her thighs, was driving her to distraction, causing an unaccountable heat, an indefinable yearning to build within her that clouded her analytical mind. To her surprise, he agreed with her, mumbled, "Aye, lass, 'tis best we dinna." But his mouth continued to dine on her flesh in the most protracted manner as if it were imperative he memorize every dip and curve of her face.

For some inexplicable reason her mouth sought his. It came as a bit of a shock to realize her body had apparently decided it would not flatten its learning curve despite her brain's protests. When he captured her lower lip with his teeth, then ran his velvet tongue slowly across it, her mouth opened to his sweet invasion. She sighed. Her heart whispered, "This man of your fantasies—of your heart—certainly knows how to kiss."

She had no idea when he'd released her left hand, none at all, but took advantage and slid her fingers into the thick waves of his ebony hair. When he started to pull away, to explore some uncharted territory, she pulled his mouth back to hers. She'd never been kissed before—not like this at any rate—and found she wanted her fill before she had to put a stop to it. Surely, just a wee bit of kissing couldn't hurt? Surely.

To Duncan's relief his once reluctant ladywife had started moving beneath him. 'Twas a most encouraging sign, but having loosened the lacing of her gown, he was most anxious to dine on her breasts. And still he couldn't get to them, for every time he tried, she'd pull him back to her mouth. He felt inordinately pleased that she wanted his kisses, for no wife before her ever had, but there were times when a man just had to do what a man had to do. And now, with her panting setting her little globes to wobbling before his hungry perusal, was one such time. He recaptured her hands.

Her mewing protest as his lips left hers played like music on his ears and in his soul, but knowing she should garner as much pleasure from his next effort, he paid no heed.

With the palm of his right hand he slipped her bodice off the prize he sought and growled in deep satisfaction. Aye, her breasts were as he imagined: perfect creamy-white cones with deep rose crests, like tiny mountains tipped with jam. As his mouth closed over the first peak, he entered heaven.

She moaned and arched her back, giving him full access. "Aye, lass," he murmured, "'tis truly wondrous, is it not?" He suckled, enjoying her texture, the way her breath began to hitch, the way her hips began to rock in response. He lapped gently at her slopes, licking his way to the top so he could suckle once again.

"Duncan...my hands...please..."

He released his hold. Her hands immediate burrowed into his hair and she arched once again.

"Perfect, lass," he groaned as he ran his tongue around the rosy crown then pulled it into his mouth. He slowly released it. "So perfect, my eyes ache."

He slid her arms free of the gown as his lips moved from peek to peek. Her anxious hands tugged at his shirt. "Help me, lass."

And she did, her eyes becoming glassy as she ran her hands over his chest. He rolled onto his side and draped a tree-trunk thigh gently over her more slender ones. His mouth again captured hers as he slid a hand down her leg and lifted her gown.

Lady Beth, now flushed and mewing, was all his heart had ever hoped for in a wife and never had.

Her skin felt oddly smooth, like new porcelain, as his fingers glided along her legs, seeking the warm moist place hidden deep within her skirts. She groaned into his mouth when his hand finally brushed the curls at the apex of her thighs. "Aye, lass, open for me."

When her legs slowly spread he slipped the clasp from his kilt, and it fell away.

His hand slowly ruffled her downy thatch, and he wondered at the color. He dared not slip the gown from her hips just yet, not until his hands were slick with her woman's dew. Aye, he wanted her on the brink of ecstasy before he stripped her naked and drank his fill.

His joy in her response knew no bounds as his hand drew slow circles on the inside of her thighs, each circle easing closer to the heat. Her hips ground against his swollen manhood, her breath coming in pants into his mouth. His fingers did as her body asked.

They slipped though the dense soft curls in search of the magic place. Finding her nub, they lingered to massage, which caused her to gasp, then groan. Her thighs started to quiver, and he slipped a finger into the pearly, moist heat.

Her cry made him pulse with need. He pressed against her hips as his finger entered the sacred pathway to her womb. With gentle, rapid movements, his thumb began to massage.

Her hips began to grind in earnest. "Please...now."

He kissed her eyelids, having found her tighter than expected. Much tighter. "Not yet, dearest, but soon." He continued to stroke her, easing her open, wanting release as badly as she apparently did.

"Now, Duncan, love...*please!*

Love? Had she said *love?* His heart tripped with excitement never having heard a woman call him thus. Aye, she had, surely. Knowing—hoping—her to be as ready as she'd ever be, he settled between her thighs. Her hips came up to meet him.

"Now!" Her hands pressed down, her nails digging into his flesh.

"Aye, lass," he whispered into her mouth, as he rubbed his swollen tip against her, once, twice, gathering as much moisture as her body would offer. He sucked her exhaled breath into his lungs and murmured, "Now."

As he thrust forward, she cried out and turned to marble beneath him.

Red pain seared through her.

Not now, God! Not now!

Rigid, unable to breathe, Beth asked God why he'd chosen this moment to take her. And why on earth had He taken a cleaver to her? Surely, she'd died just a heartbeat from ecstasy.

She'd never forgive Him. First, He gives her this face, then takes her parents, and then ends her life using mind-bending pain and neglects to give her the bright light at the end of the tunnel? How cruel could He get? She hadn't done anything to deserve this. Nor ever. She began to cry.

She felt a light touch on her cheek and opened her eyes. "Oh." Duncan hovered above her. She mustered a tiny smile. She hadn't died, after all. She'd merely been impaled. Dear God above.

"Ssh, dearest, dinna cry. 'Twill pass in a moment." She still couldn't speak, and it certainly didn't help when he amended, "Or two. Mayhap three, but 'twill pass."

God, I am literally screwed to a mattress, here! Are you listening? I'm serious! HELP!

Duncan caught a tear as it slid down her cheek. "I swear before God, lass, I didna ken ye to be a virgin." He looked as dejected as she felt. "I thought ye a *widow*, was told so, in fact. Had I known..." He closed his eyes and rested his forehead on hers.

They were still physically engaged, but she could feel the pressure lessening, the pain easing within her hips. He hadn't moved—not by so much as a millimeter from the waist down since entering her. She appreciated his restraint more than words could convey, but...

"Duncan, is this hurting your shoulder?"

He shook his head.

And pigs fly, she thought, seeing beads of sweat multiply rapidly across his forehead. She ran a fingertip along his finely crafted lower lip before closing her eyes to focus on where they were joined. The pain had eased considerably. "Duncan?"

"Aye, lass?"

"Could we roll onto your right side?"

"But yer pain..."

"It's fading." When he continued to look skeptical, she touched his cheek. "I knew this would happen. I'd been forewarned. You did well."

"Nay, lass, ye dinna reach the stars. Ye wept."

He looked dejected. Rachael had been right. Men apparently did have very fragile egos, at least when it came to making love. And he had done everything right. He'd been slow, careful, had brought her to the brink of madness. She'd been ready—past ready if the truth were told—when he entered her. How could you fault a man because he's—what's the expression?—hung like a horse?

He looked humiliated and in obvious pain. She had to get him onto his side. Hoping she sounded naïve, she asked, "Is this all there is to making love?"

He heaved a sigh. "Nay, lass, 'tis much more...or should be."

"If that's so, please, hold me tight and roll onto your right side."

He shook his head again. "Remain still and soon matters will return to their normal state. Then we can separate without ye being hurt further."

148

And meanwhile your shoulder's probably tearing apart. "But I want to see these stars you spoke of. You want me to, don't you?"

"Aye, but not this night, ladywife." His expression told her it might be never.

She studied his mouth and furrowed brow as her body adjusted to its new reality. The *dreaded deed* was done, her virginity a thing of the past. She couldn't have stopped returning his kisses, nor banked her growing need, nor squelched her enjoyment in feeling his solid masculinity quaking with pent up need for her—plain ol' Beth—had there been a gun to her head.

She knew to her marrow she'd done exactly what she'd sworn never to do.

She'd fallen in love. Hopelessly, head over heels in love.

With that admitted, she could see no logical reason not to seek the gold at the end of the virginity rainbow, and in the process get her handsome but reluctant hubby off his damn shoulder.

"Roll with me."

"Nay, ye dinna ken what ye ask. 'Tis best to wait."

She tipped up his chin, bringing his lips within range, and then slowly ran her tongue along the crease as he had done to her. From his surprised expression, she decided she must be a good student, a quick study. She stroked his jaw, "Husband, I don't understand the rules here, but where I come from, the show's not over till the fat lady sings.'" He scowled in confusion. "I'm *going* to see yer stars, Duncan, or ken the reason why. So roll me over..." Thinking it must be the wine, she hummed, "*In the clover, kiss me hard, and do it again.*"

Duncan did as Beth bid, much to his own surprise,

and she didn't cry out as he did it, much to his relief.

He brushed a lock from her face and brushed a kiss across her forehead. "Ye are a wonder, lass."

"No, just a woman who likes to be kissed."

And so he obliged.

Thinking he best get to where he need be before matters got rock hard again, he lifted her right leg and draped it over his hip. He deepened his kiss as his hand pushed her buttocks. She sighed as she eased down on him fully.

"Oh, lass." She felt so tight, warm. It took all of his willpower not to start thrusting. He didn't dare breath. "Are ye comfy?"

She wiggled a little, as if testing a chair seat for size, making him groan. "Easy, lass. 'Tis too soon for ye to be riding such."

To his utter surprise she brought his hand to her breast and whispered into his mouth, "Then you better get me ready, husband."

Chapter 13

Beth awoke feeling warm, fuzzy, thoroughly loved, and more than a little sore. *My oh my.*

Spooned against him, she craned her neck to study the man who'd shown her the stars. Who would have thought just a month ago that she, "plain-as-pudding-Pudding", would have such a lover? Or rather *husband.* Certainly not she. He was everything she'd ever dreamed of in unguarded moments, a gentle, decidedly handsome man who touched her with reverence, who whispered endearments, and brushed away her fears with his kisses.

Her pulse escalated as she watched him sleep in the faint morning light. She studied the slow steady movements of his chest, the way the air fluttered his lower lip occasionally, and marveled at the rapid eye movement behind his heavily fringed lids. What was he dreaming about? She loved the way his shoulder-length hair waved down the sides of his face and curled up on the ends, and really loved the softness of the fine dark hair that made a dark wedge across his heavily muscled chest and abdomen. Tears welled in her eyes as she memorized the rugged plains of his face.

Thank you, God. He's the loveliest thing I've ever

beheld. And he was hers. She still couldn't believe it.

In the wee hours of the night, after their need for each other had been satiated, she'd told him the rest of her story. He'd held her and clucked and stroked her back and told her not to fash—worry. He would take care of everything. No one had ever said that to her before.

She glanced toward the covered windows on her left and saw pink daylight peeping around the mustard-brown wool. Before he woke she needed to attend to one or two of life's little duties. Privately.

Naked, she reached for the chamber pot, did her business, and then poured cold water from the ewer into the pitcher's matching bowl. She glanced at her container of crushed seaweed and oats and then picked up the fine sliver of Rachael's soap. She'd rot in hell before she'd use her seaweed concoction after suffering through Duncan's last reaction—at least, while he was still within a hundred miles of the solar. "Humph."

She ran a hand over her legs. Stubble. Her underarms were in similar condition. If she and Duncan were going to 'tup' on a regular basis she'd best get adept at using the blade. She sighed resignedly and took it out of the closet. What used to take three minutes with a safety razor now took close to a half-hour.

Hearing water splash, Duncan slowly stretched. For the first time in his adult life his body and mind felt completely relaxed. He yawned and picked up the scent of their joining. He smiled. What a night. Given their shaky beginning, a miracle had occurred.

Had anyone had told him a virgin could—would— enjoy kissing, exploring, and out right fornicating as his bride had, he would have called them a liar.

And she did see the stars. Oh, aye, she'd made that

verra clear, quite loudly, in fact. She'd even called out to God! Amazing. Truly amazing.

What was more, she'd understood when he'd pulled away before spilling his seed. In the wee hours he'd asked if she wanted children and she'd assured him she did, not now, but eventually. That immediately put his mind at ease.

And he liked her. Verra much. He would enjoy giving her a child if he learned her addled mind was simply due to injury.

And speaking of addled, while curled in his arms like a kitten, his ladywife had finally finished her tale. Ack, the poor lass, believing in sky scrapes and in him becoming a ghost, of all things. 'Twas so sad he wanted to cry for her, for she truly believed her tale to be true. Believed it wholeheartedly, which made it all the more heartbreaking.

But for not knowing whether or not she could give him an heir, she would make a bonnie wife. Bonnie indeed. She was soft spoken, had a wry sense of humor, lovely breasts, a lilting voice, and liked to tup. What more could a man ask?

He rolled and reached for her. Finding the bed empty, he opened his eyes and saw her silhouetted in profile against the morning light.

Tall and slim, draped only in sheeting and with her little breasts reaching for the sky, he thought her a sight to behold. She raised an arm over her head still unaware of his perusal.

Then light bounced off metal and he saw the blade in her hand.

"*Naaay!*" His roar echoed in the solar as he vaulted out of bed and knocked the blade away. He'd used such force he'd knocked her to the floor as well.

"*Why, woman?*" Why would she take her life? His heart pounded a furious beat as he picked her up by the shoulders and shook her. Shook her so hard, she started to cry. And well she should. Christ's blood!

He shoved her toward the bed and retrieved the knife. When he discovered who had given it to her, he'd slice their throat with it.

Why? Had last night meant nothing to her? Had her kisses meant nothing?

"Ye are *Wode*, woman!" he roared. "*Wode!* Do ye hear me?"

Had he awakened a moment later, he'd be again standing ankle deep in a ladywife's blood.

She cowered against the headboard sobbing as he approached.

"Duncan? I don't understand—"

"Close thy mouth!" His entire body quaked with pent-up rage at her betrayal. He grabbed her arm and yanked her to her knees before him.

"Why?" she sobbed, "Why are you so upset? I was only—"

He raised his hand and she screamed.

"Augh!" He dropped his hand. "Christ's blood. Ye're making me as wode as ye be." He'd never hit a woman in his life. The realization that he'd nearly done so—coupled with the fear that filled him seeing her trying to slice herself open—made him nauseous.

Heart aching, blood roaring in his ears, he grabbed his kilt and stormed out. Her plaintive "Why...?" and sobbing followed him like a witch's curse.

He stormed into the great hall and all went tomb quiet. God's teeth! Had everyone heard? He had little doubt everyone in the bailey certainly had, since nothing in the solar windows would have muffled his furious railing. Ack!

With his face still hot with infused blood, he scanned the hall's rigid and silent occupants for Angus. Not finding him, he settled on venting his rage on Isaac.

Pointing to his financial advisor, he hissed, "In the library. *NOW*."

He crossed the hall with Isaac—now ash gray—following. Passing Flora, Duncan growled, "What the hell are ye grinning about?"

"Nothing, my lord. Nothing."

On the stairs he turned to see her eyes still followed him, her snide, all-knowing grin still gracing her deceptively lovely face, and his anger grew.

In the relative privacy of the library—the room, like most in the keep, still had no door, Isaac murmured, "My liege, have I done something to offend ye?" He started to pace. "For if I—"

"Lock yer jaws, Isaac, and heed." Duncan collapsed into a chair still not believing it could be happening again. He couldn't believe he'd begun fancying himself in love with Beth. "Just moments ago, I awoke to find my ladywife trying to kill herself." He threw the blade onto the table. "Do ye ken who owns this blade?" He'd racked his brain and couldn't picture any of his men carrying the *sgian dubh*. Made of silver and quality steel, the six-inch knife would have been well beyond the purse of most within the clan. And it was not Beth's. He'd been present when Beth, still unconscious, had been placed in the solar. She'd not carried it on her person. Nor would a blade of this caliber—of such great value—be left about so she might find it. Nay.

Someone had given it to her.

He pushed his hair off his face with both hands. "Isaac, I swear I have never been as frightened nor so furious in my life as when I saw the wee daft lass holding that blade to her armpit."

"*Armpit*, my lord?"

"Aye. A truly odd place to slash, I grant ye, but 'twas where the blade's edge pressed." His friend looked as ghastly as he felt. "Isaac, sit. Ye look about to faint."

Duncan hadn't wanted another wife, but if God and Albany in their infinite wisdom lusted it so, then why in hell hadn't they given him a sane one? Now he would die without an heir, his beloved castle, his lands, and clan would all be taken over by a Bruce or Stewart, no doubt. He toyed with her knife. Mayhap, Beth had the right of it. He should just slit his throat and be done with it.

Isaac held out his hand. "May I have that, my lord?"

"Relax Isaac."

"Aye, but just give it here."

He handed it over and heard Isaac sigh in relief.

"Where's Angus? I want the labor resumed on her apartment at once. I cannot watch her every moment, nor can I have her slipping, slicing, or jumping to her death so long as Albany lives."

"Angus is with the MacLean as ye ordered... the arrangement for the tournament tents?"

"Ah." He'd forgotten he'd sent Angus to barter fish for canvas. "Then find Brian and order the work started." Angus's second in command could deal with it. "And summon yer ladywife."

Ashen, Isaac nodded. "Rachael is in Drasmoor at present, my lord." He looked at the blade in his hands. "As soon as she arrives I shall send her to ye."

Seeing the marked distress on his friend's face, Duncan heaved a heavy sigh. "Isaac, I've no plans to rail at Rachael, but ask for her help. The only lock I have is on the dungeon grate, and I cannot place Lady Beth there, much as I'd like. Nor can I truss her like a goose in the solar for she will scream the walls down, surely. Nay. I want yer ladywife joined at the hip to Lady Beth, day and night, until I can cloister her for her own safekeeping. And order every knife not strapped to a man's thigh taken out of the keep. Take them to your croft, take them to the sea, I care not where, but take them away."

~#~

Tears coursed down her cheeks as Beth vomited into the chamber pot. When the painful retching finally stopped, she wiped her mouth with the back of her hand and cursed. Since childhood, every damn time she became terrified—felt that familiar overwhelming heartache—she'd vomit.

Why, God? Why has he done this?

Her breath hitched and hiccupped as she staggered to her feet. With her neck and shoulders sore, she looked at her equally aching arms and saw his handprints around her biceps.

She'd married a madman.

Beth limped into what had once been her bathroom, now her closet, and rummaged through the trunks. She uncovered her jeans and sweater, but no underwear. She could live without them.

This could not be happening. Not again. God, not again.

Just fifteen minutes ago she'd been contentedly musing over the realization that she'd fallen in love with a beautiful man, and he with her. How stupid could one woman get?

Sniffing, she yanked up her zipper and went looking for her sneakers. She didn't know whom to be angrier with; herself for believing in the unbelievable—that a handsome man could love a plain woman such as she— or with him for his painful deception and blatant use of her. That she'd brought it all on herself by opening her heart to him didn't bear thinking about. She'd known better.

Dressed, she scoured the sparsely furnished solar for a weapon. She'd not be caught off guard again. Not physically and never again emotionally. If the son of a bitch dared come through the door while she plotted her escape, someone was going to die and it wouldn't be her. She hadn't fought all her life for respect to become Duncan MacDougall's punching bag. No way.

Her gaze settled on the cast iron fire poker. She hefted it, testing its weight and balance in her hand. It would do.

At the window, firer poker in hand, she studied the boats leaving the quay. She had to get on one to leave, but how? The few times she'd asked to be taken to Drasmoor just to see the village, she'd been told to seek out her husband or been given some excuse as to why now wasn't a good time. Duncan had apparently ordered his men to keep her here. But she wouldn't stay. Couldn't.

She continued pacing. Haunting images of Duncan's tenderness in the wee hours of the night and his later inexplicable brutality constantly interrupted her thoughts of escape.

"Why?" she kept asking aloud. Why had he bothered

to show her such consideration and warmth to only yank it away come dawn? Was he schizophrenic or something?

The twenty-first century certainly hadn't invented madness, so yes, he could well be clinically insane, and no one here would dare lay a hand on him for fear of reprisal. He was, after all, the MacDougall—the Black. No wonder she's wife number four! Had he killed wives two and three? Probably. Had he lived in her time, he'd be the one kept in isolation on an island, not her.

Heart pounding erratically, she walked the keep in her mind. If she could get down to the third floor unseen, she could circumnavigate the fortification on that level to the portcullis stairway leading to the quay. There'd be guards above and below, but most would be busy. She crossed to the window overlooking the bailey, hoping to spy something to hide behind until everyone went to the hall for the midday meal. Nothing appeared large enough. Fine. She'd just have to find a storeroom to hide in until all but the tower guards went to the hall. She could be in a boat and pulling away by the time a tower guard could reach the quay. So long as the guard didn't give immediate chase in another boat, she might be able—

The solar door swung open and Beth spun, poker held over her shoulder like a baseball bat.

White faced, Rachael raced to her. "Madame!"

The poker fell from Beth's hands as fresh tears welled. Arms out, she rushed to greet her friend. "Oh, Rachael, I've been so scared!" Sobs ripped from her throat as Rachael's arms embraced her. "He...he threw me on the bed...and after all we'd shared...and then he screamed..." She sucked in a deep breath. "And I didn't know what to do...I couldn't get away and then...he raised his fist and I...I..."

"Ssh. Ssh, my lady, come." Rachael wrapped a protective arm around her and led her to the foot of the bed. "Sit and tell me all, but slowly."

Beth buried her face in her hands and continued to sob. "I don't know...what happened. One moment he was..." She hiccuped. "We made love last night. He'd been so gentle and I'd been so happy. And then I got up..." she grabbed a lung full of air, "...and started getting ready for the day and the next thing I know he's shaking me like a rag doll and I'm sure I'm about to die...and..."

Rachael brushed the hair from Beth's face and whispered, "Tell me about the blade, *mon ami*."

"The blade?" Beth sniffed as she studied the concern etched on Rachael's finely boned face. What blade? "Oh, your pretty knife. I'm sorry. He took it. I don't know where it is now." Beth wiped the tears from her face, heaved a heavy sigh, and hiccupped again. "I didn't even get a chance to finish shaving my damn armpits."

Rachael stood abruptly. Her voice rose as she waved in agitation. "Are ye saying all this—all yer crying and himself storming about like the wrath of God—is because ye wanted to shave yer *ARM PEETS*?"

Why was she upset? "Rachael, all I know is that one minute I'm as happy as a lark and the next I'm facing a madman."

Rachael shook her head and collapsed on the edge of the bed. "My *petit chou*, the MacDougall isna wode— mad—as ye think, but terrified. He thought ye about *se suicider*—to kill thy self."

"*WHAT?*" Beth bolted to her feet, mouth agape. "Why would he think such a thing?"

"*Oh, mon ami.* 'Tis a wonder he *isna* wode with thinking it happening again." Sensing Beth's confusion, she said, "Ah, I see ye ken not." She heaved a huge sigh and patted the bed. "Sit. 'Tis a sad tale of deceit and deception I am about to tell ye. When we have this sorted, ye can then tell me of the tupping."

~#~

Still upset, in part because of his brutal handling of Beth—in the past he'd been the one pounding sense into men for beating their wives—and in part due to his great disappointment, Duncan returned to the fourth floor.

Outside the solar, he scowled at the guard. Why were peals of laughter coming through the door? What in God's holy name could Beth possibly find humorous about their current state of affairs?

Women!

He kenned them not and would go to his grave in the same ignorance. Growling, he turned away.

Mayhap, God had placed women on earth to drive men into their cups and then into early graves. He had certainly consumed enough whisky in the last three hours to support the conclusion. He stomped down the stairs. He had to get to the carpenter before the man started crafting the chapel pews. There was nay hope for it; the precious wood would now have to be used to make a verra sturdy door for Beth's cell.

In the kirk, after speaking with the carpenter, Duncan ran a gentle hand over the chiseled words on his first wife's simple two-foot square stone marker. Tears formed then threatened to spill.

"I'm so sorry, lass. I did not appreciate ye full well while ye lived." This woman, who had never sought him out, who had never returned a kiss, had been the best of the lot.

His throat tightened as he whispered, "Someday, Mary, ye will have the fine bronze effigy I promised. Yer likeness will hold a lily in yer right hand." She'd ken the reason he would choose the symbol of the Blessed Virgin. "My shield will be on yer chest, and our babe in yer left arm. Aye, and yer father's shield will shine above ye. All who look upon it from then until forever will ken ye were the only jewel in my thorny crown of wives."

He ran a slow hand over the letters again then backed away. He blinked, removing the wetness blurring his vision and took a deep breath. He had to find his blacksmith.

The new door hinges the smitty labored over would have to be turned into brackets so a beam as wide as his palm could be dropped across the door the carpenter now grumbled over.

"My lord!"

Halfway across the bailey, Duncan turned to find Isaac running toward him, Rachael being dragged behind him like a dingy in a ship's wake, flopping and stumbling, her short legs no match for Isaac's length of limb or speed.

"Slow, Isaac! Dinna be abusing your ladywife in such a disgraceful manner."

When they came abreast of him, Rachael could barely catch her breath.

"My lord, Rachael has something of great import to tell ye. Ye must pay heed." Isaac looked about, his gaze settling on the hay barn. "We can talk in private over there."

Twenty minutes later, Duncan shook his head in disbelief. "Ye mean to say she does this scraping of her body with a blade daily?"

"Aye, my lord," Rachael mumbled. "'Tis the way of her people."

"'Tis foolishness in the extreme," Duncan growled as he searched through the night's memories seeking the truth of Rachael's words. He had thought it odd his ladywife's legs felt like porcelain, and had been most aroused finding her underarms naked and had licked. "Humph!"

He turned to Isaac. "Tell the carpenter he can stop grumbling and use his precious oak for the pews, and then release Young Kevin from guard duty." As Rachael turn to follow her husband, Duncan stayed her with a hand. "Nay, lady, I want another word with ye, if ye dinna mind." He could see that she did, but she stayed as he commanded.

With Isaac gone, Duncan stepped close enough to Rachael to bury his boot tips beneath her skirts. He then puffed out his chest and stretched to his full height. Rachael immediately blanched.

Good. He had her attention.

"Now, dear lady, will ye be kind enough to tell why I—being completely overwrought with grief and horror—heard ye and my lady laughing to kill yerselves just moments ago?"

"Uhmm..." Rachael's face turned the color of whey. "We...umm...we were discussing ye finding her with a green face, my lord."

Narrowing his eyes, he crossed his arms and waited. She couldna lie any better than his ladywife.

Rachael chewed on her lower lip. Apparently understanding he wasn't about to let her go until he had the whole of it, she finally blurted, "'Twas about yer manner of tupping, my lord."

"And this is a matter for laughter?" Outrage infused his face with heat.

"*Nay, my lord!* 'Twas just the manner of Beth's telling..." She looked to the floor. "...about her flowers and ye snuffling and sniffing her skirts, my lord."

He cocked his head to better examine Rachael's face, and as he suspected, found her flushed and struggling not to laugh.

Exasperated, he cautioned, "One word of this—"

She held up her hands. "Oh nay, my lord! I would never think to do such a thing."

He had little doubt she'd already told Isaac, but he waved her away. Hopefully, 'twas the end of it.

Until he faced Beth again.

And how on earth would he do that? Ack! He'd been brutish to the extreme in his treatment of her—though given his state of mind at the time, surely 'twas understandable. But she'd not understood his terror at the time and that was the most important point. Rachael had done well in telling Beth his whole sordid history with regard to his past wives, but what if Lady Beth still harbored resentment? And there was still the matter of her believing her bizarre tales of ghosts and living in the twenty-first century. Augh!

Pondering his approach to Beth, he studied the activity of the bailey. He watched the bairns at play, a few deliberately tripping their harried, unusually quiet parents to get attention as they carried casks of dried fish. More casts were off-loaded by more quiet men and carried past him and into the keep for storage. He looked above the battlements to see distant fields looking like coats of arms, white stripes against green, as newly made, urine-soaked cloth bleached in the sun. Aye, all was as well as could be expected outside, but not so within. He heaved a heavy sigh. He'd put off facing Beth long enough.

Climbing the steps to the solar he harbored little doubt his lady wanted to cleave his head from his shoulders.

He garnered his courage with a deep breath and cautiously pushed open the solar door. Marked disappointment filled him finding the room empty. Thinking he might find her in the library, he retraced his steps and turned at the second floor corridor. As he rounded a corner, he collided with Flora. He reached out to steady her, and she fell into his arms.

Chapter 14

Hunger drove Beth to the great hall. She'd spent a futile two hours in the solar hoping Duncan would come and apologize. Her monumental relief in learning she hadn't made love with a raving lunatic had bolstered her spirits and her hope for their relationship. She just wished someone had had the foresight to enlighten her about Duncan's second and third wives earlier. Had she known, she definitely would have responded to his fury differently.

Deep in thought she stepped into the unusually quiet hall, and found all eyes turned toward her. All but the children then developed a sudden interest in the trenchers or ale before them.

They know. Everybody had apparently heard the argument.

Appearing before them for the first time with a naked face couldn't compare to the embarrassment she now felt. Duncan owed her for this. Big time. And where is he?

Back straight, she crossed the hall to the tightly wound staircase that would take her down to the bailey.

Outside, people again stopped what they were doing

to stare. When she stared back, they quickly averted their gaze as if she were naked. Feeling an outcast just by being among them, her discomfort grew as she made her way toward the chapel, the place Duncan had spoken of with fondness during the night, in the hopes of finding him there. She wanted—no, the operative word here was *needed*—him to apologize and then he had to rectify the good people of Blackstone's opinion of her. Once that had been accomplished, he could kiss her if he liked. But only once. She was still mad at him.

Not twenty feet from the chapel's arched doorway a blond child of three or so darted out from between two casts chasing after a huge gray cat and nearly tripped her. Apparently unaware of the danger, the child followed the cat out the open portcullis. Expecting to find a frantic mother chasing behind, Beth scanned the women and realized no one had noticed the child's exit.

She ran after him, hoping one of the guards had already captured the dirty-faced urchin and given him a good dressing down while at it.

But outside the gate she saw to her horror that no one stood between the sea and the child as he raced after the cat. Not knowing his name she yelled, "No baby! Get back. Baby get back!"

She ran. Only feet from grabbing him, the cat jumped onto a tethered boat and the child, reaching for the boat, lost his balance and toppled over the quay's edge and out of sight.

Beth heard a woman's scream just as she plunged feet first into the frigid water after the boy.

Slipping below the churning waves, Beth felt the icy cold hit her with the force of a solid fist. She almost gasped from shock and hoped the child had enough sense not to. Tossed between the quay and the boat, she felt rather than saw the frantic child. She latched on to the wavering fabric of his shirt and kicked for the light. A breaking wave knocked her against a hull as she broke the surface with the child, his shirt still locked in her fist.

Someone lifted the child up and out of the water and then strong hands reached for her. Beth heard the child's wet cough and then a mother's cooing and admonishing as she made it to her feet. Teeth chattering, Beth pushed dripping hair out of her eyes to find the child—now wrapped in tartan—a bit blue around the lips, but otherwise okay. Relief flooded her.

She tipped her face to the sun. *Thank you, God.*

Deciding the child was none the worse for the experience and in good hands, Beth hunched against the wind and pushed through the crowd now gathered on the quay. One man silently offered her his cloak as she passed. She gave him a wane smile, shook her head, and hurried toward the keep. She desperately needed to get out of her clothing before she turned to a block of ice.

Before she made it to the keep's door someone tapped her shoulder.

"My lady?"

Beth stopped and managed a grin for the panting, apple-cheeked woman holding the drenched boy.

"Thank ye for saving me lad."

"You're most welcome." She studied the chattering child clutched to the woman's chest. "What's his name?"

Double dimples bracketed the woman's semi-toothless grin like quotation marks. "Miles."

"Hello, Miles." To the woman Beth said, "He's a lovely—bonnie lad. How many years is he?"

The woman's chambray eyes assessed Beth for a

long moment. "Soon four, my lady."

"An inquisitive age." Several more women edged closer to them, obviously curious. Beth held out her hand. "My name is Beth, Mrs....?"

The woman hesitated for a brief moment before taking Beth's hand. As she did, one woman gasped and another giggled nervously.

"MacDougall, my lady, Kari MacDougall."

"Kari, it's a pleasure meeting you. I just wish— luste—it had been under more pleasant circumstances." Beth's teeth began to chatter in earnest. "I'd love to chat, but I need to change." She gave the child's arm a pat. "Bye, and no more chasing kitties onto the quay, you hear?"

The child smiled, displaying dimples identical to his mother's. Beth waved and ran up the stairs, her goal the solar. Climbing on stiff legs, she pondered the possibility—should she remained locked in this world— of she and Duncan someday having a child so easily identifiable as theirs. Would her son have Duncan's steel blue eyes and black hair? She prayed if she had a daughter the child would have her height and build but her father's features and coloring.

As she rounded the second floor landing, Beth came to an abrupt halt. Her hands flew to her mouth.

Not fifteen feet before her in the darkened hallway stood her husband and Miss I'm Too Sexy for My Clothes Flora Campbell locked in an embrace. Something sharp contracted around Beth's chest seeing Flora leaning into Duncan, the woman's palms splayed on his chest as he casually leaned against the wall.

When they turned as one to look at her, Beth's body infused with blistering heat. She didn't wait for an explanation. Matters were clear enough for a blind man to see. Her husband loved another.

Without a word, she spun and tore up the stairs wanting only to get behind a closed door before she shamed herself by allowing him to see that he'd made her cry.

"Beth! Wait! This isna—"

Duncan grabbed Flora's upper arms and shoved her back. "God's teeth, Flora, back off with ye!" Damn all and the little fishes. Beth's expression had turned from startled to painful recognition in only a heartbeat as she had stared at them. Damn!

"Oops," Flora murmured tightening her grip on his sleeve. "Ignore her, my lord. As I was saying—"

"Flora, away with ye. Now!"

Beth already thought him a beast after he'd tossed her about the solar in a rage. He had nay doubt that her thinking she'd caught him in an adulterous clutch would do naught for his plea of understanding about his earlier behavior.

He raced down the corridor after her and then flew up the stairs, taking them two and three at a time. Why was fate so determined to blast his life down the garderobe slew? All he needed now was a raid by the Bruce and his life would be a total ruin.

At the top of the stairs he found the solar door closed. He lifted the latch and shoved. It didn't budge. He pounded a fist on the thick wood.

"Beth, open the door." He could hear her muffled sobbing.

"*Go to hell!*"

He raked his hands through his hair and growled in frustration. He'd not been able to lock her *in* for lack of a lock, but she'd locked him *out* by simply propping something under the latch. He pressed his forehead to the door. "Lass, please. 'Tis not as ye think. Flora waylaid me, 'twas all. I wouldna do that to ye."

He waited for a response and heard more muffled sobs.

Damnation! And why did she cry so? 'Twas naught as if she loved him. Women! They'd be the death of him.

A great murmuring rose from the hall and Duncan's attention began to vacillate between his sobbing wife and discovering what now had the clan in an uproar. He should stay and plead his case, but what was wrong below? The conversation escalated in volume and he stared down the hall toward the stairs.

Surely, if given time to ponder his words, Beth would see he spoke the truth. No? He had, after all, pledged his fealty to her before God and his clan just a week past, and all knew him to be a man of his word. Aye, 'tis best she found the right of it in her own good time.

He cast a final glance at the barred solar door before starting down the steps. Mayhap, he could coerce Rachael into helping Beth to see reason. He was, after all, a peaceful man and did not want his life at sixes and sevens any longer than need be.

In the hall Duncan couldn't make heads or tails of what his clansmen were saying about Beth whilst everyone talked at once. To all he shouted, "I just left my ladywife. She's in the solar so how can this be?"

"'Tis true, my lord," Clive MacDougall, an able solider chimed in. "I was up on the battlement, above the portcullis and saw the bairn racing after the cat with ye lady fast on his heels. I shouted as she did, but to no avail. The lad toppled in. By the time I got down to the quay Lady Beth had jumped in after the lad. Ye can understand my distress; the wee lad canna swim and me not knowing if yer lady could?"

"'Tis as he says, my lord," Kari interrupted.

Duncan waved the bairn's mother forward.

"Just moments ago..." Kari wrung her hands, "...I looked about for Miles and then saw yer lady running through the gate yelling, 'No, baby, no!' With my sweet babe gone, I gave chase. I near died seeing him fall into the sea." Tears sprang into her eyes. "Drown he would have if not for yer Lady Beth. I canna swim and Clive couldna have reached him before..." She gulped as tears coursed down her ruddy cheeks. "Yer lady just disappeared into the sea after my Miles and then rose with him in her hands."

All who claimed to have seen the astonishing event nodded as one. Someone muttered, "Like in the tale of the Lady of the Lake, my lord. Only 'twas not a sword but the bairn she rose up with clutched to her breast."

Duncan mentally pictured Beth standing in the hall—beyond the shock and dismay he'd originally noticed on her visage, he now realized she had looked like a ewe caught in a hard rain. Why hadn't he noticed before this?

Ack! 'Twas little wonder she'd told him to go to hell. He'd not be the least surprised if she now plotted his demise. Good thing he'd ordered all the *sgian dubhs* away or he might find one buried to the hilt between his ribs. What a dreadful day his poor addled Beth has had.

'Twas past time for him to humble himself before her and beg for reconciliation. On his knees, if need be, before the solar door.

As he turned to the stairs, he heard Angus hail him.

"My lord, a word if ye please."

Duncan studied his second in command's stern countenance as he approached. "Ye return earlier than expected. Is something amiss?"

Angus dropped his voice to a whisper. "'Tis the Bruce. We need speak of in private."

Duncan, irked by life's timing, nodded. He would just have to speak with Beth after discovering what his enemy planned.

~#~

God, if you don't get me out of this time warp soon I'm going to kill him.

Of all the woman in the keep, why Flora? Why not someone with a sweet disposition, some widow with six children she couldn't hate so much? But no. Instead, "plain-as-pudding Pudding" has to find her man in the arms of a woman with a snide attitude, a supermodel face and great boobs. *And lest we forget, one who also speaks fluent French. Talk about finding oneself on the short end of life's equation!* She mopped away her tears with her palms.

Enough!

She'd done nothing but cry herself sick for two solid hours. She'd been foolish to think she could have life otherwise. And worse than foolish for letting her guard down while in Duncan's arms last night. She'd acted stupid, pushing aside the harsh lessons she'd learned growing up as she was shuffled from one disastrous situation to another. "Lesson Number One," she muttered, "Love is beyond your grasp. Lesson Two; nowhere is it written that you're guaranteed fairness. And Three; there's only right and wrong."

And Duncan was, by God, in the wrong.

At the windows she hiccupped, sniffed and studied

the activity in the bailey and across the bay in Drasmoor. All of it—the keep, the castle, even the village—belonged to her by marriage and by law, both in this time and in her own. Amazing. Dashing the tears from her cheeks, she marveled at how life went on all around her, without her, while she huddled above it all.

Get a grip on your heart and pride, girl. Nobody has or ever will give a damn whether you're happy or not.

She heaved a sigh. She couldn't continue to lick her wounds in the solar. If the fates had decided she was to remain here indefinitely, then for her sanity's sake things had to change. For starters, she would not live in a pig's sty.

Marshalling her pride and installing what she hoped was now an impregnable shield about her battered heart, she straightened. Though her body felt like she'd gone three rounds with a prizefighter thanks to the abuses she'd suffered at Duncan's hand and the battering she'd taken by the waves, she rolled her shoulders and took a deep breath. None of that matter.

The only thing mattered. She, by marriage and heredity, was the lady of the keep—the mistress of Castle Blackstone—and it was about time she let everyone know it. It was time to kick ass and take names.

Chapter 15

Margaret Silverstein kept one eye on the parlor's wall clock timing her contractions and the other on her anxious husband as he paced before her with Lady Beth's diary clutched in his hand.

Fretting day and night, Tom hadn't eaten or slept since Lady Beth's disappearance. And daily he went to the castle and called to the ghost. He'd tried everything he could think of from bring a telly over and turning it up full blast to leaving a letter stating the Blackstone estate was bankrupt in his effort to get a response—even a furious one—from their laird and still Tom could find no evidence of their ghost about the keep.

"I've a bad feeling, Margaret. Lady Beth is ill-prepared for what she's facing."

"I dinna agree." Margaret wiped a damp curl from her brow, the day's unusual heat and humidity making her even more uncomfortable. "She's a survivor."

"Did ye not read this?" Tom slapped the fabric-covered journal he'd found under her pillow as he continued wearing a trench in their carpet. "She poured out her heart in this book, laid her soul bare. She's never been loved and craves it desperately. To make matters more worrisome, she's lived a pampered life, even by our standards, never mind the Black's." He stopped before her. "Ye were not there. Ye dinna hear her going on about the blasted water heater, for heaven sake! What will she do having no plumbing and no knowing the language as the MacDougall rails?"

"No doubt, ignore him." Margaret shook her head at her husband. She was worried, too, but for an altogether different reason. Having spent time with Lady Beth and having read the diary, she'd come away with a totally different picture of Katherine Elizabeth MacDougall Pudding.

Sure, Lady Beth craved a man's love and attention as any healthy woman might, but Beth wasn't one of those foolish women dependent on a man's opinion to feel good about herself. She was tough, had never allowed herself to be vulnerable simply because she wanted love.

"Tom, dear, ye're fashing is understandable, but ye forget that she made a comfortable life for herself without anyone's help. And she's brave."

Beth had stood up on more than one occasion for co-workers when she felt they were being treated unfairly at the risk of her own job security, and she'd thwarted a mugger. In a verra unorthodox manner by kicking him in the jewels then vomiting on him, but she'd done it.

Aye, if anyone could get his lordship's undivided attention it was Lady Beth, which was precisely where Margaret's worry lay.

Margaret kenned Tom didn't agree but she believed Lady Beth would try to hold her own against their laird. As Tom continued his fretful pacing, Margaret shifted and tried to get comfortable. She glanced at the clock as another contraction started. With a mixture of excitement and dread, she decided they were definitely coming closer together.

"Tom, how will we know if all has gone well?"

"Perhaps..." He stopped and grinned for the first time in days. "I've got to go to the castle." He raced to the hall and slapped on his hat. As he shoved an arm into his coat, he said, "I must get *his* diary, the original one."

"Tom, stop." Margaret grimaced as she levered her ponderous body into a standing position. As she did, a puddle of amniotic fluid formed at her feet. "Yer babe has finally decided it's time, dearest. Our laird's diary will have to wait."

Chapter 16

Dressed in jeans and armed with the poor excuse for a broom that she'd found in the kitchen, Beth chased two mangy dogs, three children, and the idle priest out of the hall. She didn't care if they all thought her crazed. They'd just have to live with it because the hall was in for an overhaul.

She swept rushes from one corner and started stacking the long benches in it. As she started dragging one of the many long tables toward the corner, Rachael appeared at her elbow.

"My lady, there's nay reason to strain." Within minutes, Rachael had summoned half a dozen women to help. Much to Beth's surprise they all smiled at her now and appeared more than willing to do her bidding.

As they grabbed opposite ends of one trestle table, Rachael whispered, "Did his apology meet yer *esperances*—yer hopes?"

"I don't want to talk about him, Rachael. If the man dies of a heart attack, I don't want to hear about it. Leastwise, not until *after* the funeral." She'd given Duncan Angus MacDougall as much thought as she was ever going to expend on him.

"Heart ah tak?"

Beth rolled her eyes and clutched her chest as she

pantomimed a heart seizure.

"Ah, *oui*. " Frowning, Rachael muttered something in French before adding, "As ye luste, *mon ami*."

Thankful her friend let the subject of her wayward husband drop, Beth said, "After we get all the furniture moved, I want the room swept clean. I don't want to see so much as a crumb on the floor." She wanted to see the wide-plank flooring gleam.

"Of course." Rachael issued rapid instructions in Gael to four of the women and within minutes everyone was amiably chatting as they swept the rushes out the door and down the winding stairwell to the bailey. While one woman went for fresh rushes and Rachael dug around in the west wing for lavender and whatever herbs she could gather, Beth scrubbed everything made of wood. As she labored, she hoped the caustic lye soap did as much damage to germs as it was doing to her hands. If so, she'd be making headway.

With most of the tables scrubbed, Beth found Kari at her side.

"Please, to help ye, my lady?"

Beth nodded. "Aye, ye may." She pointed to the soot-coated fireplace on the east-facing wall. "I think the stone work used to be cream-colored, or at the least beige." In her time the fireplaces had elaborate white marble facades, but not so in Duncan's. He had built them of etched sandstone with broad mantels. From his diary, Beth knew the keep to be ten years old. How the fireplace facades had become so disgusting in so short a time, she couldn't fathom unless the chimneys needed cleaning. If so, she could address it later. Right now, she just wanted to dine in a clean room.

"Can you take a scrub brush to them and find out?"

When Kari only smiled then shrugged, Beth had to wait until Rachael returned to translate. Once Kari understood what was being asked of her, Beth set Rachael to rearranging the tables.

"But the rushes, madame. They are not yet spread...down."

"We're not putting them *down* Rachael. We're putting them up."

Rachael's sable, almond-shaped eyes grew round as quarters. "Pardon, *madame?*"

"You'll see in a bit. Just get the tables aligned like so..."

As they labored, Beth thanked God Miss I'm Too Sexy Flora never showed. Had she the nerve, Beth would have set her to cleaning the chimney flues. With a short-handled broom.

Three hours later her helpers stood looking about with mouths agape, then slowly, one by one, they all started to smile. Beth, admiring their labor, smiled for the first time in hours, too.

She congratulated them, and then asked, "Are the fresh rushes on the lowest level and the sign nailed to the door?"

Rachael translated and Kari grinned. "'Aye, my lady."

"And the dogs—lymers—are washed?" They nodded again. "Great. Now to the kitchen."

~#~

Duncan's stomach growled and his eyes burned. Isaac and Angus had been sequestered with him for what felt like a lifetime, as they sorted out their dilemma.

Albany had ordered the clan leaders to pair up in teams of two for the first rounds of the tournament. He paired them not friend with friend but foe with foe in an effort to keep the peace, teaming Duncan with the Bruce, which to Duncan's mind just tempted fate. He still wanted the man dead.

"So 'tis agreed," Duncan said, coming to his feet. "We'll invite the Bruce and a limited contingent here." It bothered him that his holding and table were not as impressive as the Bruce's but Blackstone offered security. "Over mead we can work out our difficulties. He'll no doubt want to ride first in all events, which I will agree to, as a condition to Isaac holding the purses. I want separate stabling and guards for my warhorses. I do not trust the man not to slip something to mine should we win the first rounds and need ride against each other for the gold cup."

"It's as sound a plan as any," Angus agreed after he'd spent the last hour inventing what-if situations they might have to counteract.

Isaac yawned. "My lord, I'm starving and 'tis past the time for clear thought. If ye don't mind, I'll like to see my wife and then my bed."

Ack! My ladywife.

The last time Duncan had excused himself to seek out Beth, he'd been met with blatant hostility as she bustled about. When he'd asked for her time, she'd glared and closed all but her middle finger into a fist in answer. Stunned, he'd laughed. Victorious Sassenach archers used the same obscene gesture when confronting the French, men fond of cutting the third finger from captured enemy archers so they couldn't fire a crossbow ever again.

Tired now, he had no desire to try broaching Beth's defenses yet again, but try he must. He'd been in the wrong.

At the keep's second level, Sean MacDonnell of Keppoch, now married to Duncan's cousin, halted him.

"My liege, I've just returned from purchasing the iron in Oban and have news."

"Aye?"

Sean shifted his weight nervously. "I've no fondness for carrying tales but..." He looked about and behind then lowered his voice. "I met a man there who, being in his cups and quite sotted, boasted of a relationship with a woman of our sept. He described her and she cannot be any other than Flora."

"Then 'tis good." The thought of marrying his sister-by-marriage off made him grin.

"Nay, my lord, ye do not understand. The man is a Munro now attached to the Bruce clan."

Duncan frowned. "The Bruce's?"

"Aye, and he's not inclined toward handfasting or marriage. He's a tinker, my lord, someone beneath her aspirations. I did not have a good feelin' just from his manner, my lord, so I bring it to ye attention."

"Thank ye, Sean." Flora, being a Campbell and in his household, had nay reason for meeting a man of the Bruce's.

None.

As they continued down the stairs, Duncan murmured, "Angus, set a man to watch her. I want to know where and when she meets this man again."

"Aye, but mayhap Rachael...?"

"'Twould be better, less conspicuous," Isaac agreed. "I'll bring it to my ladywife's attention."

Duncan nodded as he came to full stop just steps inside the hall. Angus, paying no heed, ran into his back.

"What in all that's holy...?" Duncan asked no one in particular. His advisors stepped around him.

Angus started to laugh. "Appears yer ladywife took it into her head to civilize us."

The great hall, normally just a clutter of chairs, tables, and benches scattered over rushes, had been swept clean to the wood and divided across the middle by a pair of waist high, open chests, their shelves still full of books from the library. The end of the hall in which Duncan stood held a long dais with a head table before the fireplace. All the other tables were arranged in neat rows, separated by a center aisle. Each table was adorned with wild flowers, two large wooden bowls, candles, and odd white fabric cones. Mouth agape, he stared at the opposite end of the hall to where chairs had been arranged in a circle before the fireplace. More seating—a half dozen benches— were positioned against the back of the book chests. One of the two colorful rugs he'd brought back from the Holy Lands now lay before the sitting area's fireplace while the second hung in the center of the north wall. Two tapestries he'd brought back from France as prizes—and which he'd totally forgotten about—now hung on either side of the hanging carpet.

On either end of the mantles and sideboards sat large pewter pitchers filled with tall reeds and lavender. His coat of Arms, its bent armored right arm holding a cross-crosslet with the motto *Vincere et morri*—"To win or die"—lounged not in a corner of the solar where he'd dropped it, but now hung above the dining end's mantle. Above the opposite fireplace hung his best shield, it's bright fields of red and gold announcing by candlelight his lineage and relationship to the King to one and all.

Two of his best pennants hung on either side of the windows on the south wall, opposite the Persian rug.

"Merciful Mother, is there naught of mine she hasna plundered?"

Isaac, looking about wide-eyed, mumbled, "I dinna think so." He pointed to his left. "There be yer heavy armor. Apparently, she couldna get yer new chain mail to stand on its own."

Angus grinned. "What say ye, Duncan? Yer best lance in his hand is a nice touch, nay?" He lifted the helmet's face guard and laughed. "'Tis full of straw."

Duncan, on the verge of bellowing for his wife, snapped his jaws closed when the bailey bell suddenly rang and people started marching up the stairs and into the great hall. The men, uncharacteristically mute, took their places at the tables while the women chatted in animated fashion and settle the bairn, who, wide-eyed, spun and excitedly extolled on all the changes Beth had wrought.

He silently took his seat at the center of the head table after checking to be sure nothing sharp lay on the seat. Angus, still grinning like an idiot, sat to his right, and Isaac took the seat to Angus's right.

"Why are the men so quiet?" Isaac whispered.

"I don't understand any of this, friend." Duncan examined the pot of heather before him, and hoped his wife would make an appearance soon. He wanted an explanation.

"What are the bowls for?" Angus asked as he peeked under the white cone.

Duncan shrugged his good shoulder as three women marched in, carrying dozens of tankards. He sighed in relief as Beth followed, carrying a large flagon of ale.

She whispered something to one of the women as she handed off the flagon, and then exited before he could get her attention.

As a lass filled his tankard, he asked, "What say my lady to ye?"

"Lady Beth cautioned that I should serve from the left, lest I be fond of scrubbing possets for a fortnight, my lord."

Having no idea why serving to the left held importance, or why posset scrubbing would be just punishment should the lass not, he said, "Ah."

The ale served, more women placed baskets of bread at each table as others arrived with platters of roasted venison, fish, eggs, and with what appeared to be weeds. Beth returned and stood by the door watching the proceedings as more women followed with bowls of sauce. When all met with her approval, the women took their seats, and Beth came to sit on his left.

All eyes were upon them as he pulled out her chair. "Good eve, my lady."

She said not a word, only lifted a brow when Flora glided into the room and took a seat in the first row, directly before them.

Beth picked up her white cone, made a show of flapping it out before placing it in her lap. The women mimicked her actions. The men, frowning, followed suit. Not a one, apparently, was of a mind to garner his ladywife's or his own wife's disapproval.

As Rachael served Isaac, Beth ground out between clenched teeth, "May I serve you, my lord?"

Cautioned by the fierce glint of steel in her eyes, he said, "Thank ye. All smells verra good, my lady." When the corner of her mouth twitched, he added, "Appears verra good, as well." Her gaze slid to his lips, but she remained mute as she slung food into his wooden trencher. He scowled when she placed the weeds in it.

Pouring an oily red sauce over the greenery, she said, "Dandelions, fennel, and crest. Eat it. You'll like it."

He glanced down the table to see Rachael, having finished helping Isaac, now served Angus, who looked none too sure he wanted weeds either.

After the rotund priest offered grace, every eye came to rest not on him but on Beth. When she smiled and broke her bread, a collective sigh rose and the hall quickly filled with the usual clamor of sixty people trying to talk over each other as they ate. Of all the women he'd known, only the most powerful of dowagers commanded the level of deference he'd just witnessed. And odd that Beth now should.

Finishing a really delicious joint, Duncan glanced up and caught Kari slapping her husband's wrist as her man tried to pitch a bone to the floor. Contrite, the soldier placed the bone in the big bowl. Duncan's gaze shifted around the room to see others doing the same. Ah. The dogs will be sorely disappointed, he thought, placing his bone in the bowl before him.

And where were the beasts? He glanced around and found his normally boisterous lymers lying at the far end of the room, looking forlorn with heads on paws. At this time of day, he was normally tripping over them. How verra odd.

Having eaten his fill—even the weeds, which truth to tell tasted verra good with the wee pieces of egg and onion, he pushed back in his chair. "My lady, all," his hand swept the table and the room, "is well done."

"Of course, my lord. It's what I do, arranging

banquets." She placed her napkin on the table. "Given adequate time and ingredients, I can put on a feast for one hundred that will knock your socks—hose—off."

He recalled her tale of life in the new York. Given he'd just consumed the best meal he'd eaten in years, he murmured, "I dinna doubt ye." In fact, he could not remember the last time he'd enjoyed such simple fare as much. He studied the room once again. It did look more impressive, as if he were a knight with an income of five and two thousand pounds instead of one with a tally amounting to little more than one thousand. The Bruce will be impressed and think twice before plotting against him. Then again, the bastard just might double his efforts to acquire Blackstone.

Duncan leaned toward her. "Lass, we need speak of matters that keep us at dagger points."

"Nay, my lord." She stood and smiled at the people who now watched her. Without moving her lips, she whispered, "We've said all that needs to be said save this." She glanced at Flora and color flooded her cheeks. "I'll not tolerate her presence another day, so you'd best find a place for her outside these walls."

He reached for her hand. "But Beth, ye dinna understand..."

A wane smile formed as she gently touched his lips. "Oh, but I do, you son of a—"

She spun on her heel and left in a swirl of emerald silk but not before he'd noted the wetness, a bright silver sheen, that coated her eyes.

To see the depth of her humiliation, and to realize she might still care for him despite it, hit him like a gauntleted fist.

Chapter 17

Her heart tripping, Beth clutched the sides of the elongated dinghy with both hands as the two silent clansmen, their heavily-muscled arms bulging and straining, powered them across the choppy water bringing her closer and closer to shore. She couldn't decide if her agitated heartbeat stemmed from being in a boat for the first time since nearly drowning, from the simple excitement of finally getting to see Drasmoor, or from finally getting away from Duncan's constant demands that she speak with him.

Since she'd yet to get through a night without dreaming of him, without seeing him in Flora's arms, she wasn't inclined to even give him the time of day. Not that she had a clock.

Kari tapped her shoulder and pointing, started naming the various burns and hills before them. In short order Beth found herself gawking like a tourist. She was so distracted by the sights, Kari had to reach out a hand to steady her as the boat ground to an abrupt stop on the gravel beach.

"Here we be, my lady."

The guards jumped out first and stood in knee-deep

freezing surf to haul the bow higher on shore, the boat's wooden hull scraping in loud protest against the rock-strewn beach.

Beth jumped for dry land but an icy wave caught her feet, reminding her once again why so few at Drasmoor knew how to swim.

She followed the men through the town. The scent of roasting venison mingled with that of pine and fish drying in the sun. Dodging chickens and small children, the guards hurried them along the wide gravel-and-crushed shell paths, past the village's stone houses. Anxious to see everything, Beth's head bobbed and spun like a midway ride as she tried to catch glimpses of the sturdy stone homes' interiors. Women, their arms loaded with babies—some swaddled in crisscross fashion, others just settled on cocked hips—bobbed their curtsies as she waved and hurried past.

"Kari, why are you racing hell bent for leather?" She really wanted to see the village, to seek a possible threshold back to her time.

When her friend's expression shifted from a smile to her *what the heck are you saying* look, Beth panted, "Why do ye make such haste?"

Kari pointed to the mid-day sun. "'Tis late."

Beth blinked. It wouldn't be dark for at least six or seven hours. "I'd really like..." She came to an abrupt halt to stare up the nostrils of a shaggy bridled pony. One of the oarsmen held its reins.

She shook her head. Cute and calm as the beast appeared, Beth's only experience with horses amounted to patting the velvet muzzles of spit-and-polished police mounts. Examining the cracked and weathered sidesaddle, she asked, "Can't we walk?"

"Nay, m'lady." Kari pointed high into the hills. "There is purpure."

Beth looked up at the groundcover tinting the steep hills purple and then at the sidesaddle. "Oh." She chewed her lower lip. "There's none lower?"

Kari laughed, "Nay. Come, my lady, the sumpter willna bite."

Beth waved toward Kari's pony. "You first." After Kari mounted without difficulty, Beth exhaled and nodded to her guard. He bent at the waist and laced his fingers. She stepped up as Kari had done, only to find herself suddenly flopped over the saddle and clutching the poor animal's mane for dear life. She heard Kari giggle and flashed a warning look. She then growled at the grinning guards for good measure.

Once she had her right leg draped over the pummel, the snickering guards mounted and led them single file into the hills. The higher they went the shoddier the homes became, some were merely stone and waddle facades placed across little caves dug into steep slopes. Wandering stonewalls kept grazing cattle from devouring the scattered fields of waving oats and rye. Seeing a painfully thin woman struggling uphill under the weight of a wooden yoke balanced by hide bags full of water, Beth grimaced with guilt. Not two weeks ago she'd been put out because she couldn't get hot water on demand.

This Scotland had nothing in common with the splendid manor homes and manicured landscapes she'd become familiar with in her time.

As they rode higher, Kari murmured, "'Tis our place for the men and women who arrived after fleeing their own septs or have nay clan. The MacDougall provides refuge, protection, and food in exchange for a pledge of fealty. None bear our name."

Half way up one steep incline Kari pointed out the tiny stone cottage, saying it had once been Rachael and Isaac's. How, Beth wondered, did people survive like this? And did Duncan not trust them?

Within a few hours she and Kari had gathered armloads of heather, thistle, pine boughs and a collection of twisting vines that would substitute nicely for curly willow.

For Beth, the ride down from the hills proved scarier than the ride up. Though the views were spectacular, full of panoramic seascapes, beautiful water falls—burns— and an eagle's view of all she could lay claim to, she could also see exactly where she'd land should her pony stumble on the shifting shale clattering beneath his hooves.

When they finally reached the stable and dismounted, her legs shook so hard she couldn't walk.

Beth kissed the pony's whiskered muzzle. "Thank you for not plunging over the cliff."

She turned for the boat and nearly collided with the priest.

He reached out to steady her. "My lady, I will ride with ye to Blackstone. We need talk about yer conversion."

Beth shuddered. "Must we?"

Scowling, he grasped her arm. "Aye, my lady, we *must*."

As soon as their boat reached Blackstone's quay, Beth bolted. She'd had her fill of the priest and his edicts. How she managed to hold her tongue as he laid out his plan for her religious enlightenment, she'd never know.

She'd rot in hell before she'd spend even one morning on her knees decrying herself for a heathen. Huh! She'd been sorely tempted to tell him if he needed something to do, he should chase down her philandering husband.

She raced through all she could downstairs to prepare for the Bruce's arrival, and then climbed the stairs to the solar, where she found a beautiful starfish on the bed.

Despite her refusal to talk with him, Duncan had been leaving little gifts in the solar all week. She turned the perfect, prickly peace offering in her hand. Where did her husband sleep now? He'd given over the solar to her without so much as a grumble, so she hadn't a clue. When Flora's face came to mind and Beth's stomach clenched, she dropped the starfish onto the mantel next to the bird nest.

Feeling maudlin and hating herself for it, she picked up her latest project, her boar bristle makeup brush. The donating boar now slowly turned on the roasting spit.

As she wrapped thread around a few course hairs, she hoped the chalices she'd found in one of the storage rooms had taken a polish. Too, she hoped the women had been able to gather enough greens.

Beth put down the bristles, too agitated to concentrate. She stood and the singular key hanging from a ribbon around her neck thumped at her waist. She fingered the wrought iron symbol of her power. Duncan had left the key on the bed along with a nosegay of wild flowers. Rachael had to explain its import, that as chatelaine—mistress of the keep—she had the honor of carrying the keys. Since Duncan only had one lock, she had only one key. The fact that it belonged to the dungeon didn't detract from the sentiment. He wanted peace between them.

But the peace he sought was a long way from being won. To Beth's great annoyance, Flora, though never at meals now, still remained within the keep. Beth had no way of knowing if he went to her at night, but suspected he did, given his appetites and the woman's blatant sensuality. Thinking about them together, making love, turned her stomach and caused a tightening in her throat. She pushed the thought aside. No easy task since Flora would be joining them for dinner tonight.

According to Rachael, Miss I'm Too Sexy would serve as a gentle reminder to the Bruce that Blackstone also had close ties to the powerful Campbell clan. Why this was necessary Beth had no clue.

Beth examined her night's wardrobe and groaned. Much to her chagrin—and Rachael's delight—her ensemble included a gold-and-pearl-encrusted headband with requisite rear veil and two jeweled cauls—nets—for holding her hair on either side of her face. Her strapless gown with its row of ornamental amber buttons down the front and back laces had been altered through the bust. It was made of deep blue and green vertical silk panels. She was to wear a jeweled girdle and a three-foot-long golden link necklace with a dangling reliquary. The locket she could have done without after learning the enameled doodad was a priceless heirloom of wife number two and held a relic—a few hairs or pieces of bone from some dead saint. Just the thought of touching it made her skin crawl.

To complete her ensemble she had to wear a bliant—a full-length, highly-prized blue squirrel-fur-lined coat with billowing sleeves. Taken together it had to be the ugliest getup she'd ever seen.

Struggling into the under dress she fervently hoped

she wouldn't expire from heat prostration before the night was through, but if she did, she'd look good doing it. She now had mascara, shadow, blush, and lip gloss thanks to beeswax, soot, charcoal, wild raspberries and umpteen hours of experimentation.

As she dropped the gown over her head, someone knocked on the solar door. Thinking it Rachael, she called, "Come in."

Duncan cautiously pushed the door open to find his ladywife wiggling frantically within a mound of silk.

"Rachael, can you please help me get into this before I suffocate?"

He grinned as he strode to Beth's side. The woman was a wonder. He silently eased the gown's opening forward so she could extricate herself.

As soon as her head popped out she gasped. "Duncan!"

"My lady, pardon the intrusion. I'd not kenned you'd still be at yer toilet." Had he, he would have remained below, but then tonight was too important for both of them. As she backed away, her arms finally finding their way out of the gown, he asked, "Will ye come with me? I've something of great import to show ye."

"Oh?" Her eyes grew wide with apprehension. "Is the venison burning or the—"

As she grabbed up her skirts readying to run for the door, he caught her elbow. "Nay, my lady. The preparations below go well. 'Tis something else entirely I want to share with ye."

"Oh." She dropped her skirts and craned her neck to silently study him for a moment. She released a hiss of air before saying, "Husband, I haven't time for conversation right now. I've too much yet to do for the banquet."

Augh. She still wasn't inclined to make this easy for him despite all his gifts. "Beth, please. 'Tis of great import and will only take a wee moment of yer time. Please? 'Twill please ye, I promise." He gave her his most beseeching look. As she eyed him warily, he kenned her skepticism. Given all that had transpired between them, he'd be reticent, too, if their roles were reversed.

She huffed. "Aye, as ye luste, but later. Right now I need to get about my work."

He exhaled audibly and smiled. "Ye willna regret agreeing, my lady wife."

~#~

Heads turned an hour later when he led Beth through the crowded bailey. As he guided her toward the thatch-covered stable, her brow remained furrowed and he urgently prayed this gift—his most prized personal possession—would finally break down her defenses and incline her toward peace.

As he pushed a pitchfork out of their way, Beth glanced about. "Duncan, if you're about to show me the kittens, I've seen them. They're bonnie, but—"

"Nay, dear wife, 'tis nay a kit I luste to give ye." He drew her to his side as he rounded a mound of hay and released her hand. "'Tis this."

Beth blinked and stepped forward to examine his pride and joy, to touch the deep green globes hanging off the wee bowed branches. "What is it?"

"A lemon tree."

"A lemon..." She faced him, eyes round and mouth agape. "But how...I mean why is it hidden here? Doesn't it need sun? And how did you come by it?"

He couldn't help but grin at her. Aye, 'twas good, her wondrous look. "'Tis brought out at sunrise but kept out of the wind and then returned at gloaming to this barn where the cattle help keep it warm." He stroked one fruit with a gentle finger. "I've been coddling the wee thing for two years, hoping it would finally bear fruit. 'Tis most precious to have somethin' so fragile thrive in this harsh place, nay?"

Beth, fingers to her lips, murmured, "Lemons. I can't believe it."

He took her left hand in his. "'Tis for you. My gift. I..." When she tried to extricate her soft hand from his calloused one, he held fast and murmured, "Nay, Beth." He fingered the gold and ruby band that bound them together and swallowed the sudden thickness in his throat. Inexplicable fear had him tripping over his well-rehearsed words.

"I...I like ye verra much, my lady. Aye, verra and I am most humbly sorry for my brutish treatment of ye in the solar. 'Tis not my normal way. 'Twas fear that turned me into a beast, ye ken?" He looked up from her hand to her face and took a deep breath, pleased to find her gaze—now questioning—firmly locked on his.

"I have cursed myself far harder and longer than ye could in two lifetimes, lass, once I kenned your true intent for the blade. And ye must ken that what ye saw in the upper hall—with Flora—'twas naught of my doing. Nay. I wouldna. 'Tis not an honorable man's way." He dropped her hands and heaved a sigh. "'Tis all I have to say."

Beth took a deep breath, stunned by the sincerity in his voice. Could she believe him? His hands shook as they'd held hers. Apologizing hadn't come easy for him, and yet he cared enough about her to do it. Now her dilemma was whether or not to believe him. Did she dare hope?

Her heart cried yes, believe every word, but her brain balked. Hadn't she been hurt enough? Didn't every man caught cheating proclaim innocence? Yes. Yet her heart kept insisting, "He said he likes you *verra much*."

She reached up and stroked the brocade jerkin on his chest. Just nights ago his chest, so broad and beautiful by the glow of the solar's fireplace, had brought her to tears. She heaved a sigh. If only he hadn't allowed—wanted—Flora to remain within the keep.

~#~

Duncan's fingers halted their exploration of the intricate design on the large Broach of Lorne, the only thing of value his father had left to his keeping. His thoughts were on Beth, his troubled heart comparing his parents' loveless marriage to his own.

Why had that all too familiar steely look returned to Beth's eyes as she coolly thanked him for the lemon tree? 'Twas certainly not what he'd expected. Indeed, 'twas far from it. Could he have been mistaken thinking her expression had softened as he spoke? Been mistaken thinking he saw a warmth in her eyes, a slight turning up of her full lips as she touched his chest? Nay. It had been there, truly, if only for a few precious moments before it vanished. So what in the bloody hell had he done or said wrong to make that softness, her interest, fade? Ack!

"Remembering old times, Duncan?"

Startled, Duncan frowned at his advisor. "Aye."

"Some things are best forgotten, my friend." Isaac held out his hand for the heavy gold broach that had once belonged to the long dead Robert the Bruce. He turned it over in his palm. "Melting this down could solve some of yer financial woes, friend."

"Give it here, ye heathen." The broach, named by a predecessor for the land surrounding him and the Firth of Lorne, had been in MacDougall hands for generations. According to family lore, Ewin MacDougall married Red Comyn's daughter. When Robert the Bruce later murdered her father in 1306, the MacDougall and Bruce clans became sworn enemies. Years later, Robert—after a hasty crowning at Scone—had been forced to retreat before the victorious English into Argyll where he had hopes of reaching his Campbell allies, but he'd been surprised by the MacDougalls at Dalrigh near Tyndrum. Robert escaped, but on his discarded cloak was found the magnificent broach Duncan now held in his hand.

As always happens, political power and alliances between clan chiefs shifted back and forth over the years—to the point of Robert the Bruce's granddaughter marrying Duncan's grandfather, but this generation now had a new score to settle.

Hearing a trumpet's blare signaling the Bruce's launch from shore he placed the broach into its temporary hiding place beneath his diary. When he had use of the solar again, he would return the broach to its proper hiding place in the headboard. None besides his intimates knew he held it.

"Come Isaac, we need meet our guests."

~#~

Duncan greeted the Bruce in the bailey. John was nearly as tall as he and well turned out in a gold collar, tall hat, ridiculously long-toed shoes, and a rabbit furred houppelande—a short fur-lined tunic—all clear indications of his status and income. By law, none with a yearly income of less than a thousand pounds sterling could don such finery. Duncan again silently thanked God for Beth's labors within the keep and was pleased she would wear what fur he owned. He wore his simple best; the blue brocade jerkin over a close fitting red tunic and high leather boots. He despised hats of any style and so greeted his guest bareheaded.

"Good eve, John. I hope ye found the way easy."

"Aye, 'twas fine weather." The Bruce looked about the bailey. "Ye've made fine improvements in these five years past, I see."

As they walked to the keep entrance, the Bruce's gaze roamed as much over the castle battlements as it did over the stables, kirk, and workshops. Duncan grinned. Many of his keep's nastier defenses like the nags—the catapults that threw fire bombs at enemy ships—and the machicolation, which allowed him to pour boiling oil onto enemy heads, were all hidden behind the innocent interior parapet walls.

Inside the keep, Duncan felt renewed pride watching the Bruce's stunned reaction to Beth's idea of a well-turned-out hall. Even he had to admit it looked like the home of a wealthy man, filled with the rich glow of candlelight, tapestries and flowers on every surface. At each place at every table lay a woven reed mat, a trencher, a two tined fork and a carefully folded napkin, so it appeared a fleet of swans floated on seventy wee green ponds. The head table overflowed with bouquets and the colorful tableware he'd brought back from Italy. The keep even smelled rich, the fresh air wafting in through uncovered windows infused with a delightful mix of beeswax, flowers and roasting meat.

Beth entered the hall. As she glided toward him

wrapped in a new aura of confidence, Duncan's mouth gaped. Not only had she transformed the hall, she'd transformed herself.

He snapped his jaw closed as she dropped in a deep curtsey before him.

"Good eve, my lord husband."

"Good eve, my lady." He swallowed the lump in his throat as he took in her now sultry eyes and rose-tinted lips. Still dumbfounded by the change, he mumbled, "Sir John, may I present my ladywife, Beth...ah...Lady Katherine MacDougall."

John the Bruce bent over her hand. "My lady, 'tis indeed a pleasure." When the man continued to hold Beth's hand for longer than Duncan thought appropriate he cleared his throat.

Beth, looking quite satisfied with the Bruce's attention, extracted her hand and waved toward the sitting group. "My lords, if you please, come this way."

Leaving the Bruce's contingent in conversation with MacDougall clansmen, Duncan and the Bruce followed Beth to the chairs before the fireplace and found a wee feast of fresh bread, smelts and cheese awaiting them. More shocking was finding the hammered bronze and silver chalices he'd plunder from Persia now polished to a soft glow and holding mead.

Once they were seated Beth said, "Supper will be served within the hour. I'll ring the bell when it's ready." She dipped in curtsey and murmured, "If you'll excuse me..." then glided away.

John's gaze followed her. "Yer ladywife's speech...I must be getting' old for my ears couldna keep up with her."

Duncan tore his gaze from his wife's fine rump to

stare at the Bruce. "'Tis naught yer ears. Her rapid and odd manner of speech 'tis their way in York, or so she tells me."

The Bruce reached across the table for the chalice sitting at Duncan's elbow. "'Tis good then that ye have a way with languages, MacDougall, or ye'd be reduced to waving yer hands like a mute." He tasted the mead.

"Humph." 'Twas nay reason for the Bruce to have switched challises. When he finally chose to kill the bastard, he'd do it like a man—with a sword.

Reaching for the more elaborate chalice Beth had intended for the Bruce, Duncan mumbled, "Ye know naught the truth of yer words."

His ladywife had been using hand gestures to show her displeasure all week. Some he couldn't help but laugh at. He liked the fist in the air and arm slap combination the best. Reminded him of the Romans' ways. And God's teeth, could the woman roll her eyes. She could go through life without saying another word and be perfectly understood. But he did miss her lilting voice and warmth, particularly in the wee hours when he couldn't sleep for worrying. About her, the Bruce, and about whether or not he should take up arms again. Unlike Isaac, he wasn't as sure his shoulder would be adequately healed in time for the jousts.

Around a mouthful of cheese the Bruce said, "My people are excited about the tournament. Will ye be bringing a large contingent?"

"Large enough." Duncan had only three tents. Many within his sept would be sorely disappointed hearing they would have to stay behind, every tournament and accompanying fair being something the clan always looked forward to and enjoyed. Well, mayhap he could sell some of their kine and find a way.

"Ye're very pensive this eve, MacDougall."

"Nay, just wondering what my ladywife has prepared for our entertainment."

"'Tis naught a wife's nature to be predicable."

"Ye speak more truth than ye know."

The Bruce's eyes narrowed as he devoured more bread and cheese. "Hmm. Ye do favor this lass."

Duncan shifted in his chair. "Though odd in her ways, I canna deny she is good-hearted and clever." Reluctantly, he wondered how her tales of York and ghosts could be reconciled with this truth. And he never would reconcile it if she continued to ignore his peace-seeking overtures. Just this morn he'd set a pretty speckled starfish in the solar for her to find but she'd said naught, and he'd climbed off a damn cliff to get it. At least, she wore the key, had exclaimed over the lemon tree, and had smiled just a moment ago. Surely, that meant he'd made *some* progress.

Around a mouthful of smoked fish his enemy asked, "Have ye thought on how we're to proceed with the tournament, MacDougall?"

"Aye." And so they discussed the broad points of the contest. To his surprise Beth had assigned Flora to supervising their needs. As she tended them, he found it odd the Bruce paid little heed to his voluptuous sister-by-marriage. Odd.

Before they started working out the finer points of the tournament, specifically who would be entrusted with the prizes they planned to accumulate, the bell rang and the hall began filling.

Beth led them to their seats at the head table. She placed the Bruce to his right then took her seat to his left.

Duncan grinned watching his enemy examine all that lay before him. He well understood the man's surprise.

Once everyone had found their seat, Beth clapped and a parade of women entered carrying course after course. Platters plied high with fragrant venison, succulent roasted boar with turnips, piping clams in broth, filets of white fish, and roasted leeks smothered in a delicious cream sauce seasoned with rosemary were laid on each table, and then consumed by all in prodigious amounts.

When he thought his stomach could hold no more, a dozen women arrived with dense bread puddings soaked in rich aqua vitae—whisky—and cream sauce.

At his side, Beth reached for her wine, and Duncan throwing caution to the wind, enfolded her hand in his before she could snatch it away. It might kill him but he would make the best of this marriage. He brought her hand to his lips.

"My dear ladywife," he whispered so only she might hear, "I have never dined so well, neither in Italia nor at Albany's table." He turned her hand and kissed her wrist. "Ye are indeed worth ye weight in *or*, Lady Kathy."

Chapter 18

Beth's heart slammed against her ribs. Wide-eyed, she whispered, "Please repeat thyself, husband."

For some reason a mischievous twinkle came into his eye as he kissed her knuckles. "'Tis apparent from yer expression ye heard me well enough."

Her pounding heart and racing blood made her body quake. He finally understood!

Duncan pushed back his chair. "Come, dearest lady, we must yet speak...in private."

Feeling herself blush for no good reason, she turned her attention to the room. "But our guests, surely..." She glanced quickly from the musicians as they readied for the evening's entertainment to her room full of guests. Her gaze, as if by its own accord, fell on Flora sitting in the middle of the second row before her. Beth frowned.

The beautiful woman's hands were at her throat, her normally porcelain complexion had darkened to a deep fuchsia, and her eyes were wide in panic.

Damn! Wondering why the woman couldn't choke to death in private, Beth jumped to her feet, yanking her hand from Duncan's relaxed grip. Ignoring his startled exclamation, she ran around the table and back toward the center isle.

As she slid between the rows, the man to Flora's left, apparently realizing his dinner companion was in trouble, slammed her hard on the back to no effect. Beth elbowed him aside to get directly behind Flora.

Adrenaline had the blood pounding in her ears as she wrapped her arms under Flora's ribs. She made a fist and pulled back with everything she had in one quick motion right below Flora's solar plexus. Within a heartbeat a large piece of meat flew out of the young woman's mouth and across the table. Beth released her own breath when she heard Flora's rewarding gasp of air.

"Are you okay—better—now?"

With tears in her eyes and her coloring returning to normal, Flora nodded.

"Good." Beth held Flora's tankard to her lips. "Now take a small sip." When she swallowed without difficulty, Beth patted her shoulder.

God, can you give it a rest? Enough, already.

Miss I'm Too Sexy was her third choking rescue in as many years. And who said food service didn't have its perks?

She looked up to find Duncan and the Bruce standing shoulder-to-shoulder staring at her. The Bruce simply scowled, but was it astonishment or appreciation lurking in Duncan's steel gray eyes? No matter. He had his lover back and had her to thank for it. And right now she needed a drink. Or two. Maybe three.

Duncan remained standing until Beth flopped down in her chair. At his side the Bruce murmured, "Ye did not exaggerate, MacDougall, claiming yer wife was resourceful."

Duncan nodded as he reached for the flagon of wine.

Silently he topped off Beth's goblet. Still unnerved by her quick and successful action—for he'd seen a good man choke to death as Flora nearly had, he handed her the goblet. "Here, lass, ye need this."

"Thank you."

Rachael came to her side and squeezed her shoulders. "*Mon ami!* I didna ken what was happening until the venison took flight."

They all glanced at Flora who, having recovered her composure, now spoke with her hapless male rescuer. Rachael whispered, "Ye must *enseigner*—demonstrer—ooh..." She flapped her hands in frustration.

"*Teach* is the word ye seek," Isaac murmured coming to his wife's side. He smiled at Beth. "'Twas well done, my lady." To his wife, he said, "Come, let our lady take meat in peace. Ye can speak of this later." He bowed to Beth and took Rachael's arm to lead her away.

Angus finally looked up from his trencher. He expelled a large burp and asked, "What? Did I miss something?"

Beth suddenly laughed. Her laughter then escalated to the point of tears and gasping.

"My lady?" Duncan eyed Beth closely.

Between gasps she managed, "I'm fine." She waved him to his seat. "Ask the musicians...to play." She looked down the table at Angus only to start laughing again. The Bruce sensing something equally amusing joined her. Giving up, Duncan did as she bid and the room filled with the lilting tones of a flute and mandolin.

Two goblets of wine later Beth began humming and tapping her foot.

The Bruce leaned toward him. "Ye lady appears ready to dance."

Beth started in surprise. "Can we dance, Duncan? Really?"

He grinned. Aye, his ladywife, looking decidedly lovely tonight, was also decidedly in her cups. He'd yet to get her alone again—to plead his case—but said, "Why not." The night was young.

He motioned the lass clearing the tables to him. "Please clear the sitting area for dancing." As she walked away he called, "And tell Sean we have need of his pipes."

~#~

Watching Beth and his liege lord whirling in circles to the deafening music, Isaac whispered in French, "What say ye, my love? Is she sane or not?"

"Odd to be sure, my dear, but saner than you and I together." Rachael studied the dancing pair for a moment. "It has been discussed that if it be His will, some do return, no?"

Isaac nodded, having heard a rabbi ponder reincarnation.

Pensive, she continued, "It would explain Beth's beliefs and different ways." She then grinned watching them dance. "She's in love with him, you know."

"Yes. And he with her, though he's yet to realize it. If she doesn't forgive him soon, he'll drive us all into our cups."

His wife frowned. "He deserves to be punished."

"Aye, but do we?" He took Rachael's hand. "He drills the men unmercifully as he works to regain his strength, grumbles incessantly and still harbors an unhealthy hatred for *him*." He nodded toward the Bruce now dancing with Lady Flora.

"There's little any of us can do to solve our liege's

problems, husband."

He studied Flora Campbell. "You have done well keeping Flora away from Lady Beth."

His wife snorted. "The witch does not comprehend the danger she courts with her constant attempts to speak with Beth. You should have seen our lady's expression when I told her Flora would be present tonight. Beth may be skilled in many ways, but she is not adept when it comes to hiding her true sentiments."

"Aye, but mayhap, you can solve everyone's problems."

Rachael gaped at her husband. "And how am I to do that?"

"Duncan has learned Flora meets with a man of the Bruce clan in Oban. He asks that you accompany her whenever she leaves the keep. Should she meet this man and you see this, then Duncan will have just cause to send her—lock, stock and baggage—back to Dunstaffnage Castle. He'll be rid of her without having to worry about a Campbell reprisal. In fact, the Campbell would need worry should Duncan hear she'd not been punished appropriately for her duplicity."

"Aye, that's all well and good, but who will care for our son as I traipse after this thorn in everyone's side?"

"I, my love." When she looked askance at him and raised a brow, he mumbled, "I know. I've been negligent in my duties to both of you of late. If you do this, I promise to begin preparing Jacob for his Bar Mitzvah." He grinned sheepishly. Rachael had been after him for months to start.

Rachael heaved a resigned sigh. "As you wish, but you'd best keep a careful eye on Jacob. He has it in his head to become a knight, and too often I've caught him wielding a sword."

Though he saw no harm in Jacob learning a knight's skills Isaac nodded to placate his wife. He then turned his attention to the hall's occupants only to spy Flora, flushed and eyes blazing, marching away from the Bruce.

He frowned. "Now what have we here?"

Chapter 19

Duncan silently blessed the man who had first created wine as Beth, breathless from dancing, laughed and collapsed against him. The wine had lowered her guard enough that she again appeared willing to listen to his whispered praise and mumbled apologies. And now she smiled at him.

"More wine, my lady?"

"Nay, husband, water."

"Ack! 'Tis night, woman. If ye must drink water, please reserve it for daylight."

Beth laughed as they returned to their chairs, leaving the rest of the revelers to finish the reel. "Are you trying to get me drunk, my lord?"

"Me?" He smiled, not innocently, given 'twas precisely his intent.

"Don't look at me like that with those big baby blues, Duncan. I'm still mad at you."

He pushed in her chair and kissed her temple. "Aye," he whispered, "but ye ken 'twas only fear that caused me to behave like a beast, no?"

"Aye." Blushing, she took off her mantel and fanned her face and chest with her hands.

Looking down into her modest cleavage, images of their only night together, of her pert breasts filling his mouth, suddenly flood his mind and filled his groin. Fearing he'd start drooling if he didn't get her away, he whispered, "Lass, 'tis too warm in here." He took her hand. "Come, let us get some fresh air."

"But our guests..."

He looked about as his thumb traced a slow circle in her palm. The Bruce and his men were occupied with women and drink. Isaac had Flora in conversation. Catching Angus's attention, Duncan glanced toward his wife then toward the door. His friend nodded almost imperceptibly as one side of his mouth curled. Knowing Angus and ten of his guards to be cold sober, he murmured, "They all appear well occupied, my lady. Come." He coaxed her to her feet and led her to the bailey.

Outside, the air barely moved, had lulled to a whisper. 'Twas the time of day when offshore breezes usually stilled. Soon the land would be cool enough for the winds to reverse and bring home the strong onshore breeze, which would make for a good night's sleep. Particularly, if he could convince his ladywife to allow him entrance into his own bed again.

He scanned the bailey and carefully aimed her toward the privacy of the hay barn. "Ye look lovely this night, Beth."

"Me? Lovely?" She made a dismissing sound. "What they say is apparently true."

"What say who?"

"Some say women get prettier at closing time."

He slipped his arm around her waist. "I dinna ken yer meaning."

"No, I don't suppose you'd have a need to." She stopped and faced him. "How do you see Flora?"

Aha! 'Twas not what he had or hadna done right, but Flora that still had her fashing.

He ran a gentle finger along her jaw. "She is like fox-glove, Beth. Lovely to look at but verra dangerous—poison—even in small amounts."

"Oh." She didn't appear pleased as she turned away.

"Do you ken what foxglove can do?"

"No, but I ken she's probably hell in bed."

He spun her, gently enfolding her into his arms while forcing her into intimate contact with his chest and hips. "I dinna ken if she is or isna for I *never have nor will I ever* bed that woman. I told ye, I pledged my troth to thee, and I am a man of my word." He ran his thumb gently across her bottom lip, enjoying its pliant fullness. "*Ye* are more than I anticipated, more than I dared hope for."

Moisture came into her eyes as she studied his face. Finally she said, "Truth be told, Duncan, I do want to believe you, but experience has taught me otherwise. And there is the matter of my being here in the first place."

He sighed resignedly for there was that. If she spoke the truth about coming from another time then he was indeed married to the wrong woman, which meant one of the dead women in the coach had been his intended. Not something he wanted Albany to become aware of just yet.

And her tale certainly explained her ability to swim, to save Flora, her attitude—her proprietary interest—in Blackstone, and her most decidedly odd but charming ways. And she knew about the diary he kept, could relate specific events he'd lived through and documented; yet she couldna read Latin.

"Lass, ye ken it takes great imagination on my part to believe ye?" When she nodded, he asked, "Then, can ye nay do the same for me?"

Deep in thought, she ran her hands slowly over the planes of his chest. Finally, she looked into his eyes. "Duncan, I want to trust you. I want it so much I ache for wanting it. I just don't know if I can."

"Oh, lass." She was asking that he earn her trust, prove himself, which seemed only fair given her previous experiences—Lady Kathy's tale—and himself railing in fury after she'd given all.

He decided the first step should be seeking permission and not simply taking, though he had the right. "May I kiss ye, lass?"

When she kept her gaze fixed on his silver collar but nodded, he murmured, "Then come."

He led her into the shadows of the barn. She offered no resistance as he cradled her in his arms. Aye, she did want to believe, and he desperately wanted her to.

Under the eaves and surrounded by the sweet scent of hay he cradled her neck and lowered his mouth to hers. To his surprise her lips were responsive. When he gently increased the pressure, her mouth opened to him.

He inhaled her sigh as he ran his tongue slowly into her lush, wine-flavored interior. When her tongue began to play across his, his heart soared.

She did want him despite her verbal protests. He backed her against a pillar.

As he pressed his need to her belly, she surprised him again by groaning and sliding her fingers into his hair.

It was all the encouragement he needed.

When Duncan's hand crept up her ribs and slowly stroked her left breast, Beth's heart pounded a rapid tattoo in response.

Her sense of self-preservation started chiding, "You really should be putting a stop to this," as soon as his thumb started circling her nipple, but God, she'd missed the feel of him, the taste of him. She had no doubt she really should stop him now before he...oh, yes.

His other hand had cupped her buttocks and brought her into intimate contact with his arousal. As he kissed her senseless, he bent his knees and gently slid his swollen phallus up and down against her. She groaned. As she tried to collect herself, his mouth started travelling down her neck and settled onto the swell of her breasts.

Nuzzling, he murmured, "Ye be delicious, Beth." Within a heartbeat he'd opened her gown's laces and exposed her breasts to the moonlight. As he laved the tip of one very excited nipple she wondered at his obvious pleasure in suckling, not that she minded. Incredibly, it caused something deep within her—no doubt, her womb—to contract with need. She groaned again when he turned his attention to the other side, leaving the first breast to chill in the soft breeze, which only underscored her nakedness. God, everything he did felt so good, his every move so gentle, yet persistent and hungry.

When he left her breast and slid his tongue down her ribs she wanted to shout, "No, go back," but then he surprised her by kneeling before her.

"Umm, Duncan..."

She lifted his face so she could see into his eyes. Like highly polished silver, they glowed. "What are you—"

"Ssh, my lady. I need pay penance, aye? So dinna

214

deprive me of this."

His hands gently slid from her hips to her ankles before gliding under her skirts and up over her calves. They settled just above the back of her knees. He watched her as his callused fingers slowly circled and stroked her now quaking thighs.

"I do like the feel of ye skin, my lady." He pushed aside the fabric of her gown with his chin and licked the interior of one thigh. "'Tis silk fine yet tastes most sweet." She pressed her back to the pillar, fearing her legs would buckle and pressed her hands against his shoulders.

Without doubt she shouldn't be allowing him such liberties. No, she really shouldn't. She should still be holding him at arm's length, demanding he apologize every hour on the hour, but my, oh my, how he could play her like a fine violin. And truth be told, she did love him despite his sometime caustic ways. And he had apologized, profusely, and she was in fact married to him...

His broad callused hands crept to her buttocks as his lips and tongue slowly kissed and stroked their way up to the junction of her thighs. Feeling his pouf of breath ruffle the curls at her apex, she gasped.

Her common sense now railed, *"Enough! Someone could come in here at any moment,"* but she didn't want him to stop. She wanted to feel what he was about to do. Wanted it so badly she could have screamed.

Duncan licked just once through Beth's curls, felt her nub tremble, and looked up. Her head now rested against the pillar as her legs continued to quake. Aye, he had his lady's attention.

He pressed his shoulders to her knees to keep them

from buckling then licked through the dense curls again. She tasted decidedly feminine and sweet. Again he licked, lingering at her nub to suck. He heard her sharp intake of breath. He glanced up to find her teeth and tongue tormenting her lush lower lip. His lady apparently didna mind his way of apology. Good.

He gently separated the curls. He lingered there, swirling his tongue around then gently sucked until her hips tipped and he heard her wee groan of pleasure. Satisfied, he licked deeper still, causing her hips to grind. When his tongue slid into her secret place her nails dug into his shoulders and she whimpered, "Oooh."

She tasted sweeter, her liquid gathering. Aye, she wanted him but 'twasna time. He wanted her shaking with need, as he had these last six nights lying alone craving her.

To that end he let his thumb attend her nub so his tongue could stroke in and out as another part of his body was want to do.

When she softly keened his name, he lifted his head and found her looking at him through passion-glazed eyes. "Ah, my lady," he whispered, "do ye luste?"

She licked her lips and managed to nod. He rose and grasped her by the buttocks as his mouth captured hers. He lifted her negligible weight into his arms. Backing up, he felt hay hit his legs and settled into a sitting position. Her arms locked around his neck as she returned his kisses with equal fervor, her hands buried deep within his hair. He pushed his kilt and her skirts away in the same swipe so he could position her legs on either side of his thighs. As she knelt astride him he adjusted his throbbing member so it settled against her sweet wetness.

He broke the kiss to say, "Now, my lady, settle," only

to realize her body was already pressing down, seeking him. She gasped as he groaned, her slick warmth sucking him in. Her mouth sought his this time, her hands settling on either side of his face as she slowly began to rock. Never in his thirty years had a woman responded in such a heated fashion.

A breeze played across Beth's nipples as she slowly rocked

on the firm, swollen flesh filling her. She opened her eyes as Duncan laid back. Sweat gleamed on his chiseled features as his steel blue gaze focused on her wavering breasts. Wondering—wanting to see his reaction—she kneaded one breast gently, teasing the nipple as he had done. His eyes flashed fire and he growled deep in his throat as he reached to cover her hand with his.

His response was all she needed. The heat in her belly exploded, her every nerve strained to throw her over some unseen pinnacle to delicious release. She collapsed to his chest.

Nearly crazed with need, Beth's final spasms loosened Duncan's restraint. Clasping her hips he rocked once, twice, and exploded against her womb.

Moments later, comfortable in the hay and well satisfied, he cradled her to his chest and listened to her pleased mewing. In a languished haze, he smiled and pushed her hair from his face. Aye, it had gone well for both of them.

Waiting for his body to regain its strength and pondering why it seemed to be taking an unearthly amount of time to do it, he realized what he had done.

He'd given her his seed.

"Beth?"

She raised her head from his chest and smiled. "Yes,

my lord?"

"Have ye ever been hit on the head?"

'Twasna that he thought her tale totally implausible for 'twas certainly more between heaven and earth than his meager brain could fathom, but...

She came up on her elbows. "Not that I recall. Why?"

Damn. 'Twas certainly too late to fret. All he could do now is pray the adage *a get is more than one-half the mare* proved false should his seed catch. But then, many a maid dinna catch the first time. His mother, for one. Vowing to take more care in the future should the good Lord see himself clear to let this time pass, he patted her rump and sighed, "Just wonderin'."

She played with the fine curling hairs on his chest. "That was lovely."

He grinned, "Aye, 'twas that and more I'd say, given ye called upon heaven and my lordly self as ye reached for the stars."

"Oh!" She slapped her hands on his chest and struggled to sit.

He was faster, rolling her over to settle between her thighs. "Ah, precious, I only tease." He kissed her gently. "I canna put into words how fond I am of ye odd ways."

"Your ways are equally odd to me, though I must say you do them well."

He chuckled, pleased.

"Can I," she asked, pushing a lock from his forehead, "expect this kind of an apology the next time we fight?"

He traced the curve of her now swollen lips, "We dinna have to fuss at each other to have this. Ye could," he kissed her slowly once again, enjoying the sweetness within her mouth, "invite me back to the solar."

"Ah." She studied his eyes and then the planes of his

face. "So it's your comfy bed you seek?"

"Ack! I'd sleep in this hay the rest of my days if ye but chose to be at my side."

Her eyes appeared to seek his soul as she placed both hands on either side of his face. "Duncan, put it plainly."

"I care naught for these silent days, of fashing, of wondering if I have the power to please ye or not." He turned her hand in his palm, examining the fine bones that created the miracles within his keep. "And I didna like seeing the Bruce drool over yer hand." He scowled, "Definitely."

"Is it just the Bruce? May another—?"

"Dinna even jest, Beth." He clamped his arms about her and spun, landing on his back with her fully on his chest once again. "Ye be mine, dear Beth, and only mine and I be yer servant till death do us part." He brushed the hair from her face. "Do ye ken?"

"Aye, my lord and husband. Just so long as you remember what's good for the goose is good for the gander." He frowned so she clarified, tapping his chest, "I'll not tolerate you casting your eyes, much less anything else, on another wench."

He smiled, liking her jealous tone, but he was human. Studying the little worry lines between her brows he decided that from this time forward he would make every effort to be most careful should he be in her sight and spy a pleasing wench walking past. "Agreed," he told her.

Her obvious relief made his heart trip. Did she really think another could truly tempt him after the way she made him feel? After all they had shared? How odd.

Laughter echoed around the bailey from the keep's open shutters. "With that settled, I fear we must return." He kissed her fingertips, liking her decidedly satisfied look and ruffled appearance. "However, those in yon hall will ken our luxurious pursuits should we return in our current states." Grinning, he pulled a large piece of straw from her now loose hair.

Her hands flew to her ruined coiffure. "Oh shi...oot!"

"Indeed." He stood and pulled her to her feet. He shook like a dog and shed the hay from his clothing. Beth, on the other hand, had all she could do to re-lace her gown.

He helped her then shook out her headdress. "I much prefer yer fair hair loose."

"Me, too, but I can't walk in there bareheaded or tongues will wag." She twisted one half of her thick hair into a coil and held out her hand for one of the cauls. He reluctantly gave it to her.

Finished pulling herself together, Beth asked, "Do I look presentable?"

He kissed the tip of her nose. "Aye, as always."

In the brightly lit hall, Duncan pulled a bit of straw he'd missed from Beth's cotehardie and tossed it behind them. 'Twas then he saw they hadn't escaped Rachael's curious perusal. He winked at her over Beth's head. A slight smile took form on Rachael's lips then disappeared as she silently directed his attention to the opposite side of the hall. There he spied Angus, Sean, and Tom chest, to chest and ready to come to blows with three of the Bruce's men.

"Damn God's teeth!"

Beth, still ruminating over the import of Duncan's earlier words, of their lovemaking, murmured, "Damn what, Duncan?"

She followed his gaze and her worry over his preference for the words "I care" instead of "I love" immediately evaporated. "Oh!"

"Stay here, my lady, whilst I see what 'tis afoot." Duncan cast a quick scathing glance toward the Bruce, who looked totally indifferent to the battle brewing in her hall.

Why the hell did the Bruce just sit like a contented Buddha at the head table when half the men threatening to tear her hall apart were his? The bloody nerve!

She then spotted Flora leaning against the wall not far from the rumbling Neanderthals and wondered if the woman's flirting had caused the men's hostilities. Given the look of indignation on her face, Beth wouldn't have been the least surprised. Damn the woman.

Having seen her fair share of bar brawls, Beth worried her lower lip as she surveyed the hall and the men Duncan approached. Picturing all her hard work turned to ruin as more agitated men came to their feet, she glanced at the Bruce. He was smirking.

The bastard *hoped* they'd come to blows! Not bothering to wonder why, and not caring if Duncan approved or not—her only goal being to defuse the situation before the entire clan became involved—she grabbed an empty tankard and clanged it hard and repeatedly against the table.

The hall went quiet. Not tomb quiet but enough so she could be heard. In as loud and dramatic a voice as she could muster, she shouted, "Hark!" As worried faces turned in confusion to see what she was about, she continued with as much dramatic emphasis as her limited talents allowed, "Once upon a midnight dreary, while I pondered, weak and weary..."

She hunched her shoulders like a crone and walked down the center isle. Eyes squinting, she beckoned those that would follow with a crooked finger, "...over many a quaint and curious volume of forgotten lore..."

She saw Kari's face light in understanding and heard her exclaim, "Listen! Our lady tells a troubadour's tale."

Beth slowly spun, her voice imitating a conspirator's stage whisper, "While I nodded, nearly napping, suddenly there came a tapping," she rapped on a nearby table, "as of someone gently rapping, rapping at my chamber door."

She almost sighed seeing many wide eyes following her every move. Too many, however, still looked torn between hearing her tale and joining the fray. She again beckoned them to follow. "'Tis some visitor, I muttered, tapping at my chamber door, only this and nothing more." To her relief, they could tell that it was in fact more, and many began following her away from Duncan and the bully-boys to the far end of the hall.

"Ah, distinctly," she confided, "I remember 'twas in the bleak December, and each separate dying ember wrought its ghosts upon the floor."

Finally standing before the sitting area with most in the hall settled in rapt silence before her, she hoped Poe wouldn't mind her changing The Raven up a bit so they could better understand. "Eagerly I lusted the morrow; vainly I had sought to borrow from my books surcease of sorrow—sorrow for the lost Lenore—for the rare and radiant maiden whom the angels named Lenore."

An excited murmur suddenly swept the group before her. Daring to believe she had them captivated with the tale of lost love, she glanced toward Duncan to see how he fared. All appeared calm, though two men still stood with fisted hands on hips in heated conversation.

She silently thanked her tenth grade teacher for

forcing her to memorize the eighteen stanzas as punishment for nodding off in class before continuing, "...and the silken sad uncertain rustling of each purpure curtain thrilled me—filled me with fantastic terrors never kenned before..."

By the time she came to an end, Duncan and the Bruce had disappeared along with Isaac. Flora and Rachel had joined the crowd before her. Seeing Flora wipe a tear away, Beth wondered at it. She wasn't that great a storyteller.

"Another, my lady!" someone called.

"Aye, another," somebody else agreed, "but this be it a tale of great joy, my lady."

Great joy? Good Lord. Her mind flashed through the movies she'd seen only to discard them, one after the other, due to their very twenty-first century plots. Then Snow White came to mind and she smiled. The children present would enjoy it, at least.

Thinking how her own life now mimicked a fairy tale she began, "Once upon a time in a land far away..."

~#~

Flora studied the Black's wife as she rambled on about silly dwarves and a poisoned apple. Aye, she could use one of those.

Nay, for surely she'd be as dead as yesterday's fish if not for Lady MacDougall grabbing her about her chest and squeezing. And she did understand the pain of lost love, if her tale of the raven were true. Even a fool could see her mistress's face couldna hold a man's attention past a fortnight. Mayhap she did ken more than most the pain of dreadful angst and grieving. Aye, she'd not have the lady killed. She owed the woman that, but no more.

Chapter 20

Sitting across from the Bruce in the library, Duncan tried hard to mask his anger at his enemy's impertinence, caring naught for what the Bruce claimed his strength in numbers to be, nor his conveniences to be.

"John, we need camp on opposing sides. I'll not be traipsing across the damn valley every time I want to work my mount, so the answer is nay to ye stabling our cattle. As for the purses, I'll not concede that either. 'Tisna lack of trust on my part for ye, but for yer man. Though of Albany's house, he is a newcomer. I ken Isaac's honesty. He has repeatedly demonstrated his loyalty, and desire to remain within my holding. Ye canna say the same of William Kerr."

"True, but what if yer man takes it into his head to weigh my portion with his finger on the scales?"

Isaac, fists clenched, came to his feet. Duncan couldn't blame his friend for feeling insulted but waved him down. "Nay." Turning his attention back to the Bruce he murmured, "By all means have ye man at Isaac's side then, but Isaac collects and holds."

"Agreed."

Duncan narrowed his eyes, wondering what the

Bruce plotted for 'twas too swift a concession. He would have to see Isaac well guarded at the tournament, which posed another problem, of leaving Blackstone with less experienced men than he'd like. Damnation. Or did the Bruce really believe him easily defeated?

"So 'tis agreed," Duncan murmured, holding up his chalice. "We willna be paired in hand-to-hand, but have our lots drawn by the List Mistress. We will pair—with ye first—in all mounted contests, arriving with face plates up, bring our own heralds, hold our own cattle, and Isaac holds the purses."

The face shield idea had been Angus's. 'Twould be a hell of a thing for him to fight hard all day only to be *challenged* by the Bruce—to have steel put on their lances tips in the final round—only to lose thinking he faced the Bruce when, in fact, he faced a fresh opponent. And the Bruce had several good men to choose from.

"Aye, 'tis agreed," the Bruce affirmed raising his own goblet. They drank deep, both parched from all the talk. "Shall we join the ladies now?"

"Why not."

They rose and the Bruce laughed, "'Twasna so bad, aye?" He then delivered a powerful slap to Duncan's left shoulder.

It took everything Duncan had to keep his face serene and not drop to his knees. Damn the man! He now had no doubt that the Bruce kenned his injury, but he could spare no energy in wondering how.

He forced a smile, hoping he hadn't gone pale. The pain radiating down his back and left arm was such that had he had a dirk on his person he would have gladly buried it to the hilt in the Bruce. Then twisted it. Thrice.

Entering the hall, they found all before his lady wife;

some in chairs, others on the floor, and some like Angus, with tears in his eyes, leaning against the wall. Apparently hearing his approach, his second in command straightened and blinked furiously. Angus nodded, thumping a closed fist over his heart. His friend's signal confirmed what his eyes could see, that all was as it should be.

He turned his attention to Beth wondering what she could possibly be saying to hold the assembly so enthralled, for Angus wasna the only one who appeared moved. They couldna ken her well, surely? Then he noticed Rachael at Beth's side.

As he approached he heard Beth say, "Alone with poor dead Elizabeth, the old crone..." Here Rachael interjected, "auld sotted widwife." And Beth continued, "...opened the girl's hand and found the prized locket."

"Did she give it to Mr. Bumble, my lady," the anxious child at her knee asked, "so the orphaned babe could find his clan?"

Beth ruffled the lad's russet curls, "Nay, lad. The crone pocketed—stole—the locket before any spied it. Since they didna ken his rightful clan, Mr. Bumble christened the babe Oliver Twist."

Wondering if only orphans peopled his lady's tales, he came to her side and cleared his throat. "My lady, what say we retire? 'Tis nigh onto midnight surely."

Many an "Aw, but she isna done," and "Oh, please, my lady, what of the babe?" went up from those at her feet.

She smiled. "This tale will take many nights to tell." She stood and placed her hand on his arm. "I promise to continue tomorrow."

Amongst much grumbling and yawning, the clan

began to disperse. He covered Beth's hand and found it cold and sweating. Frowning, he placed a palm to her forehead. "My lady, are ye ill?"

She grimaced as she threaded her arm through his. "Nay, Duncan, just terrified. I've just spent two hours trying to keep your clan well-occupied by telling stories only half remembered from my childhood."

"Ah." He watched mothers collecting their ale-besotted husbands and sleepy children, while others cleared the tables. "Ye apparently did it well."

Nodding toward the Bruce who remained in conversation with his men at the far end of the hall, she asked, "Did your meeting go well?"

"As well as could be expected given the man's predisposition to maneuver all to his advantage."

Beth studied the Bruce for a moment longer, suddenly wondering about the attack on the night of her arrival. Even Rachael had said little about it. "Was it his men who attacked the coach I was in?"

Duncan nodded. "But the men were mercenaries, not of his clan. In the fray, I'd not thought to keep one alive to question, so I canna prove what I feel in my gut to be so."

"I'm sorry if my arrival caused a further rift..." She stopped as the Bruce men inexplicably settle around the room in twos. "Duncan?" She clutched his arm. "Are they *all* spending the night?"

He patted her hand as they ambled past families settling around the hall. "Aye, but dinna fash. We've guards aplenty." He kissed the tip of her nose. "And ye already ken how to bar yon solar door if ye have a mind."

"This," she mumbled through clenched teeth and a false smile as she nodded to the child who wished her good sleep, "is not something to jest about. You just said you believe the man to be a *murderer*."

To make matters more untenable, all the weapons had been put away as some sort of peacekeeping gesture.

She could picture waking—if she hadn't been killed in the night—to the hall looking like a monument to carnage.

He patted her hand. "Some would say the same of me."

She huffed. Even if only half the tales she'd heard at supper were true, some might call her husband bloodthirsty or even a mercenary, but *never* a murderer. She knew to her bones that his honor had—and always would—hold him in check. But the same, she suspected, could not be said for the man Rachael now guided toward the third floor chamber designated for their elite guest.

Just the thought of the Bruce lurking only feet below their bed pushed any desire for romance out of her head.

Her hands started to perspire again. As she twisted the ring on her left hand to ease the itch beneath the band, she knew she'd get no sleep tonight.

"My lady."

Beth turned to stare straight into Miss I'm Too Sexy's huge brown eyes. The thought of taking shears to the woman's long kangaroo lashes made her smile. "Yes, Flora?"

"*Madame*, I regret not having had opportunity earlier to thank ye for saving my life. I am most assuredly grateful, for I ken few would have made the effort."

"You are most welcome, but I'm sure any here would have done the same. I just happened to see your trouble first."

"Nay, my lady." Flora cast a quick glance toward Duncan then about the room. "I fear..." She shook her head and dropped into a deep curtsey. "I humbly thank ye and am at ye service."

As she glided away, Beth asked, "What do you make of that, husband?"

"She has the right of it. Had it been left to me, she'd have choked to death."

"*Duncan!*" She swatted his arm. "Don't even say that in jest."

He captured her hand and brought it to his lips. "Lady, I must attend to matters before retiring. Can ye find yer way to our bed without me?"

"Yes, but hurry." She didn't care to be alone with the enemy just paces away.

He ran his tongue over her knuckles causing her to shiver. "Ah, 'tis gratifying, yer impatience."

She gaped at him. Here her stomach churned with worry—that their throats would be slit as they slept, and he's got his mind on sex? God love a duck! Had she known he'd stop thinking with his head and start thinking with what dangled beneath his kilt, she never would have acquiesced to following him into the barn, let alone made love to him.

"Duncan, just do whatever it is you need to do in record time and get your butt up those stairs."

When he wiggled a brow, she just rolled her eyes and hurried toward the solar.

She kicked off her ridiculous long-toed slippers as she rushed into their room. Dropping to her knees, she routed under the bed and pulled out Duncan's heavy claymour. In the process she heard metal clanging to the floor and found a jeweled, ceremonial dirk. Great.

Heaving them onto the bed, she wondered how her husband managed to swing the huge sword with one hand for minutes on end. It had taken both of hers just to lift the damn thing.

Satisfied with her defenses, Beth lifted the window's woolen drape and studied the guards on the walls. Seeing none slept, she heaved a sigh and scratched at the skin around her ring.

Damn. Between all the cleaning she'd been doing and being nervous all night, she'd developed another rash. With no hydrocortisone ointment on hand, she'd likely claw herself raw by morning. Within a day, thanks to her unconscious but relentless nighttime scratching, the inflammation and swelling would spread across the entire back of her hand. She twisted the ring.

She had little doubt removing a wedding band had to be some kind of sacrilege, but she didn't have a choice. If she didn't get air to the area beneath the band, her entire hand could be swollen and stiff within days.

She carefully twisted the ancient gold and ruby treasure over her knuckle to examine the flesh beneath and felt a flash of stinging cold. Before she could draw her next breath, her skin, inexplicably, became luminescent. Heart pounding, she turned her hands and examined her now glowing palms. Her breath caught; her heart stopped, then kicked hard against her ribs as she stared through her diaphanous hands and saw the floor.

Chapter 21

Beth's scream rent the midnight stillness of the bailey then rolled like thunder off its walls. It caused the hairs on Duncan's neck and arms to stand. He spun from the guard he'd been questioning.

"Please, God, dinna let me find her bleeding, or worse yet dead by a Bruce blade." He charged into the keep.

Racing across the hall, he ignored the startled expressions and questions of those who'd also heard Beth's cry. He took the stairs to the solar two and three at a time. The heavy pounding of many footsteps followed him.

Whoever, he swore silently, dared cause his lady to scream in such a fashion now breathed on borrowed time. He would slit the man from ear to ear as soon as he could lay hands on him.

Heart beating a frantic tattoo he forgot the latch and threw his weight against the solar door. It crashed against the wall as he came to a sudden halt and stared at the ghastly visage of his wife.

"Duncan!"

Tears coursed down her cheeks as she held out her arms to him. He scanned the room for the intruder as his long strides ate up the distance between them. Thankful she was quite alive, he snatched his claymour from the bed. It would better serve him than the sgian dubh in his hand.

She fell into his arms. She felt as cold as the stones beneath the keep and shook like the shutters during a gale. "God's teeth, woman!"

He ran quick hands over her. Discovering her whole and unscathed, he clutched her to his chest. "What hath wrought such angst that ye screamed to stop a man's heart?"

"I pulled off my—" She glanced behind him as men piled into the room. "I...I...saw a rat," she flung out her arms to the breadth of his shoulders, "this big."

He gaped at her while his heart struggled to catch a steady rhythm. "Ye nearly killed me over spying a rat?" How one could survive around the prowling lymers and cats he hadna a notion, but she adamantly nodded and pointed to a far corner.

The Bruce's laugh caused him to look to the crowded doorway. Short steel flashed in every hand. So much for the stowing of arms.

As the fifty-year-old Bruce gasped for air, he slapped Angus on the back. "Yer laird certainly can pick 'em."

Glaring at the crowd, Duncan bellowed, "Out! All of ye!"

Beth jumped, and he tightened his hold at her waist. Angus stepped aside so the Bruce could take leave, and Rachael slid into his place.

"*Madame*, are ye all right?"

"Yes, Rachael." Beth's voice was little more than a

hoarse whisper.

"Shall I chase it down, my lord?" Angus bent to peek under the bed. "Nay. The poor beasty has nay doubt escaped if he hasna already expired from fright." He waved Angus out.

He patted Beth's back until she released the death grip she had on his tunic. "I swear, Beth, ye will be the death of me." He tipped up her face. "Dinna rats abide in the new York?"

She went wild-eyed again scanning the room. "Are you telling me there *are* rats in the keep?"

Scowling, he forced her to arms' length. "What the hell are ye then so frighten of, if nay rats?"

She blanched and started biting her lower lip. "I couldn't tell you while they were here." She waved at the door. "Please lock it. I have something to show you."

The door secured, she paced the middle of the room twisting her wedding band. "Duncan, I don't really expect you to understand this, because I sure as hell don't. But one minute I was itching and as solid as you and the next I'm glowing and turning into some sort of wavering gas..." She started to weep. "Oh, just watch. Then tell me if I'm losing my mind or if what I'm feeling truly happens."

She twisted his ring from her middle finger and slipped it forward, keeping it poised at the tip.

To his utter amazement and horror, she started to shimmer from head to toe like the undulating lights that occasionally lit the northern sky in winter. When the air in the room began to vibrate, to shift, he backed away, a hand before his face. As she slowly faded before his disbelieving eyes, becoming so transparent he could see the window at her back through her, he saw her usually calm visage reflected the awe and fear he felt.

"Holy Mother! What doth..."

Words eluded him.

Then, just as suddenly, she became as solid as the floor beneath his feet, or as it had once been, though now he'd not have sworn it so.

He'd listened to her tales of Lady Kathy and one hundred story sky scrapes, but what sane man would have believed it all? Yet, just now she nearly vanished before his eyes!

Pure instinct brought his broadsword to her heart.

Her teeth chattered as she held out her left hand. "Duncan, it's your ring. The ring brought me here and can take me away."

Heart bounding, he shook his head still not believing.

She stepped to within an inch of his blade and whispered, "Duncan, please. Put down your sword."

"Hold!" The claymore's tip vibrated with his fear and he had to grasp it with two hands to stay it.

God's teeth! What kind of specter 'tis Beth that she can come and go thus? And what did she want? Was she a fairy? Had she come to charm him, to take his seed as fairies were want to do whenever they wanted a human bairn, and God help him, he'd obliged? Or, God forbid, had she come from some other place to claim his soul?

"Duncan, please..." She held out her hands in supplication. "It's the ring."

"BACK WITH YE! I dinna ken ye or why ye be here, but *leave*!"

Fear he understood and routinely dealt with in battle, but the terror now surging through his blood and causing his muscles to quake and his breath to catch felt altogether foreign. As foreign as his ladywife's ability to disappear then reappear at will.

Fresh tears slid down her cheeks. "I don't understand this anymore than you do. But I'm still me, just plain ol' Katherine Elizabeth MacDougall Pudding who belongs in New York with her roaches and Chinese take-out, and I'm as frightened by this as you are." She wrung her hands. "Actually, I'm way past frightened, Duncan, I'm truly terrified." She reached out.

"Nay!" He used the claymore to keep her at a safe distance, and then circled the tip at her heart for good measure.

To his utter surprise she leaned into it, piercing the tender flesh over her breastbone. Before he could think— to either press his advantage or wonder why she did it— she uttered a wee cry and backed off the gleaming steel.

Shaking and pale, she looked down at the wee scarlet burn that flowed down her chest. "See, I'm just flesh and blood."

Dumbfounded, he growled and raised his shaking blade over his shoulder.

She searched his face for only a moment before collapsing at his feet like a dropped puppet. Her shoulders shook as she buried her face in her hands. She started to sob. As she rocked on her knees, her arms now clutching her middle, his blade hovered above the fair skin of her long exposed neck.

Self-preservation caused him to inhale deeply, his body readying to wield his sword.

His heart jolted when she keened, "*Why God? Why, when all I ever asked out of life was for someone to love?*"

Chapter 22

A gust of air swished past her cheek and the claymore dropped with an ungodly clang to the floor.

"Ah, Christ's blood, Beth."

Slowly she raised her face to look into Duncan's eyes. Not seeing death staring back, she released her breath. He kicked the broadsword away and settled on his haunches before her as she dashed her tears away with the heels of her hands. He reached for her, but then pulled back.

"Be ye alright?" His face was still flushed and dotted by sweat. "The cut, lass." He pointed to the spot where his blade had pierced her chest. She looked not at her wound but to the sword. "Yes."

Heart still thudding, she reluctantly shifted her gaze from the gleaming harbinger of death now lying impotent on the floor to her bloodied bodice. The once white crewelwork was now a rusty burgundy and probably ruined beyond all hope. Rachael had told her it had taken a master tailor and his three apprentice six months to make the gown. "Did you spare me so Rachael could now take my head?"

"Ack, lass." To her surprise, he reached out

tentatively, first to brush the hair from her cheek and then to trace the path of her tears to her jaw. He examined his fingers. "'Tis soot. Did yer unholy light burn ye?"

Soot? She'd only felt a bone-fracturing cold when she started to disappear and still felt chilled. She hadn't felt any heat, no burning. She sniffed and hiccuped again as she examined his fingertips more closely. Suddenly she wanted to laugh, and would have, had she had the energy. Her homemade mascara had cascaded south with her tears. It was too much to hope that she only had raccoon eyes. More likely she resembled a chimney sweep. Could she do nothing right in this world?

"Duncan, I wasn't burned. It's just lamp black—lamp sable."

Obviously confused, he frowned but only said, "Ah."

She wiped her nose with the back of her hand. "I wanted to be pretty, so I used the soot..." She heaved a sigh. "Hell, you wouldn't understand."

While she struggled to her feet, surprised she wasn't nauseous from fright, he sheathed his short blade to his calf. Not looking at her but toward the window, he quietly asked, "Will ye be leaving?"

She shrugged.

Yes, she wanted to return to her old life where threatening steel meant only a racing taxi, where she could speak normally and be understood, where she had friends, coffee and real make-up. But then again, no. For *home* would also be bereft of hope, for love or for children. She'd have her ghost but not the real Duncan. She took a deep breath and confessed, "Not right now, unless you want me to go."

Not wanting to watch as he made his decision, she walked to the window. Her head and heart continued to ache as she studied the movement along the battlements in the light of oil torches whipping like horsetails in the errant wind.

The burning in her throat defeated her effort to sound matter of fact as she confided, "I never expected to wear a wedding ring, much less be married to a man such as you. To discover the ring—something I'd hoped would hold such promise—could terrify me so..."

She heard him come to his feet. "I dinna suppose any woman should expect it."

"Three wives wore this ring before me. Have you ever been in love?" Why had she asked? What difference could his ability or willingness to love her matter now?

She placed a hand on her stomach. Did a new life already hide in the deep recesses of her womb? That possibility—not whether he could love her—would have to be the deciding factor in her staying or leaving.

He took a long time in answering. "I grieved for Mary."

Yes, he had written of his guilt, that he hadn't loved her, but had he lied to himself about loving her? Why else would he be so obsessed with the chapel?

And what, if anything, would he write of her, Beth, should she decide to slip the ring off for good? Would he grieve? And for what? The loss of a potential heir, a good meal, or just an efficiently run keep? One or all of the above? In any event, it certainly wouldn't be for her. He'd never mentioned the word love. And knowing that certainly shouldn't cause the burning at the back of her eyes and throat, much less the fissures now spreading across her heart. She was, after all, plain-as- pudding Pudding.

When she'd sent her silent plea to God for an honest

answer, Duncan had been so close to cleaving her head from her shoulders she'd seen her life pass before her. What staid his hand she might never know, but she thanked God all the same. At twenty-four, she tearfully acknowledged, she'd yet to earn the right to die.

Duncan studied his wife's straight back as she stared into the night and tried to gather his wits.

He'd never been so unnerved in his life. Aye, her turning specter before his very eyes had nearly stopped his heart, but that dinna compare to the last.

The verra worst occurred when—kenning his fear and possible intent—she'd pleaded *not* for God's mercy nor for his, but had used what could have been her last breath to demand an explanation from God for what she truly believed to be His betrayal.

No faint heart, his lady.

He'd seen many a brave man die and never before had heard such. Ack! His skin still pebbled like a plucked fowl just thinking on her temerity in calling God to task. 'Twas also at that very moment—when she keened her demand—that he kenned fully that she had spoken nothing less than the truth from the first moment he'd laid eyes on her.

He had no need to fear his enemies. He would be the undoing of himself.

And he couldna blame her if she decided to disappear for all eternity. Nay, given all the angst he'd caused her, he could only expect it.

Why the thought caused a dreadful tightening around his chest he'd not dwell on. He had yet to tell her a painful truth and he owed her that much before she left him.

He stepped forward to stand at her back. "Beth, I do

believe all ye have said." He heard her sharp intake of breath. "Aye, I ken ye are not wode but from another time and place." He studied the stars as he gathered courage to say what must be said.

"'Tis been difficult for me to accept yer tales. For if I believed in sky scrapes and plum mink, then I had to believe I willna be laid to rest when my time comes, but will haunt these halls for all eternity." He took a deep breath. "'Twas far easier to believe ye coddled in some fashion than to admit I am doomed for what I have done, for the lives I have taken."

Beth spun and found him rigid, his gaze glassy with unshed tears as he stared blindly over her head into the night.

Oh dear God!

She placed her hands on his chest and felt furious beating beneath vibrating muscle. He was terrified—not of her—but of the future.

She hadn't thought him a religious man, but given the time and the Church's influence on their everyday lives—the in-house priest, the daily vespers so many attended—she should have seen this coming. Should have understood the impact her words would have on him.

"I'm so sorry. I never meant..."

He slowly, gently, brought his powerful arms around her while his eyes remained on the stars. "Nay, Beth. Ye've not done anythin' to be sorrowful for. Ye told only the truth." He then looked at her, a small grin playing at one corner of his mouth. "'Tis by my own doing—my own hand—that I shall have no peace."

"But it makes no sense. You're honest, a man of character. Surely, there must be more to this—"

"Sweet Beth." He kissed her forehead. "Ye wish to ease my mind, but why? I am nay digne of ye forgiveness." His tears escaped the confines of his thick lashes. "I nearly smote ye with my sword."

"You were upset. Fear of the unknown can—"

He pressed a finger to her lips. "Too, I'm a widower thrice and carry that blame. And lest we forget, I've killed in battle more men than we—together—have digits."

She hadn't meant for her eyes to grow wide in shock but they did, and he murmured, "Aye, lass. At last count the number is close to sixty."

"Oh." It came out as a squeak. What more could she say? That isn't so great a number? Or he really shouldn't worry because he'll be a relatively pleasant ghost, who only has a tantrum now and then and has much more mourning yet to do? Oh God.

"My lady?"

"What?" She'd been woolgathering.

"I asked if I had issue. Did I at least leave an heir?"

Matters were definitely going from bad to worse.

She ran a tentative finger along his finely crafted lips then caught a tear as it trailed down his smooth well-chiseled cheek. He'd kept his face shaved only because she preferred it.

Please, God, let what I'm about to tell him be so.

Aloud she whispered, "I suspect that very problem is the cause for my being here."

His moan escaped before he could collect himself. He then nodded resignedly and threw back his shoulders. It was an admirable job of sucking up, but defeat still lurked deep within his eyes as one corner of his mouth quirked into a grin. "So be it."

She took his right hand in hers and examined his long, well- shaped fingers and heavy calluses. With it he had brought her to the heights of ecstasy and the pits of despair. Whether she chose to stay or not, he had forever changed her view of life.

"Duncan, I honestly believe everything happens for a reason. I could have drowned in my time, but didn't. I could have died in that coach, but was spared." She didn't add he could have severed her head just moments ago, too. He had, after all, apologized and was upset enough.

She took a deep breath. "I believe I'm here to give you an heir."

Chapter 23

Without warning, Flora began walking along Oban's rutted roads at a fierce pace. Rachael growled as she tried to keep up, doggedly dodging harried wives, venders, dogs, and waste along the town's sodden ways.

To her relief Flora finally slowed before the market stalls. When Flora came to a full stop before a woman selling flasks of perfumed oil, Rachael, gasping, sent a thankful prayer to heaven. Flora started negotiating with the vender and Rachel relaxed, her attention drifting to the next cart overflowing with fresh greens.

She finally held up a nice clump of watercress to ask Flora's opinion and found her gone.

Rachael's panic quickly shifted to aggravation. How Flora had slipped away unnoticed mattered naught at this point. She was gone. Finding her without asking their guards for help—for they could not know of Duncan and Isaac's suspicions—would take precious time from her shopping. Oban might not be London or even Glasgow, but it did have merchants and peddlers on market day that she normally had no access to in her little corner of the world.

Teeth gritted, Rachael cursed Flora, lifted her skirts

and raced along the rutted roadway fronting the loch. Here she could no longer wear her stylish French pattens—her high wooden overshoes to keep her feet dry and her hems clean—for fear of twisting an ankle. Stepping into a puddle, she cursed Flora once again.

She peeked in every window and doorway she could find. Not seeing so much as a glimpse of her wayward charge in the obvious places, Rachael began a methodical search of all the mews and stables.

Thirty minutes later, annoyed beyond words and desperately thirsty, she entered a public house and heaved a sigh of relief. There sat Flora in a dark corner across from a man Rachael didn't recognize.

"'Tis here ye be!" Out of breath, Rachael didn't remark on Flora's startled expression but wiggled in beside her on the bench. She caught the tavern maid's attention as she set her basket of greens at her feet.

She smiled at Flora and the pox-marred man across the table. After waiting a respectful amount of time for an introduction and receiving none, she said to the man, "I am Madame Silverstein, and you be...?"

"Richard of Oban."

"'Tis a pleasure to make yer acquaintance." The tavern lass appeared at her elbow. She ordered a tankard of ale and wondered why the man neglected to mention a surname. She dabbed at the perspiration on her forehead with her handkerchief. "Flora hasna mentioned that she has been keeping company with a gentleman." She elbowed her charge playfully. "Naughty girl." To the man she asked, "So how did ye come to court our full fair and fetish friend?"

He turned scarlet at Rachael's question and well he should, she thought. From the sour odor wafting across the table, Rachael could only deduce he'd not bathed since her son, Jacob, had been born. Too, half the man's teeth had hied off with most of his auburn hair, no doubt in an effort to escape the stench she now labored under. What remained had a decidedly yellow cast.

"I met Mistress Campbell..." He blinked and brought his tankard to his lips, apparently seeking the answer to her question on the pewter bottom.

"If ye must know," Flora interjected, not quite masking her annoyance, "I commissioned Richard to make our liege and lady a marriage gift."

"Ah." Rachael waited expectantly. When nothing materialized she asked, "May I see it?"

Flora heaved a resigned sigh as she delved into her pocket and pulled out a fist-sized packet. "'Tis a small token." She uncovered a brass enseignes—broach—with two doves carved into it.

"'Tis lovely! What fine craftsmanship."

Thank heaven, Flora thought. She'd purchased the piece from a peddler only a week ago in the event she got caught with the odious man across from her. She had no choice but to come today. Had she missed this rendezvous with the Bruce's man, she would have been forced to wait almost a fortnight before she could pass along her information, and then 'twould be too late. The tournament was set for the next full moon.

She had hoped to get through all this intrigue and keep the broach for herself, but better to lose a pretty than to lose her life. "Thank you."

She did have exquisite taste.

"Our lord and lady will be verra pleased." Rachael said as she turned the piece in her hand then smiled at the man. "'Tis truly fine. Yer talent is such, ye should be abiding in a major city, not hiding here where only a few can appreciate ye labors."

When Richard blushed and remained mute, Flora mumbled, "He does travel extensively to sell his wares."

"Ah." Rachael handed back the broach. "Have ye been to Edinburgh, sir?"

Looking uncomfortable, Flora's hapless partner mumbled, "Aye."

"Ye made him shy with ye teasing, Rachael." Not kenning if he'd been to the capital or not she said, "Richard was just telling me how difficult 'tis getting his cart up the steep ways of Edinburgh." When he remained mute, she kicked him under the table and ground out, "Is not that so, sir?"

"Oh, aye," Richard agreed. "'Tis verra steep the streets. The castle sits upon a mountain, ye ken? And the high street runs from the gates to the valley below."

When Rachael asked, "Has the great tower started by King David been completed yet?" Flora nearly choked on her brew. Why on earth had she foolishly encouraged talk of Edinburgh? Arriving in Scotland, Edinburgh was the first place the Silversteins had sought refuge, only to discover the city filthy and full of pestilence.

Flora glared at the Bruce's man. He had the plan to bring her brother-by-marriage to his bloody knees, so why in hell was he still sitting here tolerating Rachael's inquisition? She kicked out again to gain his attention.

This time he kicked back—hard.

Ignoring her, he smiled at her companion. "Nay yet, Madame, but the chapel has been restored."

Rachael smiled. "How nice."

To Flora's relief the Bruce's man then emptied his tankard. He had manners enough to wipe the foam from his mouth before saying, "Talking with ye has been most pleasant, ladies, but 'tis time for my leave taking." He bowed to her. "'Twas a pleasure doing business with ye, Mistress Campbell."

She forced a smile. "Good day, sir."

When he disappeared Rachael murmured, "We should be finding our guards. 'Tis past the appointed hour, non?"

"Aye." Flora came to her feet and noticed Richard had neglected to pay for his ale. She reluctantly dropped extra pennies on the table. Revenge was becoming more expensive by the hour. "If we hie home, we may be in time to hear what happens next to Oliver Twist."

"Ah, the poor wee lad." Rachael picked up her basket and frowned at her purchases. "Can ye imagine selling a bairn? And to learn the Sassenach starve poor laddies to keep 'em wee so they can force them down chimneys and then chase after them with lit brooms should they be slow at their task. Ack! 'Tis abhorrent."

Flora readily agreed as she headed for the door. Not spying the Bruce's man lingering on the street, she heaved a sigh.

Chapter 24

Hearing her husband's call, Beth quickly ducked behind the enormous wicker baskets at Angus's back. She held her breath and silently cursed her big mouth.

Duncan MacDougall was a man on a mission, while Beth had never been the brunt of so many jokes in her life.

It wasn't that she minded her husband's attention—Duncan was an incredibly considerate lover—but she'd been spending more time on her back than on her feet of late and things were falling apart in the keep. And Duncan's time would be better spent at the lists rebuilding his strength readying for the tournament. If she'd explained ovulation once, she done it a dozen times and still she'd not had a moment's peace or a solid night's sleep since that fateful evening.

"Have ye seen my ladywife?" Duncan asked as he approached.

"Ye ladywife, my lord?"

"Aye, ye twit!" Duncan paced before her hiding place. "The skinny lass with the fine arse."

Angus cleared his throat, no doubt in an effort to cover a chuckle. They'd all seen her carried away over

Duncan's shoulder often enough in the last two weeks to know the laird of Blackstone was intent, to the point of obsession, on making an heir. To her infinite relief Angus responded, "Um...she was in the distillery an hour ago."

"Well, she isna there now."

"Have ye checked the chapel?"

"Why would she go...*Ah ha!*"

Duncan's heavy footsteps receded and Beth peaked out from behind the basket. "Is he gone?" she whispered.

"Aye, but ye'd best be away. If ye linger, he'll be wondering why the fish are still sitting here." As she came out of hiding, he said, "Now dinna ye be forgetting the pie ye promised me."

"Angus, I'll make two if you can keep him occupied for that long."

Angus called, "I'll try," to her back as she trotted across the bailey, keeping well away from the chapel and to the shadows.

She'd almost made it to the keep's door when she heard, "Hold ye, lass, right where ye be!"

Damn.

Whipping the door open, she waved over her shoulder. "Can't dear! Something needs my urgent attention." She then ran for her life.

"Oh, nay, ye sweet thing!"

Chickens scattered and men laughed as Duncan raced after her.

~#~

"Ye heard nothing?"

"I was too late, Isaac, but I feel certain the ensigns is Burgandian, not crafted by that sloth."

Isaac, aware she was familiar with the fashion wars

raging on the continent between the powerful and wealthy Germanic princes and the French, didn't question her opinion. He started pacing the library. "Where is Flora now?"

"In her chamber."

"Mayhap she commissioned the piece in good faith and this Richard of Oban was merely taking the credit to turn a fast profit."

"Possible, but..." Who was she to say what was or was not possible, though she doubted Flora could be so easily tricked. Too, the man's hands appeared coarser than those of a fine artisan. "In any event, she spoke only kind things about our lady on the way home."

"Hmm. Do you think she might be dissembling?"

Rachael shrugged. "Mayhap she now finds our lady's odd ways more acceptable since Beth saved her life."

"A strong possibility given Flora is nothing, if not self-serving." He took her hands and pulled her to her feet. "Then we can do little but watch and wait."

Her beloved appeared none too happy about the prospect.

"Nay, husband. We pray, and while I continue my vigil, you can keep Duncan occupied and away from poor Beth."

Isaac grinned. "Did she tell you what has set him on his current course?"

She shook her head. "Did Duncan tell you?"

"Aye." He studied her for a moment. "Ye were right, my dear. She is a reborn, a spirit from a distant place and time made flesh again."

"Oh my." When she'd mentioned the possibility, she'd been thinking on a philosophical plane, never truly believing it could be reality. Wide-eyed, she asked,

"How has he taken this?"

"He'd slit my throat if he heard me say this, but he's frightened she may leave him, for she has the ability. I've no doubt he loves her, but with the possibility of her deserting him hanging over his head he'll never acknowledge it to himself nor to her."

How stupid could men be? "Saying he loves her might well meld her to him."

"He believes a child will do that."

She sighed. Some men were apparently more foolish than she surmised.

~#~

James the Bruce smirked as he read Flora Campbell's missive. Her plan for kidnapping Lady MacDougall could be arranged— not easily for the MacDougall had placed his sentries well—but guards had never deterred him before and would not now. He had too much to gain.

And who would have ever thought Duncan the Black's Achilles heel would prove to be a wife?

He tossed Flora's missive, with her plea that no permanent harm come to Lady Beth, into the fire. He marveled at the woman's stupidity. He would, as always, do what suited his purposes and clan. And he had other plans for Lady Beth.

Once captured and placed in his dungeon, 'twould take but a week, mayhap less, for Lady Beth to die. He would then order her body tossed over one of the many crags that bordered Bruce-MacDougall land so 'twould appear she fell. The carrion crows will, nay doubt, lead a MacDougall clansman to her, but by then 'twill be too late. For Lady Beth *and* the MacDougall.

Looking at the missive's ashes, he shook his head.

God, spare me from a woman bent on revenge.

~#~

Tears crept into Tom Silverstein's eyes as he looked upon his ebony-headed son sucking and gurgling at Margaret's full breast. 'Twas the loveliest, most heart-warming thing he'd ever witnessed.

His perfect son, just five days old, had already taken over the household. Everything turned topsy-turvy on his slightest whim. But how long would his self-determination last?

Despite Margaret's coaxing, Tom had yet to garner the courage to reread the laird of Blackstone's diary, to look for changes, for Isaac's predictions.

Too, he still worried about Beth, regardless of his wife's assessment of her tenacious spirit. Fifteenth century Scotland had been a brutal place, where pestilence, constant squabbling between chieftains and religious fervor made everyone's life a misery. Assuming she had survived her arrival, how was she faring under those circumstances? Could she survive long enough to fulfill the prophecy?

He'd tried but couldn't squelch the deep-seated fear that all he'd been led to believe, to hope for, would prove to be only lore. That nothing would come to pass, nothing would ever change.

"Tom? Are you all right, love?"

He smiled and took his sleeping son from his exhausted wife's arms. "Aye. Is there anything I can do to help ye get ready?" Today their son would be officially welcomed into their temple, named, and circumcised.

His wife's lovely china blue eyes had sunk deep into darkened sockets since his son had set himself to feeding every two hours around the clock, but she smiled and shook her head. "All but yours truly is ready. Can ye keep an eye on him while I change?"

"My pleasure."

As he rocked his son, Tom tried to put away his worry. He wanted nothing to overshadow the joy he should be feeling on this blessed event of his son's naming, yet worry he did, and he picked up the diary. With a shaking hand he then put it down. "Nay, I canna look. Not on this day."

Chapter 25

The moment Beth keened and collapsed to his chest, Duncan halted the mind games he'd been playing for restraint and exploded deep within the warm confines of his wife's lithe body.

Holding her close, he inhaled the fresh scent of her hair as it veiled his face. He grinned. His ladywife would no doubt deny it with her dying breath, but the poor wee thing was verra easy to arouse.

He only had to hold her close and stroke the side of her breast, nibble at the junction of her neck and shoulder, or kiss her softly while playing small circles on her lower back to capture her interest, to make her groan.

That's all he need do, but then he did have to catch her first, which was becoming a bit of a problem.

He stroked her small, firm buttocks. "Did ye enjoy?"

"Uh huh." She nuzzled his neck.

"Good, then can ye kindly explain why I'm having to chase ye to ground every time I want ye?"

He felt rather than heard her laugh. She rose up onto her elbows and ran a hand through her hair to get it off her face.

The way she tipped her head as she did it sent his

blood racing.

"I've already explained I'm either already with child or not. And all the tupping in the world at this point will not change that."

Duncan snorted. He knew for a fact that some women took a good deal of attention to get with child. Others ye merely had to look at crossways and they were with get. Since he had no idea what kind of woman he had, he intended to be thorough. Verra.

"Besides,"—she crawled off his chest and motioned for him to roll over so she could examine his shoulder— "you should be working the lists, and I should be in the kitchen." Prodding his new flesh, she murmured, "You're truly amazing. It's almost completely healed. Is your shoulder stiff?"

He flexed. "A wee bit."

She kissed his back. "You can roll back now." She cuddled into his side. "What will you do should you lose the tournament?"

"I'll not." Even the suggestion made his blood run cold.

"Yes, I've no doubt. But, God forbid you should lose, what will you do for money—coins?"

He had hoped she'd not put the two together. "Then I will go to France for a short while."

"*France?*" She came up on her elbows to examine his face.

"Aye, I will sell my arm to Louie."

She blanched lily white. "You'd become a mercenary again, after everything you've seen and done?"

"'Tis nay need to shout." He brushed the hair from her lovely face. He'd forgotten she'd read part of his diary. He sighed. 'Twas odd, knowing his writings were of such import they'd been translated. Twice. When she settled on his chest again, he wrapped his arms around her.

"Ye ken I dinna like it, but will do it again if need be to keep what is mine."

He felt something warm and wet on his chest and lifted her chin to see her tears. "Hush, 'twould not be so bad. Ye'd have a free hand here and nay need to fret over me chasing ye with a gleam in my eye."

She slapped his stomach. "Do not joke about war, Duncan Angus MacDougall. You could die or be maimed—"

He pressed a finger to her lips. "I'll not do it again if it upsets ye."

She settled onto his chest again. "Damn straight, it upsets me."

It came as a bit of a shock to realize his wife truly cared for him. Mayhap she'd not leave him after all, even if she couldn't have a child.

"Beth, what do ye want most in the world?"

She studied his face for a long moment as fresh tears filled her eyes. In answer she kissed him gently on the lips but said no more.

~

The next morning, unlike the rest of the clan who cheered and hooted as Duncan and Angus went at each other on the lists, sending the sounds of crashing wood on steel echoing around the bailey, Beth grimaced and silently bit her nails. She sorely regretted suggesting Duncan practice for the tournament. How the men could still laugh and call out obscene taunts as they tried to decapitate each other was beyond her.

"Dinna fash, my lady," Flora whispered at her elbow.

"Yer man is well-skilled at this. See, he has not been unseated, and Angus is verra strong and wily."

Making room for Flora at her side, Beth smiled for the first time in hours. "Good morn, Flora."

"Good morn."

Beth's smile faded into a cringe as Angus's lance struck her husband's shield with an ungodly thud and the wood shattered. "Just the thought of him falling and getting trampled by that enormous beast..."

The massive white Percheron Duncan rode weighed a ton.

Flora shook her head. "Ransom is fond of his master so he willna stomp upon our liege should he be unseated."

"I pray you're right."

Duncan had told her he'd acquired the animal in France six years ago and swore the stallion was intelligent and the best he'd ever had.

"I see ye wear thy broach," Flora whispered.

"Yes, it's lovely, Flora. I thank ye again."

"Ye are most welcome. I've come to ask if ye would like to see the new woolens Sean's wife has been weaving. So soft and fine, 'tis wondrous."

"I would love to see it." Beth had been dying to see what home industries Duncan had at his disposal. Surely, with her twenty-first century perspective, she could come up with something lucrative that would keep him home, keep him from becoming a mercenary again.

"Then let us go after the men are finished here, my lady. Sean's wife and the loom are just above the village, there." Flora pointed toward the hill just to the right of Drasmoor.

"Yes, and thank you."

Flora's attitude toward her had changed since the banquet. This last week, she'd been pleasant and the first in the hall to assist in readying the mid-day meals. Pleased that Flora had extended her hand in friendship in yet another way, Beth said, "I've always wanted to see how a loom works."

"Grand. We can cross to Drasmoor with one of the fishermen and be back by mid-day meal."

As she watched her husband dismount, Beth said, "Thank you for offering to take me."

"'Tis my pleasure."

"Ah, my ladywife!" Duncan pulled his helmet off. His hair was plastered to his head with sweat. "What say ye? Am I fit enough to carry yer token into battle?"

He was obviously so pleased with his performance she answered, "Aye, my lord. You are a splendiferous example of manhood, if ever I saw one." And he truly was, gleaming and clanking in armor as he bore down on her in the morning sunlight.

He pulled off his gauntlets and scooped her into his arms.

In a whisper, he asked, "Have I allayed yer fears, woman mine?"

"Aye." She kissed him soundly, knowing he wouldn't mind her confirming his prowess before one and all. The clan's very livelihood and security depended on his ability. Yet she worried. As strong an opponent as Angus was, the Bruce was bigger still.

Lowering her to the ground, he called to Rachael's son, "Squire, fetch yer weary knight a drink."

The skinny lad, twelve, all joints and ears, preened. "Aye, my lord!"

"You ken Rachael will have your skin," Beth

murmured, "if you continue to encourage the boy's ambitions to knighthood."

Duncan laughed. "The lad needs learn how to defend himself and Isaac agrees."

Seeing Rachael's dour expression out of the corner of her eye, Beth muttered, "Don't say I didn't warn you."

"Ye fash too much, dear lady."

She rolled her eyes. "Someone around here has to."

He laughed as Jacob handed him a flagon of ale. After downing it, he called, "Angus, ye sorry excuse for a man, are ye ready for a wee bit of sword play?"

"'Fore ye pick up yon claymore again," Angus called, "ye'd best go fetch a few brawny men, ye braggart. Ye'll be needing help walking off the field."

Duncan laughed and kissed her nose. "Later, wife. I need put that heathen on his back."

~#~

Beth and Flora had just taken their seats at the bow of the long boat when they heard, "Halt! Wait!"

Beth wondered why Flora swore under her breath seeing Rachael, flushed scarlet, racing along the quay with a man close on her heels.

"Thank ye," Rachael gasped as one of the oarsmen helped her in. She tossed her satchel onto the floor. "I feared ye had already left. 'Tis wee Mary, my lady. Her birthing isna goin' well." Pointing to the man at her back, she said, "'Tis her husband, Alex." The man, unlike Rachael, was deathly pale and obviously close to tears.

Beth nodded to the man. "Hello. What is wrong?"

"I dinna ken, my lady. The midwife wouldna tell me. She just said to summon ye soonest." As his tears began coursing down his cheeks, Flora blanched.

The oarsmen needed no coaxing to put their backs

into every stroke.

Totally out of her element, Beth whispered, "Do either of you know what to do?"

Flora, obviously horrified, shook her head.

"Mayhap I do," Rachael whispered, "but if we canna help, then our presence will, at least, be some comfort." She lowered her voice even farther. "Such a wee thing is Mary. She's had trouble from the verra first. This be her third babe."

As soon as the boat hit the beach everyone tumbled out. With their skirts soaked to the knees, the women raced after Alex.

Beth's fear that they'd lose sight of him evaporated as a blood-curdling screech rent the air. It came from the second stone cottage before her.

Rachael entered the small two-room home ahead of her and settled on her knees before a pale, sweat soaked woman on the pallet. "Shh, Mary, 'twill all be well, dearest."

The midwife, though probably only forty, looked a hundred as she whispered in Gael and Rachael translated, "She said 'tis the shoulders. The head is out but she canna bring forth the rest."

Beth, easing to the far side of the cot, felt the blood leave her head as she looked between the laboring woman's shaking legs. The child's cone shaped head was indeed out, dark and swathed in blood.

Feeling light-headed, she mentally chided, *Get your shit together. This woman needs what little comfort you can offer.__*Beth knelt, brushed the woman's russet curls from her face and placed a cool compress on her brow.

Rachael whispered to the midwife, "Ye have nay choice, mistress. Ye must break the babe's shoulder or we lose mother and child both."

"But I had hoped..."

Rachael shook her head and reached for Mary's hand and right leg. "My lady, take Mary's other hand and leg as I." When Beth had imitated Rachael's hold, Rachael murmured to the midwife, "Do it, now."

Tears sprang into Beth eyes as the walls echoed with Wee Mary's stomach-churning agony.

Before Beth could think to pray, all went deathly quiet. Beth looked to the midwife. The woman held a stout but silent babe on her forearm. With a well-practiced hand, the midwife swabbed the babe's face and mouth and then slapped the baby's feet. Beth's heart gave a mighty thump when the child, a boy, finally bellowed for all he was worth. The new mother, her arms reaching for the infant, laughed and praised God while Beth silently slid to the floor.

Excited by the simple prospect of having a child, she'd given no thought to the dangers of birthing in this primitive world. Her fingers instinctively sought her wedding band.

Chapter 26

Duncan frowned studying his wife as she sat huddled at the far end of their wee isle with her arms clutched around her bent legs. They'd not tupped in days.

Wishing Beth hadna witnessed Mary's birthing was of little use now. More worrisome was her endlessly twisting of her wedding band.

In a flood of tears, she had told him her people would have sliced wee Mary's womb and taken the babe, so the babe wouldna have had a damaged arm as he did now. Though he had heard it done when a woman was lost, he had difficulty believing both mother and child could survive such barbaric treatment. But she swore it was true, and he worried even more.

He knelt behind her and wrapped his arms around her shoulders. Believing he already kenned the answer, he still asked, "Lass, what are ye fashin' on now?"

Staring at the sea, she leaned back against his chest. "Whisky."

"Pardon?"

"Do you know how to make it?"

"I dinna ken the art myself, but Ol' John does. Why?" If he lived to be one hundred, he wouldna ever understand this woman.

"Whisky will make you rich."

He chuckled. "Ladywife, 'tis nay a way in hell John's wee still will make me a wealthy man."

"Exactly. You need bigger stills to make more. And some of the whisky needs to be put up in oak barrels and stored for five years, some even twenty."

Ack! The poor wee thing had gone totally daft from fashing, just as he feared. He stood, lifting her as he did so. "Come, lass, ye need rest."

She spun in his arms. "Listen to me. The longer whisky ages, the better it gets. Where I come from and in England, a rich man thinks nothing of paying fifty dollars—pounds—for a bottle of aged whisky this big."

His jaw dropped as he studied the small space between her hands. "Ye canna be serious?"

"Aye, Duncan, I am. As serious as your priest is about his sacraments."

He expelled a great whoosh of air contemplating the possibilities. He had heard rumors some English were quite fond of *the water of life*. Of course, he'd not tasted aged whisky because they drank John's brew as fast as he made it, but...

Then there was the problem with the land. His wouldna support large crops, but he could negotiate for grain or finished whisky from the lowlanders. He could sell a bit and put away the rest. Too, he'd have to engage in a bit more smuggling, something he'd been reluctant to do of late, but better that then going to France. Hmm.

"Lass," he kissed her soundly, "we need go speak with Isaac."

~#~

Flora grinned as Beth settled in the boat. "My lady,

we're finally off to Drasmoor."

Beth nodded. With her husband sequestered with Isaac, Rachael engrossed in mending—Beth's idea of purgatory—and the keep in good order, she'd been in sore need of a distraction. "Thank you for suggesting this outing."

"My pleasure. We shall visit the babe and Wee Mary first, then go to Kari's cottage and watch her work the Eire loom."

As they drew closer to Drasmoor Beth asked, "Do you look forward to having children?"

"Nay." Flora's gaze shifted out to sea. "I watched my sister die trying to birth and heard too many tales to want such."

"I'm sorry." She placed a hand of Flora's arm. "I hadn't meant to open wounds." After a long pause she garnered enough courage to ask, "Is that why you refused the men who have asked for your hand?"

Flora's brow furrowed. "In part."

Lost in their own thoughts, they didn't speak again until the boat beached.

At her cottage door, Wee Mary wobbled a curtsey. "Good day, my lady. And to ye, Mistress Flora." She ran a worried hand over her plain and spot-stained kirtle. "I hadna expected visitors. Please come in."

Beth smiled and handed Mary a basket laden with a beef stew, bread and jam. "I just came by to see how ye fared."

"Well, thank ye." With her free hand, Mary waved to the cottage's one chair. "Set ye and I will fetch ye a drink."

"Thank ye, but nay. I just wanted to see your beautiful son again."

The worry in Mary's face dissolved at the mention of her babe. "Come then."

Beth's gaze drifted over the soot-covered rafters, the unadorned whitewashed walls and settled on the wooden cradle in the corner.

The child was wrapped snugly in a woolen blanket so Beth could only make out his face. But such a pretty face he had now, all the swelling and redness had vanished. "Is his shoulder healing?"

She nodded. "We keep him bound but he can now move his hand."

Beth sent a prayer of thanks heavenward.

"Would ye like to hold him, my lady?"

"Umm..." Her fear of possibly hurting the child must have been apparent for Mary chuckled.

"He willna mind, my lady."

When the child had been placed in her arms, Beth marveled at how light he felt and how good the infant smelled. "What did you name him?"

"Clyde, after his father's father."

The babe chose that moment to open his deep cobalt eyes. When a bubble made him grin, Beth chuckled, "And it's a pleasure to see you again, too, Master Clyde."

She rocked him as they chatted about the upcoming tournament. When the child became restless, anxiously alternating between fist chewing and trying to rout at her breast, Beth murmured, "It must be dinner time."

She handed the baby back to his mother and she and Flora readied to take their leave. At the door Beth said, "Thank you for letting me hold him."

"Ye are most welcome and come again."

As they approached the weaver's cottage, Flora, who'd been silent during most of their visit with Wee

Mary, became animated again. "It takes Kari nigh on a year to make enough cloth for one cotehardie, but 'tis worth the wait."

"A *year*?"

Beth soon found out why.

Kari's cottage was much like Mary's, only in this home a tall, narrow loom that produced eighteen-inch wide cloth occupied the corner by the window.

Kari, a small, middle-aged redhead with a wide grin, told her, "'Twill take twenty-five yards of my wool to make a gown such as ye wear now, my lady."

"My word." Beth ran her fingers through the fine warp threads. "Will you show me how you do it?"

Kari sat on a backless stool before the loom. Beth—knowing she barely had the talent to walk and speak at the same time—gaped as Kari made the shuttle fly across the weave while her foot controlled the vertical threads. Kari then demonstrated how she created patterns.

"This is amazing."

"Nay, my lady. 'Tis only a matter of havin' practice, good eyesight, and a strong back."

"Do others in the village work a loom?" The beautiful fabric would be highly sought in major cities.

"Nay, some ken how, but this be the only loom."

"Hmm. Are looms expensive—dear?"

"Aye, my lady, but another could be crafted by a skilled carpenter."

"Wonderful." She might have found yet another way to garner income for the clan.

Seeing Flora becoming impatient, she thanked Kari again and said good day.

Outside, Flora asked, "My lady, while we are here, would ye mind if we went to Bryce Burn in yon glen?"

She pointed between two nearby hills. "'Tis only a short walk where I found kale and fern fiddles peeking up last week. They most surely are ready to harvest now. If we hurry, we may even have time to hunt mushrooms."

"Wonderful."

An hour later Beth began to wonder if Flora had lost her way. She could no longer see the smoke from the village chimneys or the harbor thanks to the dense, head-high foliage and young pine.

"Flora," Beth puffed, "how much further?"

"'Tis just around these boulders, my lady."

Stumbling over her skirt, Beth muttered, "Thank God," and continued on, climbing over the myriad of tree roots clinging tenaciously to the steep hillside.

"'Tis here," Flora said as she came up beside her.

Thirsty, Beth looked about the small, sun-dappled clearing for a brook. "Where's the burn?" Her gaze shifted from the hard ground to Flora's stony expression. Inexplicable fear made the fine hair on the back of her neck and arms stand up.

Instinct made her turn to run, only to slam face first into a massive leather chest shield. "Whoa, Lady MacDougall!" Heavily callused hands slapped around each of her wrists like manacles. Mouth agape, Beth stared at the man's familiar face. She didn't know his name but did recognize him. The night of the banquet, he'd arrived with the Bruce.

"FLORA?"

Flora calmly stared at her as a second and then a third man came into the clearing, and Beth's fear solidified into fury. She kicked the shins of the man holding her. "Let go of me!"

Her kicking only resulted in bruising her feet, and she

sought Flora's help again. Seeing her new friend backing down the path, realization dawned. Incensed, Beth screeched, "YOU BITCH!"

A gag was forced between her teeth before she could hurl another expletive. Her fury turn to liquid fear when Flora only waved and the two men holding her arms dragged her backward, kicking and crying into the foliage.

Chapter 27

*"**W**hat in bloody hell do ye mean 'YE LOST HER'?!"*

Flora didn't have to fabricate her fear or her tears. She'd never beheld such fury in her life. The Laird of Blackstone was beside himself, ready to tear her throat out and only Angus's sturdy arm kept him at bay.

Good.

Her brother-by-marriage would now lose everything he held dear just as she had. To keep steady before his wrath, she held tight to the knowledge that he would now feel all the pain and humiliation she lived with every day since realizing he would never take her to wife.

Oh, aye, she knew that her father had offered her hand to Duncan. She'd witnessed her father and Duncan slipping away and had followed. She'd listened from a darkened alcove, curious and hopeful, to their whispered conversation in the library. When Duncan had refused her father's offer saying he could not marry for grieving, she'd wanted to believe him, though she suspected it was more for the lost child than for Mary, but then she had loved her sister and him. Not a season later, however, she'd been forced to face the humiliating truth—he did not want her—when he married that pathetic nun creature, and then another and another without giving her, a well-connected and rare beauty, so much as a backward glance. That all the marriages had been ordered by Albany mattered not. Duncan had no need for more land, and he knew, had he wanted her, that her father would have done all in his power to see them wed.

That he had convinced her father she should remain trapped within Blackstone, where she'd been forced to face her humiliation daily, only added to her pain and fury. But Duncan sealed his fate the day he further debased her by trying to foist the first of several suitors on her. That he didn't care if another held her, tupped her, had been the most hurtful insult of all.

Her heart held no pity for him.

"Answer me, woman!"

"'Twas I said, my lord. She trailed behind me one moment and...was gone the next." She dropped to her knees, sobbing. "I swear...I dinna ken where she is. I sought her for hours to nay avail."

Flora could read the disgust and disbelief on his face and did not care. She had accomplished what she'd set out to do six years ago, and had succeeded beyond her wildest dreams. He had lost his heart and his holdings, all in one blessed moment.

"Throw her in the dungeon."

Two men grabbed Flora's arms, much as the Bruce's men had grabbed Beth, and yanked her to her feet.

"And she's not to be given food nor water until Lady Beth is found!"

As the men hauled Flora away, Duncan muttered, "She lies. God damn her soul into perpetuity, she lies."

To the men before him he ordered, "You two, take

ten men apiece and scour the ridges and crags. Report back immediately if you see tracks or find someone who has knowledge of Lady Beth's whereabouts." To Jacob he said, "Ready the war horses and armor."

Rachael appeared at his elbow with a goblet. "Drink this, my liege."

He took the wine from her hand and tried to swallow, but his throat had closed completely. Tears blurred his vision and he put the goblet down. "I canna lose her, I canna."

Isaac patted his back. "We will find her."

"Ye ken this stinks of the Bruce."

"Aye."

~#~

Beth awoke in a dank, black-as-pitch place. She blinked as she tried to see, and her eyelashes caught on something close to her face. She gasped and something collapsed against her teeth. She cried out. Instinctively she tried to brush it away and realized to her horror she was trussed like a turkey, with her hands and feet bound behind her back. She writhed and screamed, praying all the while that she was having a nightmare. Nothing changed.

After minutes of struggling, her heart thudded so painfully, she feared she might die. She forced herself to calm. She held her breath, refusing her lung's demand that she continue to pant. Slowly she exhaled and then eased a lungful of the fetid air back in. Her eyelashes again caught on something, and—now calmer—she realized she wore a hood. A second later, her memory came back to life...Flora leading her into the glen, the Bruce's men grabbing her, and then one of them slamming a fist into her cheek, rendering her unconscious. Against her will, she started to pant again.

Oh, God. Please, God help me.

She opened her mouth to scream. Before it could rip from her parched throat, she heard heavy footsteps. She snapped her jaw shut and listened. The footsteps—out of synchronization, telling her two people approached—grew louder, and then silence.

She nearly jerked when a man's mirthless chuckle echoed directly above her.

"Should the lady wake, give her naught." She recognized the deep voice. It belonged to John the Bruce, who apparently studied her from above.

A different voice, this one gravelly, "Aye, my liege."

The footsteps, again out of sync, sounded and then grew faint.

She took a deep breath, jerked at her bonds. A second later, fresh air seeped into her mask. Her heart lept with the realization that the hook wasn't secured around her neck. She shook her head repeatedly, dipping her chin, and was relieved to find she was able to see a glimmer of light.

Her tears flowed as she twisted and squirmed on hard packed dirt, aggravating an already miserable headache, until the mask finally slipped off.

She took a deep lungful of air, craned her neck and saw damp stonewalls in every direction. She looked toward the light, up through a narrow tube, and saw a metal grate. She was in a bottle necked dungeon. But why?

This cell was larger than Blackstone's dungeon, could easily have held four big men. The only keep of any size within two days ride of Blackstone was the Bruce's. It made sense, but she couldn't be sure. She

could have been out cold for an hour or for a day—
perhaps two, from the feel of her head—but then she
couldn't be sure. Without windows she couldn't tell if it
was day or night.

She took a second, deep shuttering breath. "Damn
Flora."

Her thoughts flew to Duncan. He had to be frantic by
now. She hoped he would see through Flora's duplicity,
but there was every possibility he wouldn't. She hadn't.
Like a naïve fool, she'd blindly followed Flora, thinking
her a friend, while picturing sautéed fiddle ferns in a
garlic butter sauce.

A sob wracked her. *Beth, you're too stupid to draw
breath!*

Her fear that something dreadful—torture or rape—
lurked only minutes away gave way to a new, far more
compelling terror; that Duncan wouldn't find her.

What if Flora told Duncan she'd fallen into the sea?
He'd search the coast, not his enemy's keep. What if
she'd told Duncan she'd run away? Would Duncan only
search the roads? Her heart stuttered...oh God...what if he
thought she'd deliberately slipped away from Flora so
she could remove his ring and return to her own time?

The very thought turned her blood to ice, nearly
made her ill.

Surely not.

Surely, he knew she loved him and would never
leave without a very good reason—and certainly not
without saying goodbye. Her fingers found his ring. Out
of habit she spun it, seeking comfort. She rubbed a
fingertip across the small cabochon rubies, the first she'd
ever worn. Her heart thudded when it slipped over the
first joint.

Good Lord! She could remove it if need be. She had a means of escape.

Her breath hitched as she pressed the ring into place, closer to her heart.

Did Duncan realize how much she loved him even though she hadn't said so?

Fresh tears made mud along her right jaw as it rested on the floor. Why the hell had she waited to say, "I love you," wanting him to say it first? And why the hell hadn't he said it?

As hour after silent hour passed, she decided she would not—short of dying—slip the ring from her finger. She would face the devil if need be, but had to cling to the hope he would eventually find her. She also resolved that if she did survive, she would declare her love the moment she laid eyes on Duncan's handsome face. Then she'd swat him—hard—for putting her through this agony.

She started to cry again. As another muddy puddle formed under her cheek, she wondered how she could still have tears. She'd not had a drop to drink in what felt like forever.

~#~

Angus pointed to the ground. "Three horses, my lord, one carrying a heavier burden than the rest." He pointed to a flat, muddy print. "One has foundered."

They were in Bruce territory. Duncan, sweat running down his back and chest, only nodded and kicked Ransom's flanks.

With every step Ransom took, Duncan prayed he'd find Beth safe. He had come to depend on her smile, her gentle hands, even her odd ways. Just knowing she would be at his side, that she'd willingly accept his babe, he'd been able to face all she'd told him of his future. But what if she was truly lost to him? Would he be able to brave his future? He didn't think so.

Hell, he wasn't even sure how much longer he could suck air into his chest if she wasn't around to breathe the same air.

Lud, why has this happened? Why hadn't he seen it coming?

"My liege, ahead." Angus pointed above the tree line toward the Bruce's stronghold.

"Line up four abreast, shields and swords at the ready. Jacob, do ye have any questions or worries?"

"Nay, my lord." The lad straightened in the saddle as he sat behind Sean and thudded his chest.

"'Tis a brave lad ye are, son." Satisfied all was in readiness, Duncan said, "Then sound the trumpets. Let the sneaky bastard know we arrive in force like real men."

~#~

"How many?" John the Bruce asked.

"Only twenty, my lord, all mounted."

"Order double their number around the bailey. Then drop the bridge and bid the MacDougall enter."

"Aye, my Lord."

Finally.

It had taken ten long years to bring Duncan MacDougall to his knees, but he'd done it. By the next full moon his enemy would have naught but the tunic on his back. No wife, no keep, no lands and no clan.

All would become Bruce holdings, though he had no use for the plain wife. He hoped Lady Beth would die quickly. He might have use for the dungeon if the MacDougall balked.

The Black, looking furious, strode into the Bruce's hall with his full contingent.

"John, I dinna want to hear dissembling. I want my wife."

"Your wife?" John smiled and picked up the tankard at his elbow. "Have ye lost yet another one, MacDougall?"

The Black growled, his hand instinctively moving for his sword. Thirty Bruce men stepped forward drawing their own steel. MacDougall men did the same.

The Bruce stood and waved his clansmen down. "We'll have no blood shed over a simple misunderstanding."

Standing before an empty hearth, he invited Duncan to sit, motioning toward the high-backed chair next to his own. "I already have a wife, who ye have no doubt heard is doing her verra best to render me wode. Why the hell would I want yer Lady Beth?"

Duncan, ignoring his invitation to sit, growled, "We tracked the men who took her onto your lands."

"Ye may well have, but they dinna stop here." He came forward. "MacDougall, think on it. If I had yer woman, would I have let the bridge down?"

The Black stared at him. "Do ye swear on yer eldest bairn's head that ye don't have her?"

The Bruce hesitated for only a heartbeat before saying, "I swear. Now, come and quench ye thirst before ye take leave to search again."

Duncan almost smiled. The bastard would rue the day he swore that oath. As planned, Duncan made a show of shedding his brilliant blue doublet and hood so all would remember what he wore. "My men need drink, as do our mounts."

276

"Of course." As the Bruce ordered the horses tended and the ale served, Duncan's men—save Jacob, who had positioned himself near a far doorway—wandered, clanging and banging around the great hall as they found places among their enemies. On Duncan's silent command Angus rudely bumped chest-first into one of the Bruce men. Growling, both reached for their dirks.

When Angus swore at the man, Duncan yelled, "Enough Angus! Stand down." As he'd hoped, all eyes turned toward the men-at- arms in confrontation.

The Bruce repeated the command to his own man.

Within minutes all had settled within the hall though it was painfully apparent none were comfortable.

~#~

"Psst!"

Beth forced opened her swollen eyelids, not sure if she'd heard a real voice or one her imagination had conjured out of desperation.

"Psst. Up here, my lady."

She rolled onto her back and stared up the shaft. "Jacob?" She started to cry. "Oh, thank God!"

"Sssh!" He looked over his shoulder before addressing her again.

"Move to the side, my lady, so I might drop a blade. Our liege will never forgive me should I kill ye."

"He's here?"

"Aye, my lady, but move quickly afore I get caught."

Relief and hope jump-started her tears again, but Beth did as she was told. Within a heartbeat she heard the blade's thump.

She almost laughed seeing Rachael's silver *sgian dubh* lying only inches from her nose. When she looked up to ask when Duncan would come, Jacob had disappeared.

Deciding it didn't matter so long as he knew she was alive, she rolled around until she got the blade into her hands.

Her numb fingers fumbled repeatedly.

God, please.

To her relief, she felt the intricate carving of the hilt. She started sawing at the bindings at her back and prayed she wasn't slitting her own wrists.

~#~

When Duncan spotted Jacob's worried countenance peeking around the far doorway, he sent a silent prayer of thanks to heaven—the lad had not been caught snooping below—and put down his tankard.

"Bruce, I thank ye, but we have imposed on yer hospitality long enough. Given the hour 'tis best we return to MacDougall land. Say a prayer my lady is somewhere safe." As if it were an afterthought he added, "And say one for the bastards who took her for they willna see another sunrise once I find them."

He stood and hit his half-full tankard with the back of his hand. As metal clanged against the stone hearth all eyes turned toward him, and Jacob slid unnoticed back into the room. When the lad thumped a fist to his chest, Duncan's heart stuttered. The lad had found Beth. Alive. Had he not, he reassured himself, surely the lad would be greeting.

It took all his control to calmly lead his men en mass through the torch lit bailey lined with watchful Bruce men-at-arms and into the stables where their horses waited.

In a dark corner of the stable Duncan yanked off his doublet and hood and threw it at Angus, who just as quickly jerked off the coiled rope he wore beneath his plaid.

"Our lady?" he hissed.

Jacob, donning Angus's cloak, whispered. "The dungeon, m'lord. She's a woeful sight but alive."

"Praise God." Duncan, breast soaked with sweat, then silently pledged to bring The Bruce to his maker at the first opportunity.

He cast a glance at Angus now dressing in his doublet and cape. Rope in hand, Duncan whispered, "Thank ye, lad. Now into Angus's helm and garb with ye."

While Jacob was hoisted onto Angus's mount, Duncan slipped deeper into the barn's shadows. He took a deep breath and prayed his men safe as Angus, now hooded and riding Ransom, led his men out into the bailey proper.

Without a backward glance Angus and the clansmen formed up into a column of three abreast and road out under the raised portcullis.

Chapter 28

The minutes felt like hours and the hours like days for Beth as she tried to rub the circulation back into her hands and feet. She started hearing heavy footsteps above her. Praying it was Duncan but not knowing that it was, she hurriedly assumed her trussed position just in case.

When she thought the guard might be peering into her cell, feeling parched and nearly frozen, she pleaded for water and a blanket.

The man chuckled, "Ah, so ye wake."

A moment later a bucket of cold, rancid water splashed on her head. As she gasped and fought to keep her freed hands locked behind her and away from the suffocating mask, she was assaulted with a long string of expletives that called hers and Duncan's paternity into question.

When the guard left, she ripped the mask from her face, sucked in some much needed air and mumbled a few rich curses of her own. She then realized she didn't feel the need to cry anymore. She certainly couldn't credit her lack of tears to courage. No. The peace she now felt came from simply knowing Duncan was close and he'd come as soon as he could.

She scooted away from the muddy spot she'd been lying in. To pass the time she pictured a calendar in her mind. She counted the days she been Mrs. MacDougall and counted the days since her last menstrual period, something she'd been avoiding since seeing Wee Mary give birth. Thirty-seven. No, that couldn't be right. Regular as a Swiss timepiece, her cycle ran twenty-eight days. Chewing her bottom lip, she started counting again.

~#~

The time passed with interminable slowness while Duncan waited impatiently for the Bruce stronghold to settle for the night. Like Blackstone and the Campbell's Dunstaffnage keep, this keep's only obvious entrance was from the bailey. Had he someone to watch his back he might have tried to find the secret entrance, but he hadn't the luxury and time was fleeing.

All finally appeared quiet by the time the moon passed the mid-point on its journey across the sky—its cool light cast only on the west and north faces of the battlements. He took a deep breath and slipped from the stable. Keeping to the shadows, he ran for the keep's covered doorway.

He pressed the latch. As he'd hoped, the door had been left unlocked for the night guards who'd been coming and going at well-spaced intervals. He pulled it open a few inches and blessed the man who kept the hinges oiled. Hearing no movement in the great hall above and none below where the dungeon lay, he slipped into the keep.

He crept to the lowest level. Assuming the Bruce had captured Beth for ransom, he'd not expected Jacob to find her below. He'd told the lad to look in the dungeon simply to eliminate it. Duncan had fully expected to spend the night searching tower rooms. That he didn't have to hunt above spoke volumes about the Bruce's intent—for which he'd pay dearly.

Spying a guard dozing on the bottom step, just feet from the dungeon's grate, Duncan slowed. Taking one cautious step at a time he stole closer. He then placed his dirk on the man's throat and pressed. As he'd hoped, the man jerked awake. 'Twas verra important to him that the cretin know who would take his life.

Grabbing a fist full of hair, he wrenched the man's head back, glared into his surprised eyes, and sliced. The man gurgled as his life's blood spewed across the stairwell coating the walls crimson. Spying the keys hanging from a hook above the man, Duncan kicked him forward and off the steps.

The way clear and the keys in hand, Duncan peeked into the dark hole.

"Psst." He worked the key into the lock and lifted the well-oiled cover of his wife's prison. "Beth." He heard no movement below and the blood drained from his head.

Please, God, dinna let her be dead.

In a voice just above a whisper he called, "For God's sake, woman, if ye be alive, wake ye."

She rolled over, opened her eyes and smiled. "It's about time."

He grinned for the first time in hours. Lord, she was a wonder. "I need drop a rope to ye. Can ye climb it?"

Crouching, she shook her head. "I don't know—ken. I can try."

"We dinna have time for tryin'." He tied a loop on one end of the rope before dropping it over the edge.

"Stick yer foot in the loop and hold tight."

Pulling seven stones dead weight straight up from a depth of twenty feet without jerking or grunting became no easy matter. By the time she was in his arms, he was drenched in sweat.

She threw her arms around his neck the moment she cleared the opening. "Oh, Duncan! I was so afraid I wouldn't see you again and I wanted you to—"

He kissed her soundly, in relief that she was alive and to hush her up. "Lass, we have much to say to each other, but now *isna* the time." He took a tight hold on her hand and started toward the stairs. She gasped and then faltered seeing the guard and pool of blood on the lower steps. He put an arm about her and forced her forward. He then led her on silent feet up the stairs.

He peeked out the bailey door. "When I tug yer hand, we run." He felt rather than saw Beth nod.

The three-quarter moon lit the north side of the stronghold. Beyond the steep south wall with its boulder footing lay the orchard and within it Angus and their mounts. But first he had to get her up onto the curtain wall where he could throw the rope over one of the crenels and lower her to the ground.

He waited until the guards settled into conversation then jerked her hand. Crouching, they ran to the right and quickly mounted the steps.

Gaining the top unnoticed, he pulled her close and pointed to the farthest point on the south wall. She nodded. Scurrying past an archer's quiver, he picked it up.

Looping one end of the hemp line around the quiver and bracing it against the battlement aperture, he threw the rope over the wall only to see it fall a good four yards short of the ground. He cursed staring at the boulders below. Even grasping the very end of the rope, he'd have to fall a yard.

He grunted. There wasn't a thing he could do about lengthening the rope now. His decision made, he glanced at the occupied guards before saying, "On my back, lady, 'tis time."

Gaping at him, Beth hissed, "You aren't serious?" She peeked over the edge. "Ohmygod."

"Make haste, woman, or all is lost."

Realizing he was right, Beth threw her arms around his neck and closed her eyes.

When she opened them seconds later, she wished she hadn't. Only his hands, wrapped in tartan as they clung to the rope, held them suspended four stories in the air. Then without warning he loosened his hold and the ground came rushing toward her.

Duncan's feet hit the boulders. He rolled to protect her but she still cracked her head and left shoulder on granite.

Dazed, she struggled to sit. "Are you okay?"

"Aye, but we best—"

"HALT! Who goes there?"

A torch suddenly flared above them, then another. Like gargoyles, the silhouetted guards leaned over the battlements as they strained to see into the darkness.

Before she could gasp in horror, Duncan yanked her to her feet. Holding her to his side, he hauled her at pell-mell speed over the rocks. She bit into her lip to keep from crying out as she twisted an ankle.

"Halt ye!" The blast of a trumpet and pounding feet echoed off the granite walls at their backs.

Clutching her by the waist, he started running across

the clearing. "Hie, now!"

She thought, "How?" He'd lifted her off her feet as dozens of arrows began raining around their heads.

With him holding her as he did, she could do little more than breathe and keep her gown out from under his feet as he carried her at a breakneck pace toward the tree line.

Though clouds now masked the moon, he didn't slow down once they reached the grove, but continued at a dead run down a well-worn path.

She soon understood why. The roar of the drawbridge crashing into place was quickly followed by the sounds of braying hounds and yelling men. Fearing they had only moments left before the howling lymers would run them down, she clung tight to Duncan and prayed.

The air was then infused with the sent of ripe pears. An owl screeched and Duncan immediately swung to the right. "This way."

Was he kidding? Her feet hadn't hit the ground once in the last three minutes.

"Here!" someone called.

Duncan immediately dodged around a heavily laden tree. She spotted Angus, mounted, holding Ransom's reins.

"Hie now," Angus whispered.

Ransom, agitated by the closing lymers and sounds of impending battle, terrified her as he pranced and snorted in place. Apparently realizing she wasn't about to get any closer to the beast, Duncan let go of her hand, grabbed Ransom's reins, and leaped. To her relief, the moment he swung into the saddle, the horse stilled.

"Beth, grab my hand. As I pull, set yer left foot on my boot." She did as she was told and with one strong tug, he hauled her before him. Before she could settle comfortably, his arm wrapped about her waist like a vice. The hounds had arrived, snapping and growling. To her horror, Ramsom suddenly reared, his from hooves lashing out at everything that moved. Duncan growled, the horse shook his head, and then spun. At the same moment a bank of clouds covered the moon.

As they raced through the orchard and then up a steep incline in total darkness, Beth clung to the saddle's wide pummel and prayed as she'd never prayed in her life, for her baby, Duncan, Angus, herself, the horse, and for the damn moon to come out of hiding.

A half-hour later they still hadn't slowed and she was hoarse from squealing with fright. How they avoided racing headlong into trees or over cliffs she had no idea. Since she could no longer hear the braying hounds, she decided for sanity's sake to just close her eyes and put her trust in the man at her back.

If they survived, all well and good, but if they didn't, she could take comfort in knowing she would go to her Maker with the knowledge her life hadn't been wasted. She'd loved a good man. Not a necessarily sane one, but a good one.

When she opened her eyes again, it was to find Drasmoor Bay and Blackstone bathed in the pearly glow of dawn. My word! She'd apparently fallen asleep.

"We are home, my lady." Duncan sounded exhausted.

As she yawned, she shivered. "Aye. 'Tis something I wasna sure I would ever see again."

He nuzzled her neck. "Ye be startin' to sound like a Scot born and bred."

She grinned, thinking of the wee Scot deep within

her, and her gaze shifted from the place she called home in this time and in her own to the ring that had given her the incredible flesh and blood man holding her. And through him, a baby.

He tipped her chin so he could kiss her. "When I thought ye lost to me..." His eyes started to glaze with tears and he looked down at her wedding ring. He cleared his throat as his fingers brushed its ruby and gold surface. "I never expected to say this to ye, but I love ye, dear Beth, more than yon keep, more than me life." His voice broke and his Adam's Apple bobbed. "I dinna want ye to go, to leave me."

Her heart soared. "Oh, Duncan." She twisted so she could touch his beautifully chiseled features. "I've loved you for so long and didn't dare hope you might feel the same. I knew—kenned you were fond of me, but to hear you say you love me..." Pooling tears clouded her vision. "I swear as long as I draw breath this ring will remain on my hand."

"Ah, Beth." His kiss told her heart all she wanted to know.

"If ye two cooing doves are quite through..." Angus mumbled. He waved his lord and lady toward home. "...yer clan awaits."

Chapter 29

A small armada of fishing boats accompanied them across the bay. As they approached the isle and Castle Blackstone, Duncan could see precious little room for another body on the quay. His sept cheered as they drew near.

Isaac and Rachael, both looking haggard, were the first to greet them as they stepped out of the boat.

"*Mon ami!*" Rachael clasped Beth to her breast then kissed both her cheeks. "I have fashed myself ill. And look at ye. Are ye hurt?"

"Nay, Rachael, just sore from the ride and in desperate need of a bath."

"Ah, *oui*." She shooed people out of her way as she raced to do Beth's bidding.

They could barely make headway as the crowd folded back on them, wanting to touch them both. Since Duncan held his lady wife in his left arm, Isaac fell in at his right shoulder.

"'Tis good ye're both home, my lord. Auld John has a surprise for ye."

"Oh?"

"Aye, it seems he took yer suggestion for whisky to

heart and we are now hip deep in the water of life. And I've had all I can do to keep the men out of it."

Duncan laughed. "'Twill be good having only the mundane to fash over for awhile, friend."

"Good for you, mayhap," Isaac grumbled. "Ye can wield a sword to get their attention. My tellin' them I dinna appreciate trippin' over sotted fools had no effect."

"Did ye hear, my lady?"

Beth turned from Kari's tearful embrace to face her husband. "Hear what, my lord?"

"Yer whisky venture has begun."

Her smile widened. "Good, because you're going to need..."

They'd entered the bailey and a great shout went up cutting off her words. "What?"

She yelled, "Later! I'll tell you later!"

~#~

Bathed, shaved, and shampooed, Beth felt like a new woman. Still a bit sore and too tired to fuss with herself, she pulled her hair back into a twist and stuck four elaborate pins into it. She didn't care if it was inappropriate to walk around bare headed. She was going to be comfortable or know the reason why.

"The pale green gown will do, Rachael." Watching her friend shake out the most comfortable gown she owned, Beth would have given anything for her comfy gray sweats.

Rachael hadn't left her side since she'd entered the keep. It had taken Beth a good ten minutes of back patting to stop her friend's tears and to allay Rachael's guilt over underestimating Flora.

When Duncan knocked then entered, Rachael kissed her once again before leaving. As she passed Duncan,

Rachael murmured, "Ye, I have yet to finish with."

Beth chuckled as he enfolded her in his arms. "What was that about?"

"Ack. She was most displeased when I took Jacob on the raid, and even less pleased when one of the men let loose with the tale of how the lad found ye."

"Ah." Just the thought of gold spurns on her only child could get Rachael foaming at the mouth. They'd have no peace around Blackstone for a while.

"Ah, indeed." He held her at arm's length for a moment just studying her. "Have I ever told ye how bonnie, how beautiful I find ye?"

Her jaw dropped. "Beautiful? Me?"

"Aye. Ye are most fair about the visage with yer bright gray eyes and sweet full lips. I even fancy the shape of yer nose. Tells all ye are a woman of substance."

She continued to stare at him, dumbfounded. No one in her twenty-four years and six months had ever called her pretty, much less beautiful.

He pulled her to his chest. "Of course, ye also have a lovely neck." He nibbled right where he knew the nerves to her knees were somehow connected. As expected, her knees buckled when he hit an especially sensitive spot.

"And then there's yer lovely white breasts..."

"Duncan..."

"Hmm?" He'd already managed to unlace the back of her gown.

"I think you need ken something." Given his words of praise, she couldn't think of a more perfect time to tell him her secret.

As he slipped the gown from one shoulder and nuzzled again, he mumbled, "What need I ken?"

She lifted his face with both hands. She wanted to see his reaction. "You, my handsome and stalwart husband, are going to be a father."

"Huh?"

She grinned at his bemused expression. "Come spring you will be a Da."

His beautiful steel blue eyes grew wide. "How ken ye? I mean are ye absolutely certain, lass?"

"Oh, aye, I'm very sure." She was late, had suffered her first bout of nausea as the sun rose, and then again right before her bath.

"Aye, she says!" His laughter exploded and rolled like barrels falling down a long flight of stairs. He wrapped his arms around her waist and swung her in great circles before kissing her soundly.

Before she could catch her breath his expression shifted to concern. "Why did ye not tell me sooner, love? God teeth! Had I kenned, I'd not have ridden as I had, jolting ye from the Bruce's to here."

She patted his check, loving the concern in his eyes. "I'm fine. Trust me. There wouldn't be so many illegitimate babes in the world if a ride could so easily dislodge them."

He continued to scowl but nodded, obviously wanting it to be so. Then a gleam came into his eyes and he stroked the top of her breast. "Would a wee bit of tuppin' hurt the babe?"

She laughed. And here she'd thought he'd been an avid tupping fan only because he wanted a babe.

~ # ~

Duncan scowled at his prisoner as she stood in the bailey before the clan. From betwixt two guards, Flora Campbell glared back, head high and dressed in the gown she'd worn when thrown in the dungeon. Why, he wondered, had he acquiesced to Beth's plea to give the damn woman food and water?

"My lady has begged for yer life, though why I dinna ken. So it is by her good graces and not mine—for I would have hung ye from the nearest mast—that ye will be sent back to yer sire in chains. Ye will be transported not by sea but by land, so all the world can see as ye pass what a foul, lying bitch ye be."

His guards had reported her ravings. She'd done all to avenge his refusal to marry her. That she swore she would gladly do worse if given the opportunity made hid blood boil. Now she wisely remained mute.

He kicked the cloth bag at her feet. "That is what ye came with and all ye take away." The elaborate gowns she favored—and he had foolishly had made for her—would remain at Blackstone, where they would be appreciated.

He turned Beth toward the keep and ordered, "Take Lady Campbell away, out of my fair lady's sight."

As he passed Angus he murmured, "Is all in readiness?"

Casting a wary eye toward Beth, Angus said, "Aye."

Tomorrow the Bruce would awaken to find fields afire, his kine and favorite child gone. No man should blatantly lie and then swear it true on his child's head.

The lad would not be harmed, but ransomed. Coffers emptied, the Bruce would be hard pressed to feed his sept, let alone pay his taxes, something Albany will not find amusing. Then in two weeks time he would humiliate the bastard before one and all.

Chapter 30

Much to Duncan's chagrin, Beth had insisted on accompanying him to Sterling, the sight of the tournament. Beth's argument—that she'd be safer with him then alone in a half-guarded keep—prompted him to give way, but they'd traveled slow and with as many creature comforts as his sumpters could haul without expiring.

If not for needing to humiliate the Bruce in public, Duncan would have remained at Blackstone. He didna need coin since capturing the Bruce lad, and had no desire to participate in a spectacle hailed as a tribute to their rightful King when Albany had yet to ransom the poor lad from Sassenach hands.

Looking at the tournament site, Beth excitedly pointed to the hundreds of colorful banners and tents scattered for miles around the jousting fields. "Oh, look! Are they the King's tents, the ones with the lion pennants?

"Aye, but 'tis Albany." Which posed a major problem. His ladywife was not the bride—the King's cousin—Albany had insisted he marry. Beth, curious to a fault, would want to experience all, and he had yet to ken how he'd keep her from Albany's view.

"There must be thousands here. Where will we make camp?"

Cradling her to his chest, he kicked his mount forward. "We settle wherever we find room." The early arrivals had seized the choicest places, which was just as well.

She pointed toward a distant hill. "Over there near the grove—copse. We'll have shade, at least."

He grinned. 'Twas a good place and a healthy distance from Albany and the Bruce, a man currently in a sore state of mind, having paid dearly for his son's return. "So be it, my lady."

An hour later they had the rudiments of a home-away-from-home set up. Beth, looking a bit hollow-eyed, kissed him. "I need to rest. Can you ask Rachael to assume my duties for a wee bit?"

"Of course." He shooed her toward the tent. "While ye sleep I will be yon." He pointed to the elaborate tent near the jousting field. "I need learn the order of events."

"Be careful."

She kenned the Bruce was now out for blood. "Aye, and ye, as well. Keep Sean in view at all times."

"I promise."

As he made his way through the throng he was hailed by many and stopped repeatedly.

Seeing his old liege lord the Campbell, Duncan—out of old habit—thumped his chest in greeting. "Sir, how go ye?"

"I could be better. These weary bones have been paired with the MacDonald." He looked about warily before adding, "I have taken Flora to task, MacDougall." He cleared his throat as his already florid countenance heightened in hue. "I apologize to ye for the harm my daughter brought to yer hostile."

Duncan kenned his friend had naught to do with Flora's scheme. "'Tis over. All ended well for my ladywife is still with child."

"'Tis good to hear. I hoped to visit with her one day."

"You will. Beth is with me." He grinned at Campbell's startled expression. Hoping it would ease the old man's mind, he muttered, "'Twas wiser to give in to her luste than listen to her complaints."

Campbell sighed in sad fashion. "'Tis often the way, if a man wants any peace."

"Aye, especially if the woman is as ox-minded as Beth." Seeing Isaac already in the long line before the Mistress of the Lists, Duncan felt no urgency to leave. "'Twould be an honor if ye'll come to meat this night." Getting ready for a guest would keep Beth occupied and out of sight. Seeing his old friend shake his head, he added, "She harbors nay ill will, Campbell."

"If that be the truth, then I will come."

Grinning, Duncan slapped the old man's shoulder. "Splendid. But I must warn ye, though Lady Beth is learning, our ways are new to her. She often speaks verra quick and odd. Dinna hesitate to ask her to repeat herself. I need do it as often as six times a day. Makes it damn difficult to have a good row."

The Campbell grinned. "Ye've not changed. Ye are still a fool."

"Nay, 'tis the making up that spurs me on."

The Campbell laughed. "Tonight then. Now, away with ye."

A moment later the hairs on the back of Duncan's neck stood. Feeling eyes boring into his back, he turned to find the Bruce ten paces away.

He nodded. "Bruce."

"MacDougall, I hereby issue a challenge."

"Accepted." Did his enemy fear they might not face off in the finals? Interesting.

The Bruce, now a thousand pounds sterling poorer, glared as he spit, "Put yer matters in order for in three days time ye die."

Duncan's lip curled. "Yer arrogance and ambition willna be the death of me, ye bastard, but of thyself." He turned his back and stalked away. In only moments he could hear a buzz, a tense anticipation of the impending challenge moving through crowd.

His ladywife wouldna be impressed.

~ # ~

"*Are you out of your mind?*" Beth paced before her husband who wisely or stubbornly remained mute as he sharpened the metal point of his lance. She cast a quick glance at Jacob, who—looking decidedly uncomfortable—tried to make himself invisible in the far corner of their tent as he studiously polished armor.

Knowing their tent walls offered no sound barrier—that all they said would soon spread through the clan anyway—Beth dismissed the youngster's presence from her mind and directed her ire back where it belonged. Toward her husband.

"You could be killed!" Instinctively she placed a hand on her swelling abdomen. "And if you are, then what? Do I point to your portrait—which, I might add, is dreadful—and tell your son, 'That was your father. As best I can recall, you favor him'? Merciful Mother of God!"

When he refused to look at her, she screeched in frustration and left in search of a saner head. Namely Isaac's. Surely her husband's advisor could talk some sense into her stubborn husband.

Ten minutes later, and witnessing no less than a dozen people placing wagers on the upcoming challenge, she found Rachael.

Hands on hips she demanded, "Where's Isaac?"

"And a pleasant good afternoon to ye, as well." Rachael put down the shawl she was embroidering for Jacob's upcoming Bar Mitzvah. "What has yer man done now? Surely he's not ordered ye back to Blackstone?"

"Nay. That fool I married has accepted a challenge from the Bruce. If I can't stop him, I want to be sure he at least left a will."

Rachael stood and wrapped an arm around Beth. "*Mon ami*, even if ye do find an honorable retreat, yer husband willna take it. He had plans to issue a challenge on the morrow himself."

The revelation knocked the wind out of Beth and she dropped like a stone onto a nearby trunk. "Why? I suffered no permanent damage. He has the Bruce's money." Tears began to cloud her vision. "We have a *child* on the way. What does he have to gain besides an early death?"

"His pride." Rachael settled before her and clutched her hands. "*Mon ami*, is it so different in yer world? Do men not have to *humilier*—humble their *l'ennemi* before all whom they hold dear?"

"He's already done it!" Tears coursed down her cheeks.

Duncan had stolen the Bruce's son right from under the man's nose. Wasn't that enough?

"Ye ken the Bruce and our liege have both held quiet about what transpired these past weeks, being uncertain how Albany would take their hostilities so close to the games, but the tale has still spread among the clans. Some believe the Bruce will attack after all this." She waved toward the hundreds of tents surrounding them. "Your husband must prove he is the stronger, the best, or all ye have becomes vulnerable to all those wishing to expand their holdings. Yer husband canna appear weak or men will die."

Beth didn't want to believe it, but she'd seen the gleam in some men's eyes as they placed their bets against her husband.

"Yer time, *mon ami,* would be better spent convincing *yer* husband that he is without peer than in trying to convince *mine* that this is madness."

Beth heaved a heavy sigh, knowing Rachael probably had the right of it. She had little understanding and even less influence over Duncan when it came to matters of clan politics.

She'd been appalled learning Duncan had stolen the Bruce's heir, a lad of only eight, and had done everything in her power to comfort the boy until his father could claim him. That Duncan had also been kind to the child, had played darts and read to the boy, helped little in eradicating her guilt over being the cause of such vengeful feuding. Had she been more alert, less gullible, Flora never would have had the opportunity to lead her into a trap and set Duncan on this path of revenge.

The fires the MacDougall clan started on Bruce land she refused to think about. She couldn't imagine the angst the Bruce women felt watching their lives' work—their homes, handmade furniture, and crops—going up in smoke. She thanked God nightly that no lives were lost. That the Bruce clan still had some resources to get through the upcoming winter—but just barely—brought little comfort. She was sure possessions were lost in the fires that could never be replaced.

She heaved a heavy sigh and brushed away her tears. "Since there's nothing I can do to stop my idiotic husband, I suppose I should start getting ready for the Campbell's arrival."

"Take heart, *mon ami*. You have a courageous and strong man who'll not take any unnecessary chances."

Beth snorted. Everything Duncan planned for the next week was—to her mind—totally unnecessary and chancy.

~ # ~

In the gallery, wedged between the Campbell and her best friend, Beth prayed. Her heart tripped as Duncan, decked out in his finest armor—carrying his gleaming red and gold shield with his family coat of arms on his left arm and his red lance with its potentially fatal steel tip glistening in his right—rode into the long makeshift arena to face his enemy.

Her gaze instinctively flew to the opposite end of the lists, her heart hoping to find the Bruce smaller—frailer—than she recalled. But the man was as she remembered; only more lethal-looking dressed in dark armor. To her dismay, she saw the Bruce's mount was dressed not in trapper—chain mail—from head to tail as Duncan's horse was, but in metal plate. The enormous black warhorse looked like something out of a futuristic movie.

Rachael tugged on her hand and Beth turned to find Duncan smiling at her. As the Bruce's herald started touting his lord's prowess, Rachael whispered, "Blow your husband a kiss, *mon ami.* 'Tis what his heart needs."

"Aye." With tears in her eyes and a pounding heart, Beth brought shaking fingers to her lips and blew Duncan a kiss. She then whispered, "I love you. God's speed."

To her monumental relief he understood and mouthed, "I love ye," in return.

In what seemed like only the time between two heartbeats, trumpet blasted. The crowd roared as the warring titan's dropped their visors, and the horses reared, and then charged.

Beth held her breath as their lances struck wood. Her heart nearly stopped when Duncan's shield, absorbing the impact of the Bruce's strike, split in two. Her worries multiplied as Duncan shucked the steel band that once held his shield and turned his mount at the opposite end of the arena.

Beth leaned over the rail. At the opposite end of the field, the Bruce's shield, though severely damaged, still clung to his left arm.

She frantically scoured the crowd for MacDougall men. "Where's Angus? Why isn't he bringing Duncan another shield?"

Duncan's shoulder had barely healed. He couldn't take a hit to that shoulder. She desperately wished she could see his face, read his expression, know if he was in pain.

The Campbell pulled her back to her seat. "Lady Beth, 'tis aught his men can do. Duncan must continue as armed or forfeit."

"NAY!"

Blood drained from her head and the world began to

spin. She felt Rachael's hand grab her waist.

"Beth, can you hear me?"

She opened her eyes. "Ya." She pushed away the chalice the Campbell held to her lips and blinked repeatedly. "I'm okay—well." She straightened in her chair. As the field became clearer, she began to make out the faces within the crowd before her. They all stood and roared once again.

~ # ~

"To win or die!" Duncan roared as he kicked Ramsom's flanks. His warhorse snorted, his blood as fired as his master's. He let loose the reins and braced his legs in the stirrups.

He had little doubt the Bruce would strike low this time, hoping to gut him with a blow under the breastplate. He rode upright, waiting until the last possible moment—until it would be nigh onto impossible for the Bruce to alter his aim—then dropped over his horse's neck.

Driving his mount to the rail with his legs, Duncan gritted his teeth and raised his lance.

The impact, squarely hitting the Bruce's right shoulder, nearly unseated Duncan. The crowd's roar made it impossible for him to hear—to know if the Bruce had remained seated. As his mount slowed, he twisted in the saddle to find the Bruce on his back in the middle of the list, covered in dust and with two feet of lance sticking out of his chest. Immeasurable joy flooded him. The bastard was completely at his mercy.

Immediately, he threw down the remains of his lance, reined in and turned his horse around. When his agitated mount finally stopped prancing, Duncan swung his right leg over the high pommel and slid to the ground. He landed with an ungainly thud, drew his short broadsword, and approached the Bruce.

Standing over his enemy, Duncan placed his sword tip on his enemy's throat. The crowd roared.

Beneath the Bruce's slotted helmet, Duncan saw fear then resignation register within his enemy's clear blue eyes. He smiled. Using his sword point, he raised the Bruce's faceplate.

"Aye, ye bloody bastard, now ye pay."

Chest heaving, Duncan glanced at the blood seeping around the wooden staff impaling the Bruce's armor. He'd struck well and deep.

Duncan, having been challenged, now had the right to end his enemy's life. John the Bruce, had he had the advantage, would certainly have pressed his sword against Duncan's throat without a moment's hesitation, yet Duncan did hesitate.

He looked at Albany, draped in the finest his taxes could buy, and found him smirking. He scanned the crowd, all now standing and screaming for blood. He then searched of Beth. He found her—staring wide-eyed and white-faced at him, with one hand on her lips and the other on their unborn child. His lips tightened into a hard line, his anger renewed.

The crowd erupted again, roaring, "To the death! To the death!"

He had to act. Fulfill his need for revenge and destroy his enemy once and for all, earning the admiration of his clansmen and his allies or drop his sword. He looked at Beth once again wanting her admiration and respect more.

He prayed he wasn't making a monumental mistake as he pressed his blade's tip into the hollow of John's neck. "I spare ye, Bruce, and only for yer sons, but should ye or any of yer sept ever again dare step foot uninvited onto MacDougall land, I promise ye, they and ye will regret it. Do we ken one another?"

When John nodded, Duncan dropped his sword. Many in the crowd hissed and booed but others cheered as he knelt on one knee and closed his fingers over John's right hand. "'Tis done then. The past is past."

His blood lust now drained away, Duncan looked up to find Angus racing toward him. He accepted Angus's help and struggled to his feet. As he made his way to his horse, Bruce clansmen raced onto the field to retrieve their fallen leader.

Over the roaring, Angus yelled, "Ye did well, Duncan."

Unsure, he muttered, "Tell that to my ladywife."

~ # ~

Entering Sterling Castle's touchier lit great hall, Beth began praying in earnest that Duncan and Isaac were right; that Albany wouldn't know Katherine LeBeau Demont—his great niece and the King's cousin—from a hole in the ground. To keep from turning tale and running, she ran sweating palms down the front of her gown while Duncan assessed the crowd.

"This way, my lady," Duncan murmured, drawing her to the right and keeping to the back of the hall. "We should be able to hover unnoticed."

Beth's eyes rolled. "You can't be serious? You stand a full head taller than most in the room. The minute Albany looks this way, he'll spy you." *And with you, me,* she thought dejectedly. God help us all.

Having won the final prizes, Duncan had no choice but to be present at Albany's evening entertainments.

When Beth had also been summoned, Duncan, Isaac, and Rachael had done their hurried best to prepare her for the inquisition she was sure to face. But would it be enough? Could she pass Albany's scrutiny? Hoping Albany would be well into his cup by the time she had to stand before him, she mentally rehearsed all Rachael's edicts; when to curtsey, when to smile, which two fingers she was to use when eating meat, which two for eating fruit, and most importantly her three well-rehearsed responses to any questions.

They'd decided she should appear excessively shy and dependent on Duncan. Under those circumstances, it would appear more natural for him to deflect questions and answer for her. Should Albany question her directly, she would then depend on Duncan to cue her into the appropriate response by winking, squeezing her hand, elbow or waist. Their survival depended on remaining in contact, never separating. That and keeping as low a profile as possible until they could escape.

No easy task considering Duncan's height and the ten pounds of headgear and the voluminous peacock colored gown she wore. Rachael had really gone over the top getting her ready for her first royal audience.

"Ah, here ye be!" a redheaded man greeted them. "His grace has been asking after ye." Smiling at Beth, he said, "Ye must be Lady MacDougall."

Duncan introduced the man as Robbie Stewart. Mutely, Beth smiled, curtseyed, and held out her right hand. As Stewart bowed over her hand, Duncan asked, "Is he in a fair mindset?"

"Aye, very. The Campbell was not only routed but ye came out the winner. Too, there were few squabbles amongst the septs. None, at least, that caused disruption.

And ye? How are ye feeling after winning?"

Duncan grinned. "Relieved and a few pounds wealthier."

"More than a few, my friend. Have ye seen the chalice?" When Duncan shook his head, Robbie said, "Come."

"Aye, but let me settle my ladywife first. I will join ye later."

"Nonsense! His Grace has been anxious to see yer lady as well. Come, the pair of ye."

As Robbie made a path for them through the milling chieftains and their ladies, Duncan clasped Beth's shaking hand and whispered, "Remember, Albany has not seen his niece since childhood."

Swallowing down a sudden swell of nausea, Beth nodded. By the time she stood before the ruler of Scotland, she couldn't keep her knees from knocking together. Keeping one hand on Duncan's arm, Beth dropped into a deep curtsey. She would have gladly stayed in that position—with her face averted—for the rest of the night had she been given the option, but Albany chuckled and took her hand. Rising, she did her best to smile.

Albany said something—what, she hadn't a clue—and Duncan responded for her. When Albany said something else, Duncan squeezed her hand. She felt heat rising in her face as she mumbled in French that she was pleased to see him again, as well, after all these years.

Duncan chuckled as Albany again addressed her. She looked to Duncan for help and he winked. She took a deep breath, tucked her chin, and murmured "Oui, tres honoree oncle."

Albany laughed.

Relieved her response apparently pleased Albany, Beth dared to glance up and study the man who held their lives in his hands.

Not a large man, Albany was handsome and clean-shaven. Had he been dressed in a three-piece suit and dropped onto Wall Street, anyone passing Albany would assume from his piercing blue eyes, bearing, and gestures that he was a man of importance. Dressed as he was in an ermine lined coat of red and green silk with its dagges— an irregular pointed hem with all the requisite little brass bells—a tall ermine trimmed hat, heavy brass girdle, and long pointed shoes, he looked for all the world to Beth like a court jester. But then, so did most of the men surrounding her.

Thank heaven her husband had better sense. Though it may have simply been his lack of funds that curbed his desire to dress as the other men did, she found his simpler garb and the drape of MacDougall plaid far more appealing.

Her thoughts of how handsome she found her husband must have shown on her face for Duncan, smiling, leaned down and whispered in her ear, "He says you find marriage to your liking."

Beth cast her gaze to the floor as heat flashed across her cheeks. She didn't dare look at her supposed uncle.

Duncan whispered, "Shall I tell him of our glad tidings and that ye be tiring, so we can escape?"

Beth cast a quick glance toward Albany before shyly turning her face into Duncan's sleeve. She nodded.

The news of their impeding child was greeted with more laughter and congratulatory backslapping before Albany reached for her hand. He surprised her by kissing her cheek. She hoped it was her imagination when she saw his eyes narrow slightly. He then murmured something in Gael. Clueless, Beth bit her bottom lip and tried to smile.

When Duncan squeezed her elbow *and* waist, she froze. Two responses were required. God help her. She dipped into a curtsey and decided to say thank you before reciting—in French—it was a pleasure speaking with him and to wish him good night. As she straightened, she saw Albany no longer smiled. Staring at her beneath furrowed brows, he asked her a pointed question in Gael.

Duncan jerked her to his sided with a possessive arm. Startled, she looked up and found his eyes narrowed, his jaw muscles twitching, and his lips compressed into a thin hard line. The blood immediately drained from her head.

Oh God! What did I do wrong?

Just as her knees began to give way and as Duncan's chest expanded and his free hand reached for the hilt of his dirk, John the Campbell, laughing and backslapping, stepped into the breach.

She couldn't hear what he said, what with the blood pounding in her ears. As John continued to speak, Duncan scooped her into his arms and carried her out of the great hall and into Sterling Castle's torch lit bailey.

"Be ye well, Beth?" Duncan features had taken on sharp edges as he settled on a low stonewall. "Ye look about to pass dead away."

John Campbell and Angus rushed toward them as she nodded. "Aye...but what happened in there?"

John Campbell answered. "His Grace asked why ye dinna ken Gael and no longer had blue eyes."

Beth's stomach heaved. "Oh."

"Dinna fash, love. 'Tis well, now." Duncan looked at

his old liege lord. "Why did ye lie to Albany for us, John? Why did ye say ye kenned Beth from the past?"

The Campbell cast a wary glance about the bailey. "Three years past I was sent to check on Lady Katherine's holdings. Albany feared she—being only three and ten at the time, couldna keep that lowlander Demont in hand." He grinned. "I discovered a shrew. The lady was of fair visage but had a wasp's tail for a tongue. Demont, on the other hand, was ill, cowered, and oft times sotted.

"'Twasna long after I made my report to Albany that Demont conveniently died and Lady Katherine was shipped off to France until a new husband could be found for her. One who could control her, her dowered lands, and now those of her husband's estate." John clapped Duncan on the shoulder. "The moment I saw fair Lady Beth in yon tent, I kenned she *was not* the woman ye were ordered to marry."

"So why did ye tell Albany Beth *was* the Stuart lass?"

The laird of Dunstaffnage shrugged. "Who is alive to naysay me? Her parents are dead. She had so siblings. No one of import—save myself and her departed spouse—has even seen her since the age of six."

Angus murmured, "So one of the women we buried that night was Lady Katherine Demont."

Seeing the Campbell's eyes widen, Duncan told the Campbell about the night he found Beth. He then made a mental note to write to the abbess as soon as possible and reassure her he had the names of the dead women with Lady Katherine. "John, ye'll hang if—"

"Ssh!" The Campbell clamped a firm hand on Duncan's shoulder. "Just keep ye ladywife away from

Stewart holdings where they might kenned Lady Katherine."

"But why—"

"Mayhap I did it because ye've been like a son to me, Duncan. Ye treated my Mary fair, and ye dinna smote Flora, though ye had every right." The Campbell then brought Beth's hand to his lips and winked. "Or mayhap I did it because I am most smitten with yer ladywife's odd ways."

Chapter 31

"Take it off," Beth pleaded, tightening the death grip she already had on his hand. "<u>Now</u>, damn it!"

"Aye, my love, my pet, in a wee minute."

Sick to his stomach, Duncan cast worried glances toward Rachael and the mid-wife. 'Twas the tenth time his ladywife had demanded he slip the ring from her finger in as many minutes.

"Is all well?" he demanded of the women tending Beth.

Both women nodded. Rachael placed a cool compress on Beth's brow. "Aye, my lord. Actually, she is doing verra well. The babe should be here momentarily."

"Don't believe them," Beth hissed through clenched teeth. She tried to roll onto her back again, but he gently held her on her side as the mid-wife had ordered.

"Hush, dearest, hush, 'tis almost over." Leastwise, he prayed it so.

Why in God's name had he allowed Beth to talk him into this? A husband's place during a birthing was pacing the great hall or out on the lists. Not here, where her every tear and cry rent his heart to shreds. *'Tis barbaric, this custom of hers!*

Watching Beth grimace yet again, he wanted out so badly he would have given his sword arm to escape. But he'd promised to see her through, and so he would. "Ye are the bravest, lass."

"Duncan, if you ever want to see the light of day again, you'll take...OOOW!" Beth's face contorted into a frightful grimace.

The midwife popped up from between Beth's legs. "That's right, my lady, push!"

As Beth's nails dung deeper into his flesh and her face turn fuchsia, his fashing turned to panic. "What is--"

Rachael placed a hand on his shoulder, "'Tis well, my lord, the head is here." To Beth she said, "A deep breath, *mon ami*, and push!"

Beth growled, and the midwife crooned, "'Tis well done, lass; now pant."

Rachael started panting so Duncan started as well. Sweat-soaked, Beth locked her gaze on his and followed suit.

"Lass, have I told ye how much I love ye?"

Before she could answer the midwife coaxed, "Now one deep breath. That's the lass. Now push! One more grand push, and 'tis done."

Apparently the promise was all Beth needed. She gritted her teeth and bore down for all she was worth.

In a heartbeat she heaved a great sigh and relaxed in his arms. When a strident cry suddenly filled the solar, he released the breath he'd been holding and laughed.

He'd never felt such relief in his life. His Beth had labored, given birth, and was still alive.

He brushed the sweat from her brow and kissed her. "I love ye beyond all words."

With her eyes still closed, she smiled. "You'd better."

"My lord." The midwife chuckled as she held up a plump, furious, red-faced babe for his perusal. "Ye have a bonnie son."

"A son." His heart swelled to near bursting as he looked upon his handsome heir. 'Twas a miracle.

Crying, he pressed his forehead to his wife's and whispered, "Ye saved my soul, my beloved Beth."

She stroked his cheek. "Nay, my love, you did it yourself."

Epilogue

"**E**nough, Tom. Sit!"

Margaret Silverstein had waited long enough. Bone weary of watching her husband pace and equally tired of fashing about her beautiful son's future, she would learn—here and now—if she could dream for her child or not. Would he have the freedom to follow his heart into medicine or perhaps music, or would her child be trapped in this wee village like his predecessors until the day he died?

She handed Tom their Laird's diary. "Open it, husband. I'll not wait another moment, let alone another day."

Tom nodded, kenning she had the right of it. Beth had never been found and the ghost and the ring had not returned. He had put off reading the diary for long enough.

His hands shook as he turned the key in the bronze lock and lifted the ancient wooden cover.

The laird's bold strokes appeared unchanged from the last he'd seen them and his heart sank.

Kneeling before him with their son clutched to her breast, Margaret whispered, "Turn to the last entry that

Isaac had made, love. The one describing the Laird's death from the infection."

"Aye." He carefully turned the frail pages one after the other, needing only to scan for he had the words memorized and then he stopped. He read for a moment and choked on a sob.

"What? Tom, for heaven's sake! What does it say?"

Tears streamed down his face as he handed her the ancient tome. An unfamiliar script in fading ink covered the last page.

"Let it be known that on this day, the sixth day of April in the year of our Lord one thousand four hundred and nine, was born a healthy son, Duncan Thomas MacDougall, to Lady Katherine Elizabeth and Duncan Angus MacDougall, Laird of the clan MacDougall, Blackstone Castle, Scotland.

Katherine Elizabeth MacDougall Pudding MacDougall

PS: Love blooms. Give Margaret and the babe a kiss for me.

Speechless, Margaret reached for Tom's hand. A plain woman with a great need and capacity for love had finally broken the curse that had shaped their lives.

Her love had set them all free.

Author's Note

This work of fiction came to life while visiting Scotland and after reading the lore associated with the Bruce's Brooch of Lorne.

My hero Duncan is fictional. In reality, this particular MacDougall line, started from Dougal, son of Somerled of the Isles, ended with Laird John MacDougall, who died without issue in 1388.

His holdings in Lorne, the area along the western coast of the Scottish Highlands near the Firth of Lorne where this story is set, passed to the Stewarts of Lorne after John's death. Fictional Castle Blackstone was inspired by my husband's clan's ancestral home, very real Stewarts of Appin's Castle Stalker.

The references made about the MacDougall and Bruce feud are true. The Bruce did murder Ewin MacDougall's father-in-law, Red Comyn in 1306.

As for the Bruce's broach; By chance, the MacDougall clan surprised the Bruce, then king, at Dalrigh near Tyndrum. The king escaped the battle, but on his discarded cloak was found a magnificent example of Celtic jewelry, which was later known as the "Brooch of Lorne". It became one of the MacDougall clan's great treasures.

Eventually the MacDougall chiefship passed to John

MacAlan Macdougall of Donollie. The MacDougall lands were again restored. The twenty-second chief, Ian Ciar, fought in the rising of 1715, at the Battle of Sheriffmuir. His son, Chief Alexander, a Jacobite sympathizer, did not join in the 1745 rising, although his brother and clansmen fought at Culloden.

The books Beth finds in the keep and those Duncan gives her were hardbound publications in circulation in Scotland in 1408. The references to the Papal Bull and Pope Clements are fact, as well.

About the Author

Award-winning author Sandy Blair has slept in castles, dined with peerage, floated down Venetian canals, explored the great pyramids, lost her husband in an Egyptian ruin (she still denies being the one lost,) and fallen (gracefully) off a cruise ship.

Winner of Romance Writers of America's © Golden Heart and the National Readers Choice Award for Best Paranormal Romance, the Write Touch Readers Award for Best Historical, the Golden Quill and Barclay Awards for Best Novella, and nominated for a 2005 RITA, Sandy loves researching and writing about Scotland's past.

Sandy resides in New Hampshire with her tall Scot husband and spoiled pup, Coco.

More Books By Sandy Blair

In the Castle Blackstone series:

THE ROGUE
A THIEF IN A KILT
(Coming June 2013)
THE WARRIOR

Other TIME-TRAVEL novels
A HIGHLANDER FOR CHRISTMAS
THE MACKINNON
MACDUFF'S SECRET

Other novels
THE KING'S MISTRESS
THE ACCIDENTAL DUCHESS

The Rogue

Be careful what you wish for, very careful.

1410, Loch Ard Forest, Scotland. To win a wager – and the keys to a castle from his liege lord, Sir Angus MacDougall must find an acceptable bride within three months. Unfortunately, his battle-scarred countenance and lack of title has made the task difficult. He has only three weeks left to find an educated and devote woman to become his chatelaine when an inadvertent handfasting binds him to the beautiful but illiterate pagan, Birdalane. The arrangement can only lead to ruin and both now rush to undo what the gods and ill-phrased wishes have set in motion.

Made in the USA
San Bernardino, CA
20 March 2017